TRUE CONFECTIONS

TRUE CONFECTIONS

A Novel

KATHARINE WEBER

Shaye Areheart Books
NEW YORK

495273388

Copyright © 2010 by Katharine Weber

All rights reserved.
Published in the United States by Shaye Areheart Books, an imprint of the Crown Publishing Group, a division of Random House, Inc., New York.
www.crownpublishing.com

Shaye Areheart Books with colophon is a registered trademark of Random House, Inc.

Grateful acknowledgment is made to Ziplinsky Music for permission to reprint "Say, Dat's Tasty," by Frieda Ziplinsky, copyright © 2009 by Frieda Ziplinsky. Reprinted by permission of Ziplinsky Music.

Library of Congress Cataloging-in-Publication Data is available upon request.

ISBN 978-0-307-39586-3

Printed in the United States of America

Design by Lauren Dong

10 9 8 7 6 5 4 3 2 1

First Edition

For Barbara Findeisen, Bright Star!

I'm an empress.
I wear an apron.
My typewriter writes.
It didn't break the way it warned.
Even crazy, I'm as nice
as a chocolate bar.

—ANNE SEXTON, "Live"

TRUE CONFECTIONS

AFFIDAVIT

I, Alice Tatnall Ziplinsky, a resident of New Haven, County of New Haven, State of Connecticut, do hereby certify, swear or affirm, and declare that I am competent to give the following declarations concerning the history of Zip's Candies of New Haven, Connecticut, based on my expertise and personal experience derived from thirty-three years of dedicated employment, and as a shareholder in the Ziplinsky Family Limited Partnership, as well as my personal history as it pertains to the Ziplinsky family and Ziplinsky family business practices, before, during, and after my thirty-three years of marriage to Howard Ziplinsky, as the mother of Jacob Ziplinsky and Julie Ziplinsky, as the former sister-in-law of Irene Ziplinsky Weiss, and as the daughter-in-law of the late Samuel Ziplinsky and the late Frieda Ziplinsky, and I do hereby certify, swear or affirm, and declare that all of my information is based on my personal knowledge and experience, unless otherwise stated, and that the following matters, facts, and things are true and correct to the best of my knowledge:

1

ON MY FIRST DAY of work at Zip's Candies, it took five minutes for me to learn the two-handed method for separating and straightening the Tigermelts as they were extruded eight at a time onto the belt that carried them toward the finishing chocolate-striping applicator tunnel. The necessary reach-shuffle-reach-shuffle Tigermelt-straightening gesture was demonstrated for me with condescending efficiency, with the belt running at half speed, by the irritable Frieda Ziplinsky, whose husband, Sam, had just hired me that morning, an impulsive act on his part that she would regret audibly every few weeks for the next thirty-three years. In the sixth minute, I had my first glimpse of my future ex-husband.

Across the whirring, clanking, chugging, sugar-caked Zip's Candies factory floor, there appeared Howard Ziplinsky, emerging feetfirst from the large, rotating drum used to tumble the Little Sammies in the thin hard-shell chocolate coating, just a little more brittle than a Raisinet's, that gave them their signature sheen.

That Little Sammies panning drum was one of the original machines still running on the Zip's lines that hot summer of 1975. It finally wore out beyond repair six years later, in late August 1981, an unforgettable time for me personally as well as a notable event in the history of Zip's Candies. I had just begun to be plagued with morning sickness, but Howard and I hadn't yet revealed to anyone that I was pregnant with our first child,

Jacob. I was working long, exhausting, split-shift days that summer, supervising the first and third shifts to meet Halloween orders, when the Little Sammies panning drum seized up for the last time. We had shut down the line twice that week because of fruit-fly infestations (the eggs probably came in with a contaminated batch of peanuts for the Tigermelts), which had required cleaning every piece of equipment on the line, including internal mechanisms. The gear shaft on the drum motor was probably insufficiently relubricated when the line started up yet again, and it broke down irreparably on that last Thursday night of August, just as the third shift was starting, causing the disastrous Little Sammies shortage of Halloween 1981.

Replacement parts for that panning drum had been fabricated as needed for thirty years, but by 1981, the very last known functioning machine capable of making those parts had become obsolete and worn out as well. The fabricator—Bud Becker, an elderly retired machinist who operated out of his Hamden basement (by then he was the last living member of the original start-up crew on the Zip's lines when Eli Czaplinsky opened his doors in 1924)—had thrown in the towel when he couldn't get the parts for his machine that made the parts for our machine. He was eighty-three, and for fourteen years Zip's had been his only customer.

A new panning drum, the one that still runs on the Little Sammies line today, was rush-ordered from Holland, making it the first-ever custom-built mechanism to grace the Zip's floor. (It would remain the most expensive single production-line element for several years, until the cost was surpassed by the overdue replacement of the entire Tigermelt line, from batch tables to wrapping machines, with some slightly newer used equipment, in 1989.) Those lost seven weeks before the new Little Sammies panning drum was installed on the line were a disaster.

We even tried hand-dipping on jury-rigged enrobing frames in finishing trays, the way Little Sammies were manufactured at the very beginning, in 1924, in those first months when Eli was still developing and refining his cherished candy inventions, well before Little Sammies were distributed beyond New Haven. But there was no chance we could duplicate the finish and gloss of the panned Little Sammies, and all we did was waste product and man-hours, because it is, of course, impossible to get that thin, hard, chocolate-shell coating onto Little Sammies any other way.

Imagine trying to finish M&M's or Reese's Pieces by hand. What we produced was perfectly good candy, but they were just little fudgy chocolate-covered figures, probably a lot like the earliest versions of Zip's signature candy. So it was useless. They weren't remotely like what people expect when they open a pack of Little Sammies.

I don't know if it is obvious even now just how catastrophic this was for Zip's at the time. Little Sammies sales have carried more than half of Zip's annual gross for decades, and almost three quarters of annual Little Sammies sales occur in that all-important zenith of candy-selling seasons, from back-to-school through Halloween. It was only the advent of the protein-bar contract work that changed Zip's dependence on Little Sammies. The Detox bar and Index bar lines have grown ever more significant for us in recent years. Every time I look at our balanced books I thank God for our nation's ongoing glycemic-index obsession.

That interruption on the Little Sammies line was a true crisis. Howard and I had been married for six years by then, and I had never before seen him cry, not even when his grandmother died just ten days before our wedding. We got through it, and I thought at the time that if we could survive the Little Sammies

Halloween shortage of 1981, we could survive anything, but I was wrong.

I HAVE BEEN instructed by Charlie Cooper, my attorney, to tell my story in as clear and detailed a way as possible, from the beginning, though what a lawyer means by "clear and detailed" and "from the beginning" is probably very different from what I prefer to make of those requirements for this account. So my recollection of events begins on the humid summer day that was the twelfth of July, 1975, when I applied for the job at Zip's out of the blue.

I say "out of the blue" because it really was just that, the consequence of picking up a discarded section of the *New Haven Register* to leaf through while I dawdled over my toasted corn muffin and coffee at the counter at Clark's Dairy, on Whitney Avenue, where I had taken to lingering each morning after I fled my family's house, my hair still wet from the shower. A classified ad with the heading "Dat's Tasty!" in the "Help Wanted" pages jumped out at me.

I had just been graduated from Wilbur Cross High School, where Miss Grace Solomon, my favorite English teacher, had instructed me in correct usage, which is why I just wrote "been graduated" instead of "graduated." Because whether or not I have a college degree, I consider myself to be a perfectly well-read and educated person with as good a command of language as any college graduate I know, including a certain member of the Ziplinsky family who considers herself to be quite educated indeed after those four years in Providence at that university named for those slave-trading Brown brothers.

It is a deeply ingrained Ziplinsky family trait to place a little too much confidence in what it says on the label without full regard for quality control. Trust me, no Ivy League diploma on the wall confers an automatic ability to discern the correct uses of the words *lay* and *lie,* nor is it an antidote to chronic split infinitives and dangling modifiers. Let us not dwell too long on the habitual incorrect deployment of the word *myself,* the use of which is apparently believed to connote superiority and classiness. Out of that smug Ziplinsky mouth often comes the cringeworthy phrase, "On behalf of myself," revealing, with those four inapt words, the truth of the matter to all literate people, whether or not they possess an Ivy League degree. I consider myself to be an autodidact. One definition of an autodidact is someone who knows what *autodidact* means.

I WAS IN the top tenth percentile of my class at Wilbur Cross, I was the winner of the Senior English Prize, and I had already picked my courses for my first semester at Middlebury College, which had been my first choice. But I had screwed up so badly a few weeks before my first day at Zip's Candies that I wasn't going to be heading off to college after all, though Middlebury was willing to consider deferring my admission to the following year, their inevitable letter rescinding my admission concluded (with a certain calculated and smug coldness that was meant to discourage me from pursuing the option while simultaneously conveying a superficial gesture in the direction of fairness), with my deferred admission depending on a demonstration of "sufficient growth of character in the interim, given the circumstances."

I already had a summer job, so there was no reason for me to be reading the classifieds section of the *Register*. But there was nothing else left to read in that particular lone, abandoned newspaper section after the horoscopes and advice columns and used-car ads, all of which I studied with a deep and pointless concentration each morning. (Plus, I had always enjoyed reading the want ads, starting in about third grade, when I would read them aloud to my mother while she made dinner, and together we would create stories about the people who applied for those jobs.)

I was at the end of my third week scooping cones at Helen's Double Dip out on the Boston Post Road in Milford, and I had come to dread putting on the claustrophobic, short, lime-green polyester uniform with its lumpy zipper and attached apron. I washed and dried my uniform every night, and it had already begun to pill. I dreaded everything about Helen's Double Dip. I dreaded the sugary slime of curdled cream underfoot, which had impregnated the soles of my bright new JCPenney sneakers. I dreaded the daily din of bratty children whining at their irritably indulgent parents, who rarely thought to tip as I labored to fill their orders while enduring a twinge in my elbow that was a direct consequence of scooping nut-infested flavors at an awkward angle with a bad scoop.

I took the job at Helen's Double Dip after three humiliating interviews for much nicer jobs had left me feeling that I would never do better and probably deserved exactly this punishment for everything that had happened. I had aimed much higher at first, when I applied for an entry-level editorial assistant position at Yale University Press. But when I sat down with an editor (a balding, middle-aged man with a stammer, whose scrawny polka-dotted bow tie heralded a vast collection of variously patterned bow ties, one of which he no doubt wore each and every day) and he leaned back in his chair and cocked one seersuckered leg over the other (exposing some hairless shin above a droopy sock) and asked me in a falsely avuncular fashion why I wasn't going to college in the fall, given that I had just finished high school, and I started to explain about the fire and the sentence and my family's money issues, he closed the file folder and stood up abruptly, even though I had been there only a few minutes and we hadn't yet discussed anything at all about the job.

My next interview was for a receptionist position at a big law firm on Church Street, but when I met with the human resources lady, before I could say a word about which job I was applying for, she took one look at me and shook her head, and then she quickly told me the job had been filled and then she started typing really fast and didn't look at me again. I stood on the sidewalk in front of the building in my dowdy interview outfit feeling waves of shame as office workers on their lunch hour brushed by me. I had just been intercepted attempting to pass myself off as a regular person.

I applied for a job at the bookstore on Whitney Avenue where my family had bought books my entire life, but the formerly friendly owner was abrupt with me and vague about actually needing anyone after all, even though there was a hand-lettered sign on the glass door advertising his need for part-time help. As I turned away I caught him rolling his eyes at one of his employees, a soft-spoken retired music teacher who had always been nice to me and who shared my mother's passion for Angela Thirkell novels. In the glass of the door, I could see her reflection, shrugging and grimacing in response as I made my way out.

At Helen's Double Dip out in deepest Milford, nobody asked me anything about whether or not I was going to college, and more significantly nobody seemed to notice or care that they were hiring a renowned pariah with a criminal record to work a daily shift from nine to six. All Freddie, the manager (with his Don Ameche mustache and his terrible acne scars), seemed to care about was my comprehension of the rules, which mandated showing up on time, thorough hand-washing, correct scooping technique, and the strict limit of three free samples per customer, no exceptions, not even for friends. I assured him I had no friends.

THAT MORNING, SITTING at the counter at Clark's Dairy, I was drawn to the quaintness of the little "Dat's Tasty!" ad declaring that Zip's Candies was seeking a "hardworking and honest individual willing to be dedicated to learning old-fashioned techniques at a world-renowned candy factory." Like the Clark's counter itself, the ad seemed to me like something from another era, an era so much simpler and nicer than my own. I wished I could make up a story about the person who applied for this job, to tell my mother while she made our dinner, but my mother wasn't speaking to me in those grim days, and it wasn't clear that she would resume speaking to me anytime soon.

Moments later, instead of driving a few exits south on traffic-clogged I-95 and going straight to work, I found myself driving under the highway ramp and navigating the desolate Krazy Kat landscape of the old industrial waterfront of New Haven on the other side of the train tracks, at the edge of the Quinnipiac River. I had gone once with my father to this part of town, years before, to buy a replacement part for the old-fashioned crank-out awning that shaded our backyard patio. Yes, we have no bananas, he would always sing as he cranked, deploying the green-and-white-striped awning to shade the table and chairs on our back terrace. In my memory, voyaging to the awning factory on River Street had been an expedition, far more of an adventure than the five minutes' drive from downtown that took me to the corner of River and James streets.

Though I had intended, out of pure idle curiosity, only to

take a quick look and keep driving, when I spotted the big, faded "Dat's Tasty!" ghost lettering embedded in the worn bricks up so high near the roof that you wouldn't notice them once you got closer, I stopped, and then I parked my car in front of the nondescript three-story factory building with the number on the door corresponding to the address in the ad. Were it not for that "Dat's Tasty!" declaration in old-fashioned italic lettering, which already felt oddly familiar to me as I gazed at it, I wouldn't have been at all certain I was in the right place. Was this worn brick building surrounded by boarded-up husks of long-gone industry at the baked edge of nothing really the home of a world-renowned candy factory?

I was not specifically interested in the candies themselves at this point in my life. Sure, I was always happy enough to find Little Sammies or a Tigermelt in my Halloween candy, who wouldn't be? Mumbo Jumbos were more problematic, as I was rather ambivalent toward licorice in those years, and I was always willing to trade away Mumbo Jumbos for something with chocolate (although my father liked them, so sometimes I would save them for him). And there was a family vacation on the Cape one rainy summer when my father used Mumbo Jumbos to replace some missing backgammon pieces in the set we found in a closet of the rental house.

But I had never gone out of my way to buy any Zip's candy with my allowance money in my earlier candy-buying years, when I would ride my bike to the newsstand on Whitney Avenue on Saturday afternoons. With my fifty cents I could buy three comic books, a pack of gum, and a candy bar. Frankly, I tended to favor Baby Ruths. I suppose I had a vague awareness that Zip's Candies was located somewhere in Connecticut, but I had no deep affection for boring and familiar New Haven, and my family was never one of those Chamber of Commerce, hometown pride kind of families. It certainly never occurred to me that I was destined to spend my life here.

There was a reason for the anonymity of the building, I would learn. Zip's had deliberately kept a low profile for a while at that point, although years earlier, especially in the 1950s, there had been a great deal of effort put into maintaining a very visible hometown identity, with local radio and television spots, sponsored parade floats, and lots of giveaways (rare Zip's memorabilia is avidly sought by collectors, especially the Zip's green umbrellas from the early fifties, a prize awarded to those willing to amass immense qualifying quantities of Zip's wrappers and mail them in, with a dollar for postage and handling; these occasionally show up on eBay for ridiculous sums).

Factory visits had never been permitted by Zip's, for reasons having to do partly with hygiene but mostly with keeping secret the specific manufacturing techniques for each line because of a not-unreasonable family paranoia about the potential loss of trade secrets. Plus, Frieda just never wanted to deal with groups of children. That woman didn't like people in general, and she really didn't like children, preferring to keep her distance unless she had a specific reason (like, if they were her own grandchildren) to tolerate them.

So, in my school years, I had experienced no class trips to the Zip's factory to see Little Sammies and Tigermelts and Mumbo Jumbos whizzing along the lines on their journey from raw ingredients to finished candies to wrapped products tightly packed into boxes for shipping. This is in distinct contrast to the way I had been marched through Lender's Bagels on three occasions by the time I was in sixth grade. In 1975, Zip's Candies was so low profile that there wasn't even an air of mystery about Zip's, unlike the fog of rumor and innuendo that has surrounded the legendary fortress that is the PEZ factory in

Orange, which no civilians have been permitted to penetrate since PEZ began American operations there in 1973. I fail to comprehend the allure of PEZ, I have to say. Even as a child, I was PEZ-resistant, more interested in the PEZ logo and the word itself, *PEZ* being a sort of Austrian shorthand for the word *Pfefferminze,* than I was in the cheesy dispensers or the actual candy (where's the charm in a stack of compressed, tooth-pastey chalk bricks?). How many PEZ bricks in the PEZ logo? Forty-four.

The Zip's building had no sign. The original sign was in storage, I would discover later that summer when I was taking a smoke break out back by the loading area and spotted it beside a bin of old wooden shipping pallets. Not that the official company history would tell you this, but the truth, according to Pete Zagorski, the old-timer on the loading dock, was that it had been removed in 1969, in haste (by Pete Zagorski himself, who had been rousted out of a deep sleep before the sun was up by a call from Sam, asking him to hustle down to James Street and take down the sign, which is why he was so authoritative on the subject), on the first of May, because of a tip-off by a friendly detective with the New Haven Police Department. He'd heard a rumor that the charged-up mob on the Green protesting the Black Panther trial in the Elm Street courthouse was planning a march across town to the Zip's Candies factory, to protest a certain candy inspired by Little Black Sambo, even if the company had for a while tried to revise history with statements about how in fact the myth that Little Sammies were named for Little Black Sambo is just one of those erroneous beliefs that circulate, because the truth is that the candy was really inspired by the birth of the owner's son, Little Sammy Ziplinsky, born the same year Zip's Candies started production.

In 1921, the Curtiss Candy Company in Chicago changed

their Kandy Kake bar into the Baby Ruth, claiming former president Grover Cleveland's dead daughter Ruth had somehow inspired the name. This was implausible at best, and it is most likely that the Baby Ruth bar was an unauthorized attempt to cash in on the popularity of baseball great Babe Ruth. It hardly seems fair that in 1931 Curtiss won their case to shut down Babe Ruth's own licensed candy bar on grounds that it was too close to their bestselling product.

Nothing happened to Zip's Candies during the Black Panther trial. There was no angry march from the New Haven Green across the railroad tracks, even in that season of turmoil when anything was possible. The whole city of New Haven seemed to be one spark away from a great big Black Panther conflagration. It was a potentially threatening time for a company known for making small, chewy, Negroid candies, no matter what the explanation for the name might be, no question. All it meant to me at the time, a couple of miles up leafy Whitney Avenue (named for that other ambitious and inventive Eli, whose ingenuity gave the world the cotton gin, which led to a vast expansion of cotton production in the American south, which of course increased the demand for the slave labor necessary to pick all that cotton), was that my parents watched the news on television compulsively and I wasn't allowed to leave our block on my bicycle.

I COULD SEE through the big mullioned windows on the first two floors that the factory lights were on. I turned off my Subaru before the engine could overheat, which it tended to do, which was why my mother was driving her new Volkswagen and I was driving this old wreck, and I sat there. I knew I needed to backtrack to the highway entrance I had passed on my way. I could get to work on time if I left now. Something kept me sitting there in the still car. I don't know what, beyond a general reluctance to face the day, to face the rest of the summer, and after that, to face the rest of my doomed life stretching out in front of me.

I harbored a hopeless vision of spending all eternity at Helen's Double Dip, where I would turn into an aging spinster furiously scooping triple Nutty Buddy cones with my by-then crippled arm while life passed me by. There's poor old Alice, people would say. The sad one, with the mustache. (I would have let myself go completely. Doomed felons don't pluck.) They say she's worked at Helen's Double Dip all her life.

The truth is, that summer, that day, that moment, I had come to the end of something. I had lost my place.

Sweat trickled down my neck in the suddenly stifling car. I opened my window. A certain burnt sugar and chocolate aroma hung in the air, that marvelous, inevitable, ineffable, just-right aura of Zip's Candies, that unique blend of sweetness and pleasure and something else, a deep note of something rich and exotic and familiar that makes you nostalgic for its flavor even though you may never have tasted it before. I have loved that smell every day of my life from then to now. Some days, I go to work for that smell. When I travel, I miss it, I long for it. On Mumbo Jumbo days there is an added spice in the air, a dark hint of cherry and anise that adds a top note of danger. In retrospect, I believe this was a Mumbo Jumbo day. The aroma wafting through my car told me what I already knew I had to do. I went in and applied for the job.

My FUTURE FATHER-IN-LAW, Sam Ziplinsky, appraised me with a sidelong glance from behind his messy desk, never taking the unlit, moist stub of a cigar out of his mouth (he couldn't smoke on the premises, so he nursed a disgusting half-smoked cigar all day long instead) while barraging me with questions about my education, about my experience, about my family, about where I lived and what I wanted to do with my life.

He didn't seem to hear my hesitant, evasive, contradictory answers at all as he rooted through untidy heaps of papers and threw out more questions, one on top of the next—Why did I think I deserved to work here, did I know it was like joining a family, am I someone who gets sick a lot, am I reliable, where do I live, am I good with my hands, am I in college, why not, do I want to marry and have children, am I a team player, do I like licorice? Red and black, or did I prefer red and hate black? Which do I like better, Little Sammies or Tigermelts? Until finally he interrupted me to exclaim in triumph, Found the sucker! as he extracted a ledger book from beneath a pile of folders.

I stopped trying to cook up plausible and attractive answers to each question, in order, since I was about three questions behind and I seemed to be talking to myself anyway, so finally I just stopped speaking altogether and waited to see what would come next. Was he listening at all to my replies? Was this a conversation, or a job interview, or what was it? I was now late for my shift at Helen's Double Dip. Freddie would be seriously disturbed that I was not there to start the morning flavor batches of the day and complete the daily inventory checklist before the lines started to form. Was I reliable?

Sam sat back in his creaking desk chair, holding the formerly misplaced ledger book in his lap, and then he looked me in the face for the first time, for a long moment. There was a metal bowl of deformed, uncoated Little Sammies on his desk, some of them undersized and missing parts, some of them all stuck together in a blob of limbs and torsos. He ate a clump absent-mindedly while looking at me, and then he held out the bowl and I took a three-headed triplet cluster and nibbled on their heads while waiting for whatever came next. At last he said, with a wry smile, all at once, not pausing for my replies, the cigar still firmly planted in the corner of his mouth, You want to work here, kid? You're what, sixteen? Eighteen? You want a job at Zip's? You want to work? You a hard worker? Sister, this isn't just a summer job. It's hard work. You like candy, kiddo? What we make here are three great candy lines, true confections, that's what my father, Eli—he founded the company—that's what he called them, true confections. You like Little Sammies? That's me, you're looking at him, I'm the original Little Sammy. I used to be little, now I'm not so little. So what do you think? You know what? You're hired. I got a good feeling.

MY FUTURE MOTHER-IN-LAW gave no indication of having any kind of good feeling about me whatsoever. Pearl Anastasio, Sam's secretary, a Zip's stalwart who had started at Zip's as a Little Sammies summer wrapper when she was in high school and Eli ran the place (in the era before he rigged up the first wrapping machine on the Little Sammies line), someone who would turn out to be a true friend to me as the years passed, though I hardly made eye contact with her that day, led me down a corridor. We reached a windowless office, where Frieda Ziplinsky sat at a desk piled high with stacks of envelopes she was stuffing with what looked like order forms. She would stuff a dozen, then seal a dozen. Stuff, seal, stuff, seal. Her hands were a blur. We stood in the doorway waiting for her to stop and look up, but she didn't stop and she didn't look up. She was a stuffing and sealing pro, a stuffing and sealing maniac. Finally

Pearl announced loudly, Hey, Mrs. Z. Mr. Z said to say to you we've got our new hire. Okay, Mrs. Z.? Frieda finally glanced up and gave me a sour look. Pearl abandoned me with a friendly pat on the shoulder that was combined with a little push so I would step into that room.

You're not twenty-three, you look fourteen! You ever even worked on a line? You got line experience? You got another job? Frieda asked me, eyeing my absurd and too-short lime-green Helen's Double Dip uniform. I shrugged and shook my head apologetically, furtively yanked on my hem with one hand, and mumbled No, I had no line experience, and No, I was through with Helen's Double Dip, and today was my last day. She scowled. Not the racker and stacker from Entenmann's, from West Haven? I thought that girl was supposed to come in this morning first thing. I thought that was you. Sam maybe thought so too. He hired you? You have any idea what the job is? He say what the pay is? You know this isn't a summer job? You ready to train right now, while I have the time?

I shook my head again, and then again, and then I nodded, feeling as if anything I said or did would further the degree to which I had inadvertently taken Sam's side in an ongoing argument and was now allied with him against her forever. Which was true.

Sighing heavily, clearly having already reached the conclusion that asking me any more questions would be useless, Frieda got up, went over to a white metal cabinet, and rummaged around on the shelves, and without looking in my direction she handed me a hairnet, which I put on, and then a white factory coat, which I also put on. As I buttoned it, she gave me a look that suggested that covering myself more modestly from now on would be a good idea in general, regardless of hygiene requirements. The lightweight white coat was a foot longer than the hem of the uniform I would never wear again after this day. I stepped out of my sneakers and pulled on, over my little pom-pom tennis socks, the pair of too-big, white, galoshy go-go boots apparently required before a civilian could set foot on the Zip's Candies factory floor, as Frieda wordlessly handed them to me, first one, then the other, with a look on her face as if I was putting them on incorrectly. She herself wore Keds.

She walked out of the room, and I waded down the hallway behind her, sloshing along in the boots, mimicking her when she paused to glove up with latex gloves from the wall dispenser by the big swinging double doors to the factory floor which have always made me feel as if I am about to enter an operating room, and then I followed her into the chaotic din and clatter of the sweet mechanical ballet of the Zip's Candies factory for the first time.

Even before my Tigermelt-handling indoctrination, I already knew I belonged at Zip's Candies. I knew it out on the sidewalk when I breathed in that burnt sugar and chocolate aroma. I knew that being here—hairnet, white coat, rubber boots, and all, forfeiting my job at Helen's Double Dip (along with my second and final paycheck, which I never had the nerve to go pick up), even as I was scornfully instructed on the nuances of straightening Tigermelts as they dropped onto the belt—was deeply, essentially right. Perhaps some people would call this destiny. Zip's Candies needed me, and I needed Zip's Candies. An inexplicable joy welled up in me as I realized that I knew that my life could start again from here, from this moment.

THAT FIRST TIME I saw Howard, thin and dark, handsome like a foreign doctor in his white lab coat (despite the stray, uncoated Little Sammies clinging to a sleeve), his face and eyebrows were freckled with a fine spray of chocolate droplets. This was the thin, glossy chocolate used to apply the final coat to Little Sammies in the panning drum from which he had just emerged, having reamed a clogged nozzle with a pipe cleaner. He had been working on the Mumbo Jumbos blending unit just before that (it was one of those days when the summer humidity soaked into everything, despite the chugging air-conditioning system; it was overdue for upgrading, but Frieda didn't want to spend the money, which was foolish, as the humidity affected every piece of antiquated equipment on the floor), and he was already dusted with the powdered sugar that had caked and clogged the feed tubes on the big licorice-blending pot. I thought he looked confectionary, like a sugared angel, and I could feel Frieda glaring at me, wanting to keep her beautiful son all to herself. And so we met.

Howdy, he said, coming toward me, not in greeting but introducing himself, because that's what he was called, Howdy Ziplinsky, and this confused me for a moment, as I sensed that nobody in the Ziplinsky family was likely to be from someplace where people said "Howdy" to one another, so I thought perhaps this was a Yiddish word I couldn't quite hear over the factory din, but at the same moment, through my confusion, I felt something completely new and profound stir in me, and I had to resist my unexpected impulse, as we shook hands for the first time, to lick him.

2

I DIDN'T MEAN TO burn down Debbie Livingston's house. Despite all the ridiculous stories that most people believed, the way people love to believe ridiculous stories, it is important to recognize that the events of that night were never fairly represented by the newspapers or the local television stations. At least the Internet didn't exist in those days. That fire took place long ago, on May 7, 1975, to be precise, and the facts of that case obviously have no specific bearing on the current matters at hand, but establishing the truth is important to me. Howard has told me more than once that I am obsessed with the truth. He himself could have a little more respect for it. But Dr. Gibraltar, my psychoanalyst, always said that the truth is overrated. Dr. Gibraltar never did say much in all the years of my analysis, but when he spoke, it was usually to utter a little kōan like that.

Ellie Quest-Greenspan, my other therapist, who was supposed to be Howard's and my marriage counselor, talked a great deal, and often spoke about how I was on a quest toward finding my truth and how I was always learning how to stand in my truth. And Charlie Cooper has more than once advised me, as we walk through the door for this or that deposition or hearing, that answering questions truthfully isn't the same thing as saying everything I know. In other words, speak the truth in as few words as possible (which, apologies to Charlie, is not really my style). Apparently everybody is obsessed with the truth, one way or another. Anyway, given that my qualifications to provide information about the business of Zip's Candies are being called into question by a certain greedy member of the Ziplinsky family who has no idea what she is talking about, it seems important to explain about that fire now.

I know that many people in the Greater New Haven area believe things about me that are untrue. Some of them will always think of me as Arson Girl. I am bitter about that. Why wouldn't I be? I didn't mean to burn down that house. It isn't arson if there is no intent. It's just an accidental fire. Call me Accidental Fire Girl.

My one-year sentence for third-degree arson was suspended and I was given two years' probation. I didn't realize that when I agreed to a guilty plea (which I did because I was a distraught teenager, and also because I caused the fire), I was agreeing to a charge of arson. That was a mistake.

My parents had to pay the Livingstons a huge amount of money as part of the deal. This bankrupted my family, and my father had to close his real-estate business, because he had not incorporated, and so his personal liabilities sank Tatnall Realty. Plus, being the father of Arson Girl probably wasn't exactly good for business. By the end of the year, my father had gone to work for the Martha Rivers Agency, headed by the calculating and rapacious Martha Rivers (whom he had always mocked), the most underhanded and manipulative high-pressure real-estate agent in town. Martha was the only one who made him an offer, and that may well have been prompted by a perverse attraction to our pariah status, given how loathed she herself was by so many people in the community. She represented everything my father hated in the business, and now he was her employee, and it was my fault.

My mother went back to substitute teaching in the New Haven and Hamden public school systems the following autumn. My parents stopped talking about their dreams of certain trips or their wish to build a vacation house in Vermont. Both my parents pretty much stopped talking to me altogether that summer, without admitting that they weren't talking to me, and the pretense that they were talking to me was much worse than out-and-out silence. I was an only child, there were no cousins for hundreds of miles, and I was really marooned. Only when Jacob was born was there anything like a thaw, and even then, they never really opened their hearts to me again. I don't know how you turn away from your child the way they turned away from me. But it's something people do.

WHEN HOWARD AND I were married in early October, only three months after we met, my parents never questioned our plan, having little curiosity about this huge, possibly disastrous, and certainly reckless leap I was making just a few weeks before my nineteenth birthday. Working at Zip's Candies and then falling in love with Howard, a Jewish man ten years my senior, were for them just the latest two things I had gotten myself into. I like to think they were preoccupied with their bankruptcy. Under other circumstances, perhaps they might have been more concerned about me. But the fire changed them as much as it changed me, and I will never know what it would have been like to have parents who would question my choices instead of just being relieved that whatever I might do next, now it wouldn't be their problem.

At our wedding, they acted like guests, or remote relatives, the sort of people who tell you they remember when you were a baby because they have nothing else to say. We were married in the backyard of Frieda and Sam's house on Marvel Road on a beautiful Sunday afternoon by a groovy rabbi known throughout the tristate area for marrying couples like us.

I had grown up attending the First Unitarian Universalist Society on Whitney Avenue a few times a year; it was a compromise place of not quite worship chosen by my Episcopal mother to mollify my atheist father (he was raised a nominal Congregationalist). It was important to my mother that we belong to a church of some kind, with services in at least a vaguely Christian format, and this was the best she could do with my father, this church for atheists. I am sure my mother was drawn to the Unitarian philosophy offering a free and responsible search for truth and meaning, which allows each person an opportunity to find an individual path. She was always really big on individual paths.

When I was about ten, my mother took up a sort of spiritual meditation habit she called "discerning," and although she never instructed me about anything remotely religious, sometimes she offered to let me sit with her in silence so we could discern together. But it made me itchy to sit with her like that, and it felt like something too private, and I didn't believe she really wanted me right there next to her when she was doing it. Sometimes she and my father discerned together, and I would walk into their room and they would be sitting in silence and I would feel as if I had walked in on something so intimate the door should have been bolted to save us all from my embarrassing intrusion.

When we did go to church, services were led by members of the congregation, and as a child I couldn't differentiate those services from the earnest political meetings that took place in the same rows of chairs at other times of the day.

Jacob and Julie attended the progressive, cooperative preschool located in the carriage house behind the Unitarian Society, a pleasant continuity for me, though by the time they went to preschool there I hadn't set foot inside the church (really just a house) since high school. The preschool didn't exist when I was a child. I didn't go to nursery school at all, though I think it probably would have been a good idea if I had spent more time with children when I was little, as I was a solitary only child who was always more comfortable around adults than I was around other children. But my parents didn't think I "needed" to go, as if nursery school was some sort of remedial treatment.

When I got to kindergarten, instead of rushing to play with the other children, I preferred to spend recess chatting with the teacher, if she would let me. And if she gently suggested that I go play with the other children, that always made me feel such shame, because I was exposed for having wanted something from her—adult friendship—which she certainly wasn't going to provide, no matter how much of a serious little savant I made myself.

When I was invited to play at someone's house after school, my playmate would become irritable when I lingered at the kitchen table long after the snack had been consumed, deep in conversation with an impressed mother. I was that child your mother always suggested for playdates until you explained to her that she liked me better than you did.

I don't really know why it never occurred to me at the height of the fire crisis to seek solace or wise counsel from anyone connected to the Unitarians, but I didn't, and as far as I know neither of my parents turned to anyone in the church either, possibly out of embarrassment. At certain times in my life I have wished with all my heart that I had a rabbi or a priest to whom I could have turned. I truly envy those with genuine faith. Their lives must be so much easier to bear.

I have chosen instead to worship in the house of psychoanalysis, which offers little solace in any immediate sense, and which in fact holds the possibility of a great deal of shame for anyone who voices a wish to be held and comforted and soothed.

You can only analyze your desire to be held and comforted and soothed, and you can discuss why it wouldn't be appropriate for that ever to take place in this room with this person you employ to listen to you talk to yourself, and you can feel waves of shame that you are in the grip of the transference neurosis that drives this attachment to the doctor, to whom you pay enormous sums of money.

This is how I started seeing Ellie Quest-Greenspan on the side. Howard and I went to her just four times, at the recommendation of my dentist, who told me that her imperiled marriage had been saved by Ellie. Perhaps that sounds silly. I thought we did good work, as they say, in those appointments, but Howard was really only showing up to humor me. It was the least he could do, he said, with that door-opening, chair-pulling-out, walk-on-the-street-side-of-a-lady, superficial gallantry of his. Nothing that was said in those sessions (though he acknowledged that he knew he was breaking my heart, which was better than if he had no idea, I suppose) was going to change his plan to leave me and go to Madagascar, where he could finally truly inhabit his other life, his real life.

Howard walked out of the appointment halfway through that fourth and final meeting, saying he would get more satisfaction out of hitting a bucket of balls, and that was it. Ellie simply held me and rocked me while I cried for the remainder of the appointment. She asked if I wanted to come back, and I said I did, and I kept seeing her, with appointments every other week, while I was at the same time still seeing Dr. Gibraltar three or four times each week.

I would like to point out that I was never a big spender of the Ziplinsky millions in any way other than this, the tens of thousands of dollars in checks I wrote to Dr. Gibraltar over those twenty-five years of psychoanalysis. For all those prosperous years with Howard, in that era when everyone around us was so frantically getting and spending, I lived modestly. For twelve years I was comfortable driving a sturdy Saab acquired when Julie was in preschool, though Howard, a car nut, was always urging me to get a fancy German sedan. (He was disappointed when the Saab finally died and I switched to a Jeep.) Unlike ordinary women (according to the magazines I read in the checkout line at the supermarket), I have no desire to own more than just one handbag, a nice one, a Coach bag in red leather, and I have only a few pairs of shoes. I have certainly never bought myself fancy jewelry or designer clothing. I have never gone to a spa to have processes applied to my body, and I have never taken vacations in the Caribbean or gone on a cruise. Wouldn't most women in my position have felt utterly entitled to do all of those things routinely?

The most money I have ever spent on myself was when I bought an original Harriet Rose photograph, a charming picture of a cat sleeping in the window of a pharmacy, for my fiftieth birthday. I have modest needs and desires.

I resent, therefore, the statements that I have recklessly squandered Ziplinsky money on neurotic quantities of psychotherapy hours. (a) My medical expenses that are not covered by the insurance provided by Zip's Candies are in no way relevant to the matters in dispute, (b) nothing about my psychotherapy has any relevance to my competence as an employee or an administrator at Zip's Candies, (c) I concede that the gasoline in my Saab was paid for with a Zip's Corporate ExxonMobil Speedpass account, though records have never been kept concerning personal mileage of Zip's employees, and this is an irrelevancy, and (d) I am angry that in the name of family loyalty Howard has apparently chosen to disclose details of my private life to his sister.

❄ ❄

DR. GIBRALTAR DIDN'T know about those continuing appointments with Ellie Quest-Greenspan. I didn't want to tell him I was still seeing her, without Howard, because I had felt his skepticism hovering like a cloud in the air behind my head as I lay on the couch reporting to him about our first appointment with Ellie. When I described her credentials (surely not everyone with a degree from an alternative modality institute in Colorado is a kook) he shifted uneasily in his chair. When you've been in analysis a long time, you know how to read things like this, and he might as well have leaned over and smacked me in the face. Despite his obvious disapproval, I went into the details of the role-playing and nondominant hand, silent finger-painting dialogues that had taken place in that first fruitless appointment with Howard, and Dr. Gibraltar withdrew his attention and stopped taking notes (his scratching pen went silent). I knew he was punishing me, waiting for me to get to more reasonable material before he was willing to engage with me again.

After Howard and I met with Ellie the second time, when I told Dr. Gibraltar that she had been concerned about my cough and at the end of the hour had given me a CD of James Galway playing that ubiquitous *Echinacea Serenade* you hear in every massage therapist's office, and that I had listened to it over the weekend and I thought it had really helped me get over my bad head cold, he made a doubtful sound in his throat, and I could hear his pen fall onto the rug, where he had dropped it in disgust.

I didn't tell him that Howard had walked out of that fourth appointment, because I knew Dr. Gibraltar would have admired him for doing so, and if he took Howard's side I would have been devastated. It was bad enough that I would have been expected to analyze why I thought he had taken Howard's side, while being stonewalled with the usual "I am a tabula rasa"–inflected interventions such as "How does that make you feel?" and "Where's that coming from?" (It makes me feel that your countertransference is showing again, Doctor, which is always thrilling, but also it makes me feel like crap, and surely you're the one who should know where it's coming from, just check the tags on your own psychodynamic baggage!)

Meanwhile, something I said to Ellie a few weeks into our work together about missing analysis made her think I had terminated my treatment, though Dr. Gibraltar was in fact only away for the month of August (every year he went to Wellfleet with all the other psychoanalysts). I didn't correct her impression at that moment, as I had only been taking a break before getting in touch with my anger at my unavailable father by doing some more screaming and hitting a pillow with a plastic bat, and I didn't want to lose my emotional momentum.

No, that's untrue. I didn't want to admit to her that I was still on Dr. Gibraltar's couch, still working away at the glacially slow process he once called "turning ghosts into ancestors." When we had our first (I thought), hopeful marriage counseling appointment with Ellie, and I made reference to my long and ongoing experience with psychoanalysis, she had gotten a look on her face that was like the expression of a tolerant vegetarian friend to whom you have just mentioned a fantastic steak dinner. So I didn't want to admit to her that I was still seeing him almost every day. Consequently, each of them thought I had come to my senses and stopped seeing the other.

I was committing therapist adultery. But what of it? I could afford it. I had the time. It helped me, and it made me feel more in control during the appointments. It pleased me especially when I was lying on the couch in that beige room with the annoying wrinkled Escher poster that attracted my gaze even when I didn't want to look at it (I get it, we cannot trust our distorted perceptions!) and I would parrot a bit of Ellie's wisdom, and I could feel Dr. Gibraltar's glowing approval of my progress as evidenced by this analytic insight, which was manifest in the way he made his little approval noise, sort of a satisfied chirp, and the way I could hear his pen scratching as he jotted process notes. It was the same set of approval sounds I loved to hear when I rambled through an especially successful interpretation of one of my fabricated dreams. Dr. Gibraltar was obsessed with my dreams. What harm did it do, paying the dream extortionist with counterfeit dreams that delighted us both?

Similarly, when working with Ellie in a feeling session, I would appropriate some of Dr. Gibraltar's interpretations of my personality, blurting them out as if they were my own sudden associative insights in the middle of a process, and Ellie would always tell me she was proud of me and hold me in a particularly loving maternal hug that meant the world to me.

I liked the way this worked. I really miss all that therapy, now that Ellie has moved to Big Sur and Dr. Gibraltar has died. He broke his neck diving into the surf last August, in Wellfleet. I read about it in the *New York Times*. He hit a sandbar. He was seventy-three, and his wife is a social worker who was born in Santiago, Chile, and there were two married daughters and five grandchildren. A secretary called me a week after that to tell me the news and cancel our scheduled post–Labor Day sessions. She said she was a secretary but I knew she was actually one of his daughters. I could hear it in her voice. I let her tell me the sad news in a sensitive, caring way, and I pretended that I didn't already know, because it was the only conversation I was ever going to have with anyone about Dr. Gibraltar's death. I had nobody to tell.

So I miss all that therapy, but also, I do miss that funny private dynamic. My only consolation is a secret little minor habit I have recently developed. Although I have the sturdy Tatnall teeth and gums and I floss regularly, and all of my dental check-ups are quite routine, I have become a patient at three different dental practices, rotating my cleaning appointments among them on a regular schedule. Whenever I go for a cleaning, each of my dental hygienists praises me for my extraordinarily pristine oral hygiene. I like this. And for someone in the candy business, I do have exceptionally good teeth.

STRANGE AS IT seems, when we met to discuss our wedding plans, Rabbi Matt didn't care that I hadn't formally converted, though in those days, when I was under a sweet spell of Ziplinsky enchantment, and grateful to have found this new and better family, I would certainly have done it, gladly and willingly. But Frieda insisted, perversely, that I shouldn't, that it wasn't at all necessary. In retrospect, it was just one more way she tried to keep me out. If I had converted, she wouldn't have been able to hold it against me that I was a Gentile; she wouldn't have been able to be such a martyr to her son's mixed marriage.

My mother chose not to walk down the aisle formed between the few rows of folding chairs on the grass. Howard's best man, Ted Thorntel (his Yale roommate), played Bach's "Bourrée in E Minor" on his guitar as my father walked me stiffly to the front. He left me there with the intimacy of a man dropping a letter in a mailbox, and then he went to sit with my mother somewhere near the back. The ceremony was more bizarre than I realized at the time, as this was my first Jewish wedding, and it wasn't until I accumulated some experience of ordinary Jewish weddings over the years that I realized retrospectively just how flaky and altogether nonstandard ours had been.

When Rabbi Matt pronounced us man and wife, we kissed a little self-consciously, and then Howard stomped on a glass wrapped in a linen napkin. We had debated skipping this ritual, but the rabbi had persuaded us a few hours earlier that it didn't represent the consummation of the marriage so much as it symbolized the unchangeable transformation of the two of us, who would be as permanently altered by the state of marriage as the broken glass would be forever beyond reconstitution. Rabbi Matt, swaying slightly as he stood before us in his off-clean embroidered shirt, offered a final admonition as we faced him. Both of us were trembling and tearful as he told us that our love would be everlasting if we remembered each day to "Sprinkle, sparkle, and do art!"

Howard squeezed my hand tightly and I caught his eye and damp sobs of laughter erupted from both of us at once. Ted picked up his guitar and began to play the recessional music we had chosen, Gershwin's "Love Is Here to Stay." I felt incredible happiness at that moment, as we turned and walked the few yards across the grass between the rows of smiling people, and there it was, like a déjà vu of a déjà vu, the faint lingering notes of a lovely and familiar tune that cannot quite be identified. It was the echo of the burst of inexplicable joy I had felt on that first day at Zip's Candies.

My parents were barely present that afternoon, at the margins of the gathering of perhaps fifty people. Neither of them met or talked with anyone they didn't already know, except when absolutely cornered. Many of the guests on the Ziplinsky side (and most of the guests were on the Ziplinsky side) didn't realize my parents were even there that day. I was Arson Girl friendless; neither of my parents had close family, and they had declined to invite as many guests as they had been offered to by Frieda, who was, to her credit, very gracious about hosting the wedding, even though the family of the groom has no such obligation. It suited her; it gave her the advantage.

There were three black people among the guests. One of them was Minnie, the bright shining light of my childhood, maker of perfect tuna sandwiches, affectionate possessor of the only bosom, and an ample one it was, that I had ever been completely comfortable snuggling against. I hadn't seen her since her retirement a couple of years before. I had glimpsed her wiping her eyes with a big handkerchief as Howard and I walked up the makeshift aisle. I didn't know the others, a well-dressed couple in their early thirties, who had come in during the ceremony and were standing at the back, near my parents. I am ashamed to say I assumed they were Ziplinsky family past or present household employees, since they weren't familiar faces. (Zip's did have several black employees by 1975, but only a few select front-office people had been invited that day.)

As the curiously vile refreshments circulated (a troll in a white uniform kept breaking into groups and thrusting trays of hors d'oeuvres up from below drink level while braying, "Corned beef twist? Miniature knish? The lox on the blinis is very moist!"—I think it's pretty safe to assume my parents ate nothing that day), the distinguished black couple headed purposefully toward us. I felt Howard stiffen, and then he said quietly, "I'll be dipped. Darwin and Miriam are here. I didn't see them. I'm sure my mother didn't think they were coming."

I shouldn't have been so surprised by their skin color. (But then, in retrospect, there is a great deal about which I should have been more observant. *Had I But Known,* the story of my life.) At this time I had heard only a few references, mostly from Sam, about his uncle Julius, Eli's younger brother, the one who stayed behind in Budapest when Eli and the oldest brother, Morris, came to America. Julius was the one who went to Madagascar during World War II and then never left. He had an unlikely and prosperous life there, presiding over his cacao and vanilla plantations until a malaria epidemic killed him, a couple of years before Howard was born. Remember, I had only known the family for three months at this point, and all I knew was what I had gleaned in passing, in fragments. Nobody ever tells you the story of a family in a coherent sequence.

I had heard a few stories about how Howard had spent many summers staying with the Madagascar cousins, mostly weeding around cacao trees and performing menial tasks in the pollination and harvesting of vanilla seed pods. Irene had gone just once and never went back, finding the accommodations too primitive and the work too hard, but it was a really important part of Howard's life growing up. The way this had been described to me in passing made it sound like some sort of fragrant family kibbutz floating out there on that unlikely island in the Indian Ocean.

I gathered that Julius had children, but not until he got to Madagascar, which was why Darwin, his son, was Howard's contemporary, though Darwin was Sam's first cousin. I knew the plantations were still in the family, and that Howard had been on Madagascar in the spring of that same year, just three months before we met, though he said more than once that he should have known better than to go in monsoon season. I wasn't even sure where Madagascar was until Howard told me he had family there, a few weeks into our romance, which prompted me to look it up in the world atlas in my bookshelf at home, where I was still technically living that summer. But until this moment at our wedding, I had simply not considered what these cousins might look like. And so I met Darwin Czaplinsky and his wife, Miriam.

Howard was clearly nonplussed by the sight of them, as their inclusion on the guest list had really been meant only as a gesture, and nobody had expected any of the Madagascar branch of the family to come on such short notice, especially since none of them had replied to the invitation. Darwin was fierce and uncanny-looking, with dark brown skin and deep-set midnight-blue eyes. Miriam was a true Malagasy, exquisitely beautiful in an unidentifiably exotic sense, with a bearing like one of Gauguin's Tahitian women. I would learn later that she was from the Merina people, from the highlands, where Julius had settled among his vast estates.

They were dressed perfectly, better than anyone else there, like diplomats among the native peoples at a rural village festival. As they bore down on us, they both arranged their mouths to reveal their beautiful teeth, and they each looked me hard in the eye as we were introduced. After a moment's hesitation, they each kissed me on both cheeks, French-style. Then they surrounded Howard, pulling him away from me, and I heard Darwin say in his low, precise, accented voice, "Howdy, what have you done?"

Miriam looked at me over Howard's shoulder and said, "You may have the use of him, my dear, but you must never, ever forget that Howdy is ours." She showed me her beautiful teeth again. It wasn't a smile. The bad fairies had come to the wedding party. In a fairy tale, there are warning signs: the sun suddenly goes behind a dark cloud, a chill wind gusts through, frolicking gnomes run away and hide, the tranquil cat puffs herself up and hisses. But this was not a fairy tale, so I didn't recognize the signs, though I do believe I felt a distinct chill.

ONCE HOWARD AND I were married, my parents evidently stopped feeling at risk for further liability consequent to whatever disastrous thing I might do next, which made them much nicer, though there was never more between us than an occasional tiny flicker of fondness. As the years passed my father grew very deaf, and my mother's arthritis worsened, and then when Jacob and Julie were still in grade school my parents retired and moved to a well-regarded continuing-care community in Chapel Hill, south of snowy winters. It was a sensible alternative to Florida, of which they shared an unreasonable horror.

We made a few awkward visits so Julie and Jacob would continue to know their other grandparents, but then came my father's stroke, and then my mother had a heart attack, and they ended up spending their final years in separate wings of the nursing facility at Woodfield Farms, each of them unwilling to make any further effort to deal with the other. According to the social worker there, this turn of events is not entirely uncommon.

And then they died, a few months apart, nine years ago. They left their modest estate to my kids, their grandchildren, in equal shares, which was as it should be, but I have to say I would have liked to have been left some specific personal object by either one of them. When I went through their few and tidy papers, I hoped to find a letter addressed to me. Something, any-thing, personal. But there was nothing like that, just all the very impersonal and efficient legal documents. The year they both died, people who heard my news would try to comfort me with the trite observation that so often in the case of couples who have been married for so many years, when one dies, the other one loses the will to keep living on alone. Usually, I didn't have the heart to disagree. So that's my *mishpochah* of origin, as the Tatnalls never used to say.

It's not the meek who shall inherit the earth. It's the ambi-tious, the passionate! How much love could I be expected to feel for these ungenerous people as the years went by? I don't believe it's just my life among the door-slamming, bellowing Ziplinskys that led me to hope for more, more of anything, from those chilly, murmuring WASPs. Dr. Gibraltar told me I had displaced my unfulfilled desire for their approval (even before they were dead, but especially since their deaths, as after that it was concretely too late for them to come through), onto the living, breathing Ziplinsky family. Is that really what I wanted most of all, Ziplinsky approval? Good luck to me.

Mistakes were made, as Nixon would say. Starting with my guilty plea to the felony arson charge. This was all consequent to the biggest mistake of all, which was my having been represented by Lou Popkin in the first place. Lou was the attorney who handled closings for my father. He had no experience with criminal cases, or much of anything else that didn't have to do with real estate, and had hardly ever appeared in front of a judge. He told me the only way I could stay out of jail for having burned down Debbie Livingston's house was if I just said yes to everything the judge asked me, and he would take care of everything else and not to worry, it was all set, I should just say yes. So that's what I did, I said Yes, and Yes, and Yes, Your Honor, and the next thing I knew I had agreed that I understood the charges, I had admitted to arson, and I had asserted that I felt extreme remorse. Moments later, I was found guilty of third-degree arson, with a suspended sentence and probation. I was a convicted felon. I was Arson Girl. And so I want to take this opportunity to set the record straight about that first fire, before I refute the allegation against me concerning the Zip's fire.

Once again I am involved in an accidental fire. People are so unimaginative. Inevitably, everyone smirks and says, Uh-huh, okay, we see, another fire, another accidental fire like the one that burned down Debbie Livingston's house, what an interesting coincidence, *Arson Girl*. Because only in novels do people accept wild coincidences without comment, let alone skepticism. Maybe it's the fault of all those plotlines on television and in movies (the same ones with music sound tracks that tell you how you're supposed to feel) that depend on coincidences always having a huge amount of meaning, and this makes the audience feel smart and insightful. The truth nobody likes to accept, out of a fear of missing something and being exposed as naive, is that sometimes a coincidence is only one of life's strange repetitions, only a coincidence. It's a funny thing about human nature, the way we resist genuine patterns and meanings, but when events form random patterns, we insist on seeing relationships and adding meanings that aren't really there at all.

THE FIRE THAT burned down Debbie Livingston's house in 1975 is not just old news, it's also new news, and not just because of the Zip's fire last month, but also because two years ago those television news clips were dredged up and aired, when Zip's made the news in the middle of June 2007. That was when Guadalupe and Hilaria Diaz, two Guatemalan sisters on our night cleaning crew (we have found Guatemalans to be very dependable workers in various capacities at Zip's, though when each was hired in the last few years we did not anticipate the collective impact of their religious devotion, which around certain obscure saints' days has required us to plan ahead so as not to disrupt our production schedules, as we were far more focused on issues of counterfeit green cards and false Social Security numbers, and we had to define a benevolent "Don't ask, don't tell" hiring policy for Zip's), attracted a lot of attention when they perceived the Virgin Mary in a concretion of hardened chocolate drippings that had formed under one of the Tigermelt striping nozzles after the line had been shut down for the night.

First Guadalupe sees a dazzling, bright ray of light beaming down on this inexplicable dark object on the belt that she immediately knows in her heart is the Blessed Virgin Mother, and then Hilaria swears on her sainted grandmother's soul that she sees it move, and then they both see a blob of chocolate drip from the nozzle and land perfectly on the Virgin Mary's head, like a halo, which is, of course, a clear sign. (Indeed—a clear sign that someone hasn't emptied and cleaned the striping applicator tank and nozzles per standard operating procedure when the line was shut down for the night. And that celestial ray? Probably a flaring high-intensity ceiling-fixture bulb in the security night-lighting system on the verge of burning out.)

Channel 3 ran the story the next day, a perfectly charming little human-interest segment to cap their six o'clock local news broadcast, the final feature before the local station switches over to the network national newscast, which was certainly a solid hit for Zip's public relations at the community level. We couldn't run the Tigermelt line for three days, not until the Blessed Chocolate Virgin (who looked to me more like a six-inch, poorly tempered chocolate version of the Incredible Hulk than like a divine manifestation, but I did not grow up in a culture that conditioned me to see images of Our Lord Jesus or the Blessed Virgin in every burnt taco or chocolate stalagmite) had hardened sufficiently so she could be carefully sliced off the Tigermelt enrobing belt and moved to a suitable place for preservation and worship. This was done two days later, with much ceremony, under the supervision of Father Carlos Asturias, the elderly priest from the church in Bridgeport to which the Diaz family belongs.

Jacob used a cutting wire to slice the Blessed Chocolate Virgin off the belt cleanly, and I was proud of him and the way he was suitably serious and professional throughout the procedure, maintaining a steady hand and a respectful mien that his father would probably not have been able to muster without cracking wise or smirking in my direction.

For more than thirty years, when things were good between us, I had a huge tolerance for Howard's unwillingness, or constitutional inability, whichever it was, to play the part of a grown-up without breaking character. I don't think Howard has ever appreciated the degree to which the way he behaves has so often undercut his authority at Zip's. I knew this about him before I married him, but I suppose I hoped he would outgrow it. He has that particular form of arrogance that can afflict those who have had all their good fortune handed to them. In inverse proportion to actual achievement, people like Howard crave credit and admiration for having reached the summit. It's definitely caused resentment among some of the most loyal employees over the years. Why would they enjoy taking orders from an idiot prince?

For years, I would have reminded myself at such a moment that Howard was essentially a good man with a good heart, and I would have had myself convinced that his clowning bid for my attention was a harmless signal in our secret code, a symptom of our closeness as a married couple, in the Mrs. Miniver sense of there being always an eye to catch.

But Howard wasn't there that June day two years ago on the floor at Zip's to swagger around his candy kingdom before deftly and casually slicing the Blessed Chocolate Virgin off the Tigermelt belt with his unique blend of competence and irresponsible insouciance, while cracking some joke about how he was just the right man for this job because innate skills for slicing halvah and lox were in his blood. Instead, Zip's was in a secret management crisis, Howard having been in Madagascar for two months at that point, living his true authentic life while a lot of urgent issues gathered like storm clouds over the business. I did all I could, with Jacob shouldering a lot of responsibility, to carry on the day-to-day business without letting anyone know how long Howard had been gone or how unclear it was when, if ever, he would be back. Instead, Jacob, dignified and authoritative at twenty-five, stepped up that day.

I was immensely proud of our son, proud of the way he presided over the situation with an appropriately respectful grace and authority that would have completely eluded Howard. Seeing Jacob take over at that moment, seeing his tender gallantry with the devout Diaz sisters, who hovered anxiously over the operation, I had a sudden revelation about just how corrosive Howard's behavior had been for Zip's. His perpetual undermining wisecracking, which I had tolerated and excused for so long, was demoralizing for everyone. I realized that I was glad Howard wasn't there, and at that moment I knew Zip's Candies would survive, that the business would be okay, better than okay, without him.

We had sufficient Tigermelt stock on hand. Let's face it, Tigermelts are a very small and stable line, which at Zip's is code for stagnant, with an ever-dwindling market share. Because of that one catastrophic new product failure at Zip's, Howard has been especially reluctant to mess with the Tigermelt line in any significant way for years now, even though he knows perfectly well that the only way Zip's can hope to hold our place in our little niche (since we can't possibly compete with the big companies and their multimillion-dollar advertising budgets and endlessly deep pockets for slotting fees) would be with modest forays into brand extensions. And of course, while we hardly like to admit it, and don't reveal this publicly as a matter of both corporate pride and industry confidentiality, it is the contract manufacturing of those two energy bars that has kept our lights burning these past few years.

So the briefly suspended Tigermelt line didn't hurt us. It would have been a very different story if this had occurred in the run-up to Halloween, but June isn't a big candy season, though God knows we need a few more occasions and holidays in the year that trigger candy consumption the way Halloween and Easter do. I am convinced there has got to be some way to penetrate the Fourth of July market much more deeply, for example. Consider what you buy at the grocery store for the Fourth of July: hot dogs and hamburgers, buns, ketchup, mustard, pickles, chips, soda and beer, ice cream and cookies, maybe watermelon—but where's the candy? There's no specific tradition for it. So that's a lost opportunity. There is an enviable reflex to reach for a Hershey's bar when you buy s'mores ingredients, but that's about it. Tootsie Roll, among others, does a Fourth of July wrapper, but I'm not sure that in itself is sufficient to create an association for the consumer.

We do well enough with theater box sales for summer movies, but it's diffuse, not pegged to a specific holiday. Oddly enough, we also do really well with the back-to-school season, especially if the heat of summer doesn't linger. Something about autumn leaves and crisp new notebooks and sharpened pencils seems to inspire the purchasing of Tigermelts and Little Sammies. Possibly it is a strong season for all the older brands, like ours, like Mary Jane, like Baby Ruth, because of a semiconscious nostalgia for their own childhood experiences on the part of parents. Or perhaps candy sweetens the loss of summer's freedom. In any case, it didn't hurt us to shut down the Tigermelt line for a few days.

Who knows, the Blessed Chocolate Virgin could have been the trigger for a whole new market for Tigermelts among the Central American immigrant population, if the company had ever been willing to spend more than a few begrudging nickels on promotions of any kind (you have to go back to the 1960s to see good Zip's merchandising), let alone creative marketing. "Strike while the iron is hot" are words that might as well be in Esperanto when it comes to our small-minded distributors, who are both satisfied with the status quo for accounts like ours and at the same time have bigger fish to fry, so to speak.

That reminds me of how desirable I have long thought it would be if we could find a way to inspire, to incentivize (as we say in the business, with apologies to Miss Solomon, who hated vulgar words like *finalize* and *incentivize*) country fairs and carnivals to feature fried Tigermelts along with all those fried Milky Way and Three Musketeers bars. I've done a little testing with Tigermelts, and as is true for Milky Way and Three Musketeers, the bars have to go into the batter frozen, and then they should be fried for no longer than two and a half minutes or you end up with fried goo. In Scotland the big thing is fried Mars bars, sometimes offered in chip shops, dessert to go with your fish and chips, and I am certain they freeze them as well, given that nougat and caramel core.

None of our distributors is willing to think through any of the possibilities for increasing the numbers on Little Sammies, Mumbo Jumbos, and Tigermelts with imaginative promotions. If I could clone myself, this was one of the times I would have worked the phones, to make the most of the Blessed Chocolate Virgin, and if I had felt more comfortable in my de facto role as head of the business at that time, I might have tried to get going with a fast production of a Limited-Edition Zip's Blessed Chocolate Virgin, using the Little Sammies production line, with a molded figure replicating that holy object sent by God to Zip's Candies, here on Earth, in New Haven, Connecticut, at the edge of the Quinnipiac River, to blorp out of that striping nozzle onto the Tigermelt belt.

We are long overdue, to the point of real negligence, to find some room in the budget for a Spanish-language campaign with print ads, bus cards, urban street-level billboards—and this would have been our golden opportunity. But we were just treading water as it was at that time, and that was before Channel 8's ambush, so there was really no chance for Zip's to cash in on the Blessed Chocolate Virgin.

And so, Zip's being Zip's, the whole Blessed Chocolate Virgin moment was only good for some meaningless local color news coverage and temporary fodder for those lunatics who apparently sit at their computers all day long and post constantly in the comments area on the strange fan blog devoted to Little Sammies that Julie monitors (she tells me the bloggers call themselves a community), and we got no bump, not even a discernable blip, on our Tigermelt numbers for that quarter.

And we probably lost any chance we had for Tigermelt traction from the Chocolate Blessed Virgin not just because of our trademark inertia (there's an idea—we really should make a Zip's Inertia bar, a glucose-saturated bar guaranteed to zap your glycemic index and keep you sedentary, unproductive, and ambition-free, and market it to the burnt-out middle management worker), but also because of what happened with Frieda when the busload of Guatemalan nuns from Queens arrived to see the Blessed Chocolate Virgin.

I was supervising the floor, with two lines running, and Jacob was trying to cover both the front office and Receiving. Jacob was on the loading dock arguing with the delivery guy for our sugar supplier about some ripped bags and consequent moisture dam-age and waste in the previous delivery. Julie had called in to say she was working from her apartment, which is code for too depressed and disorganized to get up and get dressed, I am sorry to say.

It was one of Frieda's good days, so instead of being at home expressing her contempt for one of the extraordinarily patient home health aides we employed in thankless eight-hour shifts to keep her out of trouble and to make it possible for her to keep liv-ing in the house she and Sam shared for the last forty years of their fifty-two years together, she was on the premises, in the old, little-used bookkeeper's office down at the end near the factory door. There she could spend an hour or two zealously date-stamping stacks of old, now-meaningless invoices from the 1980s in a kinetic parody of the actual work she did at Zip's for so many decades before that well-tempered mind grew softer and duller, losing its snap and gloss. I have a mental picture of what hap-pened to Frieda's brain as it gradually lost its deep crenellations and became smoother and smoother and duller and duller, like what happens to the Tigermelts when there's a pileup on the belt running through the enrober and some bars get stalled under the nozzles and become heavily overcoated.

Five years ago, Frieda's loosening grasp of reality forced us to maneuver her gradual withdrawal from any genuine responsibilities at Zip's. Irene knew about this shift, and she cer-tainly knew about her mother's faltering mental state, so it is hardly legitimate for her now to characterize the way her mother was treated as a power grab on my part. Irene knew what we were dealing with. It was very clear at the time that the only interest she had in the management issues at Zip's was her uninterrupted income. Those who did all the work continued to do all the work. Those who sat back and cashed checks continued to sit back and cash checks.

We carefully eased Frieda out of the daily workings of the business inch by inch. It helped with the transition to set her up on her good days with something familiar to do, though the tasks grew smaller and smaller until they were only gestures, and then finally they had no meaning at all. At times it took a lot of effort to make her feel useful, but it was the right thing to do. Even with Howard AWOL, I wanted to do everything I could to see to it that she was welcome to come in when she was up to it, no matter how much energy it took to accommodate her, until the incident with the nuns. Are these the actions of a gold digger?

On those good days, after checking in with her keeper to see what kind of night it had been, Jake would go pick her up at her house in Westville (he carried a milk crate in the back of his Jeep so she could step up to climb into the seat), drive her to Zip's, park in the visitor's lot, and walk her in the front entrance (instead of parking out back and going in through the loading dock area as he would otherwise begin his workday). Then he and I would arrange everything for her, the way you would organize a busywork activity to harness the energies of a competent toddler visiting an office, with a few tall stacks of old useless paperwork that had been set aside for recycling and the big, heavy chrome date stamp we used to use for logging invoices, and she would go to work.

THE NUNS WERE just two hours too late. Renee Cohen, the front-office manager (she's my age and has been with us seventeen years, and for just one small example of the way we treat our employees like family, I'll mention that in 1996 Zip's helped her with a low-interest loan for the down payment on her little Cape in Short Beach), politely told them they had missed it, and explained that the Blessed Chocolate Virgin had left with Father Asturias and was by now presumably ensconced in the church in Bridgeport, where they could go see it. The nuns just milled around uncomprehendingly in our dingy reception area, though the ones with sufficient English were tearful. You would think that the Blessed Chocolate Virgin had been scraped into the trash instead of transported to Bridgeport to be worshipped and venerated, but apparently they had their hearts set on seeing the miracle in the place where it had occurred.

Renee had wisely paged me off the floor, and I had just invited them into the factory for a quick, consoling glimpse of the actual Tigermelt striping apparatus from which the holy object had been extruded, when Frieda, having either completed or lost interest in her morning's task, came shuffling down the hall. She got one look at the nuns and began shouting that they couldn't set foot in her factory, it would violate hygiene regulations, those dirty habits could catch on the machinery or spread germs, she would call the health department herself, they all had to leave, no tours, no tours, no exceptions, get out of here, all of you, go in your *schvartze shmattas,* vamoose!

As I signaled to them to disregard her and keep following me, she became agitated and yelled at them, Ignore her! That woman is not family! She has no authority here; she is just summer help! Then she ran out of steam and just stood there in the doorway to Howard's office, panting and looking pitiful, trying to catch her breath after her strenuous shouting. Sam, where is Sam? Sam? Howdy? Where's Dad? Howdy! She kept calling out, looking around in a new kind of panicky confusion that was the herald of further deterioration. This was the last day we ever had her come in to "work" at Zip's.

Frieda wouldn't let me touch her, let alone steer her to a chair, and fortunately her beloved Jakie arrived on the scene at this point. I tried to coax the nuns past her and down the hall to the factory doors while he strong-armed his grandmother into Howard's office, but they were frightened and confused, and clearly troubled by her indignant muffled cries, so they fled in the opposite direction, to the sidewalk out front. I followed them to their bus and gave their driver directions to the church in Bridgeport, and the driver waited while I ran back in so I could fill a bag with Tigermelts, Mumbo Jumbos, and Little Sammies to sweeten their disappointment.

ALL OF THIS is to say that the Zip's Blessed Chocolate Virgin story would have played out quickly, if not for that damned producer at Channel 8, who apparently had a mother who recognized me—Arson Girl!—in the Channel 3 report for which I was taped out in front of Zip's (we don't allow photographs of anything on the floor, because, no joke, this is how the competition can figure out how you do what you do), unwrapping a Tigermelt and explaining to that idiot reporter, whatever her name is, the one who looks like a guppy and dresses like a flight attendant, who kept calling me Alice Zip instead of Alice Ziplinsky and then she overcorrected and referred to Ziplinsky's Candies instead of Zip's as she ended the interview, so they had to do the whole segment over again, twice, which was surely not my fault (she got very irritable with me), and I had to unwrap two more Tigermelts while explaining each time in the same way how a combination bar is made and how the Tigermelt bar gets that final signature dark-chocolate tiger stripe from the nozzles from which dripped the little chocolate miracle.

The producer's mother had lived on that same block on

Canner Street and had been friendly with Mrs. Livingston. And so, when Channel 8 ran their catch-up story the next evening, featuring Father Asturias entering his Bridgeport church in a solemn procession with the Blessed Chocolate Virgin carried aloft behind him, it was heralded by a teaser promising an exclusive shocking surprise revelation about how a member of the prominent (in New Haven, maybe) Zip's Candies family, Alice Tatnall Ziplinsky, had a dark history (those were the words, *dark history,* which sound now, as I write them, almost pleasingly bitter, like dark chocolate) and a criminal record.

And then, not that it had anything whatsoever to do with the Blessed Chocolate Virgin story, after maybe only ten seconds (at most, for all that fuss and bother) of me squinting into the camera and unwrapping a Tigermelt and explaining the dark-chocolate tiger stripe all over again for the Channel 8 reporter the way I had done it for Channel 3, there was footage of the 1975 fire that burned down the Livingston residence on Canner Street, and guess what? Arson Girl, so called because she pleaded guilty to this terrible crime of arson and yet she never served a day in jail, what about that? She grew up to be a member of the prominent Zip's Candies family! Are your children consuming candy made by a convicted criminal? Several people interviewed on the street expressed their determination not to buy candy made by felons. And now, in other news.

The shock of that unexpected exposure gave me a sick, punched feeling in my gut. Just remembering it now, I am feeling waves of nausea all over again. (I have never liked the word *prominent*. It always means more than it means.) I have felt that kind of panicky free-fall horror only a few times in my life. The day of the fire, the day of the sentencing, the day I got the letter from Middlebury telling me to never mind. Life has been much kinder to me for a long while, with many joyful experiences, and it was not until the dawning of the whole truth about Howard's other life in Madagascar that I felt such blackness again.

I certainly had a doomy feeling the day I first saw Frieda exhibit symptoms of dementia and had to admit to myself what I had known for a while, that she was losing it, but I suppose that was a different shade of black, in the pantheon of my darkest moments. Our relationship was always tricky, and she made it hard for me to love her, but there was something really admirable in her toughness and her loyalty to the family, and to the business, even though she was pretty hard on me over the years. She did soften a little toward me after Jacob and Julie were born (I once overheard her telling one of her Hadassah cronies that the problem with me was that I was a dumb goy with two smart Jewish children). Given that my purpose in these pages is to say everything I can about Zip's Candies and to give history and background to establish my knowledge of the facts about the current issues, and given that every piece of Ziplinsky family history is also Zip's Candies history, and also given that I have just described an instance of Frieda's dementia that was potentially harmful to the business, I might as well describe that first incident now, given that Frieda's behavior in her final years could have exposed Zip's to very damaging liabilities, for which I could have been blamed.

I documented this incident at the time, seven years ago. I was helping with a pour and blend for a big batch of Tigermelt nougat. People are amazed at how much is still done by hand at Zip's. Creating the necessary machinery to automate some of these functions on the line would cost a fortune, and our batches are so small, it just wouldn't pay to automate each of these steps unless it was part of a bigger plan to increase production and distribution in a substantial way. And it could be surprisingly difficult to get it right, to create efficient machines that would duplicate precisely every step of the unique processes that are integral to production on our three lines.

Ironically enough, Tigermelts contain no butter. We all know what happened to the competitive tigers in *Little Black Sambo*— "they all just melted away, and there was nothing left but a great big pool of melted butter . . . round the foot of the tree." For the Tigermelt centers, when the marshmallow nougat (a proprietary blend of egg whites, sucrose, and corn syrup) and the caramel (dried milk solids, sucrose, molasses, and vanilla) are cooled to just the right temperatures in their blending pots, they are then poured and swirled together in a partial blend, not a fifty-fifty blend, more like seventy-thirty, with more nougat than caramel, and then the hot fried peanuts are stirred in. This all takes both physical strength and coordination and also really specific timing, so it requires teamwork. You are rushing to beat the clock as you blend this beige goop just a certain amount in a very precise way, on a big, sinklike batch table.

Time and temperature are two key ingredients in every candy line. Time and temperature, Sam used to say, they're your friend, or they're your enemy. If you don't control the time and the temperature, you will have no quality control, you may ruin your product, and you will never have a smooth-running line. You have to own the time and the temperature, or the time and the temperature will own you. Eli cared about tempering, and it was a point of pride for Sam that Zip's Candies has always had a high standard for well-tempered chocolate, and it is a feature of the Tigermelt coating. Tempering is chocolate alchemy, mechanical manipulation plus precise heat in order to force chocolate into the desirable crystalline form so that when it is properly cooled it forms a stable solid with a smooth and shiny surface.

When the Tigermelt center mixture is sufficiently blended

and cooled, you have only about a seven-minute window to stir in the hot fried peanuts. It has to happen at just the right time as the temperature of the mixture cools, so the peanuts are blended all the way through the nougat, so they get mixed in with the caramel swirls instead of sinking too quickly or failing to penetrate and getting stuck all bunched together on the surface, which creates enrobing problems and leads to misshapen bars. (It's like baking *shmura* matzo; to prevent inadvertent leavening, within eighteen minutes the flour and water have to be mixed, the dough has to be kneaded and rolled, and the matzo has to go into the oven.) The average number of peanuts in a Tigermelt is twenty-eight. Other than Baby Ruth, I defy you to name another combination bar with national distribution that has such a high proportion of whole peanuts. (Not peanut halves or pieces, whole peanuts.)

It's simple enough, but if the blending isn't done correctly it throws off the texture and the consistency of the Tigermelt bar. Most popular combination bars are made of these same ingredients and the same inclusions, more or less, in varying proportions and consistencies. What gives each bar its unique flavor and texture are the recipes—the established proportions and protocols that guarantee predictable results and uniformity, batch to batch. When you take a bite of an Oh Henry!, a Baby Ruth, or a Tigermelt, you know what to expect. That's what makes you take your favorite candy bar off the rack at the supermarket checkout and put it on the belt with your grocery order week after week, even though you would never write it on your shopping list.

Your mouth and taste buds have their own kind of sense memory. You have a deep, semiconscious anticipation and desire based on experience for what's going to hit your tongue and your teeth first, and then what happens after that, how it's going to blend when you bite down and start to chew and the flavor hits the roof of your mouth and then the back of your throat as you begin to swallow. If there is no consistency to the consistency, then there is nothing on which to build loyalty. And loyalty is a fundamental key to success in selling candy bars, along with creating in you, the consumer, certain deep feelings of desire, cravings that can be reinforced and triggered in calculated ways by branding and advertising.

Loyalty is the key. The successful candy bar is supported by a consumer belief that he or she is honoring family traditions, so that loyalty is all bound up with nostalgia for childhood experiences either actual or longed-for. Ideally, too, the consumer has a sense of entitlement to self-indulgence driven by an ambivalence toward guilty pleasure. I mention all these things because my knowledge and experience in the candy manufacturing business in general, and with Zip's Candies in particular, should be above question, but they have been questioned, so it seems necessary for me to provide ample evidence that will establish my credibility in these matters.

To give one more example of my role in the business over the years, Sam told me many times that I was a smart cookie for advising him long ago that Zip's could do better at Easter, a holiday with which I had personal experience. Consequently, Zip's Candies ended up in more Easter promotions and in more Easter baskets. I loved being able to provide that valuable insight. I love the candy business.

So, THE MOMENT: Frieda, who was kibitzing as usual, telling everyone to hurry up or be careful or slow down and then hurry up, the way she always did, suddenly went quiet, which was, for her, unusual. We finished the pours, without her customary admonition about squeezing out the last caramel sludge from inside the nozzle so as not to be wasteful, and then I looked across at her in time to glimpse an expression of confusion sweep across her face, as if she didn't quite know where she was, as she backed away from the batch table. She immediately bumped against a rolling rack that holds the wooden mogul trays for Mumbo Jumbos, but the rack, being empty, this not being a Mumbo Jumbo day, wasn't chocked, so it rolled back, causing her to lose her balance a little. Then Frieda took another step back, and now she was at the edge of a worktable against the wall. All this happened in just an instant, a few seconds, and it was really nothing, but some tiny sense that there was something wrong kept me watching her. Sally Fernstein, one of the steadiest line workers at Zip's, passed just then, pushing a stack of Tigermelt wrapper boxes on a dolly, and she eyed Frieda quizzically, also sensing something awry, then looked over at me with a raised eyebrow.

On the worktable behind Frieda was a coffee can (Maxwell House, I can see the blue can with that tilted cup in my mind's eye even now) filled with small pliers and wrenches, greasy bolts and brads, pins and washers and screws, and stubs of little pencils, along with some pushpins and a couple of rolls of electrical tape and little springs and hinges and coils of wire and who knows what else. That can of essentials was part of our arsenal for keeping the ancient equipment chugging along for one more day (and of course it shouldn't have been anywhere near an active production line, but hardly a day passes when something isn't being tightened up or readjusted, if not flat-out jury-rigged, at some point in the shift).

Just as Petey Leventhal (who came to Zip's in 1978, when Cadbury took over Peter Paul in Naugatuck) returned on cue, lugging the ten-gallon stainless-steel pail of hot fried peanuts and calling out, "Hot soup! Hot soup!" over the factory din the way he always did to clear his path to the batch table from our medieval-looking peanut fryer (it's a repurposed vat originally designed for use in a poultry processing plant, when freshly electrocuted chickens are dipped briefly into boiling water to loosen the feathers before being processed through the plucking machine), I saw Frieda pick up the coffee can and peer blankly at the contents.

As Petey poured the peanuts into the mixture and I began stirring with a big wooden mixing paddle that looks like a small rowboat oar, and then Petey set down the empty pail and picked up his paddle and began stirring even more vigorously, Frieda (who should have been dabbing at the mixture by now as well with the third paddle), as if mimicking his gesture of pouring out the peanuts a moment before, emptied the contents of the coffee can into the mix in one big sweeping motion. Out of this cornucopia of hardware remnants came a cascade of nuts and bolts and screws and springs and cogs, all instantly deployed in a perfect parabolic wave across the surface of the peanut-studded Tigermelt nougat and caramel mixture. The metal pieces sank down and were instantly and inextricably bound into the cooling sweet and chewy, salty (we salt the fried peanuts) and crunchy secret blend that gives Tigermelts their irresistibly delicious Tigermelt taste. Most people can taste this core of the bar and recognize the Tigermelt identity instantly, even before the two applications of enrobing milk chocolate and the final dark-chocolate signature tiger stripe have been applied.

Why on earth did I do that? Frieda murmured under her breath before walking away from the batch table, still holding the empty coffee can. Petey and I just stood there for a moment and watched the shrapnel glistening in the blend, stupefied. Both of us had kept stirring for one more moment, as if keeping on with our routine could in some way override the reality of what had just happened. We had to shut down and throw away that entire batch, of course, and sterilize the batch table. When I told Howard what Frieda had done (he had been out on the Yale golf course with a grocery-chain buyer from New Jersey most of that afternoon), he laughed it off, and went around the rest of the day singing an adaptation of that pernicious and effective Peter Paul jingle, so his version was about how sometimes you feel like a nut, sometimes a bolt. But we both knew it was a turning point, even if no one ever said another word about that incident.

AND TO FINISH about that ambush of a Channel 8 evening news report on the Blessed Chocolate Virgin story two years ago, by the time the eleven o'clock report rolled around, they had expanded their coverage. Having broadcast teasers for the story in the little newsbreaks between commercials all during prime time, they led off with a breathless intro about a developing story uncovered by their team of investigative reporters. I kept expecting my phone to ring at any moment with a call from a friend, a family member, an employee, but either nobody had caught it or everyone had.

The piece began with the Zip's Blessed Chocolate Virgin story recap, with a good exterior shot of Zip's and a few words from the generally incoherent Diaz sisters, then there I was with the Tigermelt, followed by a nice little sidewalk interview with Jacob about the history of the family business, and then came some footage of the procession into the church, led by Father Asturias, with the Blessed Chocolate Virgin on a platter, held aloft by a throng of worshippers. This was followed by a dramatic candlelit glimpse of the Blessed Chocolate Virgin safely ensconced in a place of honor inside Saint Thomas's, on her own blue velvet altar. Then the story shifted back to 1975 and there were dramatic captions and dramatic scenes of the blazing Livingston house, ornamented by useless streams of water pouring from the firemen's hoses into the smoke and flames.

They cut to overexposed daytime courthouse exterior footage, and there I am, a zombie of a teenager in a peasant blouse and a denim skirt, my tear-blotched face masked by a huge pair of sunglasses that aren't mine, my unruly hair bunched into an indifferent ponytail, shuffling in Dr. Scholl's wooden sandals into the courthouse under a harsh glare that is probably a combination of relentless summer sunshine and the bright lights of the news cameras. I am flanked by my grim, squinting parents (they are willing to appear supportive in public) and our lawyer, the hapless Lou Popkin, with those sideburns, sweltering in his regrettable orange corduroy suit with the pointy lapels (he will commit suicide a couple of years later, for no apparent cause), and suddenly this stupid thing I did by accident a lifetime ago, when I was a child, something having nothing whatsoever to do with Zip's Candies or the Blessed Chocolate Virgin, this rancid and bitter piece of the past, becomes inexorably blended into the present.

I KNOW I will never be able to clear my name completely. I will always be Arson Girl, and nothing can be done about that. I am especially sorry that Julie and Jacob have to live with it. I can only say once again that while my actions did cause that house to burn down, I was a foolish high school kid, and it was an unpremeditated, freakish accident for which I was then and am now truly sorry. (I am not entirely sorry about the Zip's fire, which I know I probably shouldn't admit, but my willingness to admit that I am not entirely sorry should be in my favor, because of what it says about my willingness to be completely truthful and honest about my statements pertaining to Zip's Candies.)

How was I to know that water pistol had charcoal lighter fluid in it? How was I to know Beth Crabtree's father always lit their barbecue that way? That's really stupid and dangerous, when you think about it. Yet he was never charged with reckless endangerment or whatever. I only took the water gun for a joke.

State of mind is important in the eyes of the law. I recall with perfect clarity my state of mind. When I saw the transparent red plastic Luger lying on the windowsill in the Crabtrees' kitchen, as I waited by the back door while Beth lied to her mother about what movie we were going to see, I picked it up, and feeling that it was loaded—what else but water should it have been filled with, I ask you?—I slid it into my fringed, patchwork shoulder bag, which I had bought on Eighth Street on a day trip to New York's Greenwich Village with a group of girls from my class a few months before. It was a spontaneous gesture, with no more than a second of premeditation before I took it, if that. (And no, I did not smell the lighter fluid, hard as that may be to believe.)

Why did I take it? I can never answer this question satisfactorily enough. Just on an impulse, to be silly, to whip it out at some point later that night as a joke. My mother used an old water pistol to discourage a neighbor's cat who liked to dig in our flower beds and shit all over her penstemon. If I had really planned only to use a water gun as a joke, the assistant district attorney, Kevin what'shisname, kept asking triumphantly, why hadn't I taken that water gun from my home? Which only proves that this was a spontaneous act, my taking the loaded water gun off the Crabtrees' windowsill, wouldn't you think? I had no plan!

What did I have in mind? Absolutely nothing. Yes, it is true that at Debbie Livingston's party I anticipated that I was likely to encounter Andy Ottenberg, who had developed a nasty habit of mocking me cruelly when I was at my most heartfelt and impassioned. He had done this all through our senior year at every opportunity. He was the managing editor of the school paper, for which I wrote an excruciatingly pretentious advice column called "Go Ask Alice." But I had no plan. And it really didn't feel like theft of a potentially lethal weapon. It was just a plastic water pistol.

After Beth's mother told us to have fun at our movie (we told her we were going to see *Dog Day Afternoon*), we headed over to Debbie Livingston's house, where there were no parents, because Mr. and Mrs. Livingston thought their little darling was still the sweet innocent who not so long ago dressed as a bumblebee three Halloweens in a row. They had no idea that these days she was famous not for her imaginative costume skills but for her imaginative and dexterous approach to certain skills of sexual manipulation, which she provided willingly to a select group of the most popular senior boys, and her parents had definitely never heard her personal motto, "It isn't a sin if you don't put it in." Mr. and Mrs. Livingston thought they had no worries at all that night, since Debbie had told them she would do homework and feed the cat, and maybe her best friend, Mara, would sleep over and they might watch some television before bedtime; meanwhile her parents should have a super great time in the city. So off they went to New York, for dinner and a musical and then an overnight stay at the Plaza Hotel. It was their wedding anniversary.

I FINALLY SAW *Dog Day Afternoon* on television one night when I was up late with Julie, who was a colicky infant who frequently needed to be held and rocked and soothed. Howard had gone to bed because he had work in the morning. (I took six months maternity leave for Jacob, and for Julie, but in fact both times I was back at Zip's before that, working a few hours a week, wearing my baby in a sling.) Watching Al Pacino grow more and more frantic as he realizes he has no good way out of the bank he is trying to rob, I found myself growing more and more regretful that Beth Crabtree and I hadn't just gone to see the movie to which we claimed to be headed, out by the mall. We would have shared a giant tub of popcorn, watched the movie, and gone home. I would have spent four years at Middlebury College, and today I would be a college graduate with many friends doing who knows what, living who knows where, and if I were to attend my Middlebury reunions nobody would call me Arson Girl.

Perhaps Beth Crabtree and I might have remained good friends over all these years. But we never spoke again after that night. If we had gone to the movie we said we were going to see, the Livingstons would have come home from New York the following day to find their spacious, five-bedroom, neo-Colonial house with its attached two-car garage and its overgrown rhododendrons pretty much as they left it, with no discernable trace of yet another of Debbie's very popular, unauthorized, parent-free parties. The Livingstons would not have returned to the Plaza after their show in a festive mood (they had a pretheater dinner at Mamma Leone's and saw *Chicago,* I read in their statements) to find four urgent messages from the New Haven Police Department, and they would not have driven back to New Haven at top speed in a panic after midnight, and they would not have returned to Canner Street to find a smoldering, blackened, three-story neo-Colonial husk surrounded by blackened rhododendron skeletons, with three fire engines still churning, police cruisers with flashing lights parked all over the street, barricades at both ends of their block, and disembodied radio-dispatcher voices squawking occasionally from the dashboards into the hot, smoky night air. I saw them arrive. I was in the back seat of one of the police cruisers, although I had not yet been arrested.

If Beth Crabtree and I had gone to see *Dog Day Afternoon* that night, then poor old Homer, Debbie Livingston's ancient orange cat, would not have been found dead three days later, wedged up high in a tree in a neighbor's yard, his severely charred tail tangled in the branches. Accidental incineration of a beloved pet is not a crime in the state of Connecticut, but it is a terrible, terrible crime. If I were Debbie Livingston, I wouldn't have forgiven me either.

THAT NIGHT IN the Livingstons' backyard, when he saw me come through the gate with Beth, Andy Ottenberg said something to the group of his friends with whom he was standing around a rusty and tilted three-legged barbecue grill, which was very close to the side of the house, right by the back steps that led up to the kitchen door. I know this sounds middle-aged and suburban and unlikely for a bunch of high school kids, but that is what they were doing. I have a very clear recollection of the way the grill surface was entirely covered with sizzling hot dogs, and there were several washtubs of ice beside the grill, filled with beer and soda cans, with more packages of hot dogs piled on top, and there were packages of buns on a card table, next to big bowls of potato chips and a stack of paper plates and napkins. I absolutely love hot dogs, and I remember distinctly feeling too self-conscious to be observed eating one at that party, although I was instantly hungry after my first whiff of that alluring, greasy smoke.

The boys around the grill all snickered and turned to look at me and I heard somebody say the words *tits* and *bitch* as Beth and I approached. If Andy had ever sincerely liked me, the feelings had curdled and gone rancid long before this night, and his merciless teasing had become painfully personal and barbed, it is true. I have never denied that.

"What did you just say?" I demanded of Andy, who was leaning one-handed with a studied casual air against the side of the Livingstons' house, chugging beer from a bottle. Maybe he was a little drunk. Maybe they all were. I was so self-righteous! Why did I care so much? Possibly I was already resenting my self-imposed hot dog deprivation. "What were you saying about me?"

"I said everybody knows you're a bitch because you're sexually frustrated," Andy said with a smirk, putting his beer down on the ground so he could thrust the curved end of the barbecue tongs up and down through circled fingers in a lewd and monkeyish gesture. His friends erupted in knowing laughter again. "You want some of this, tat for tits?" he added. (And you question why I took the name Ziplinsky gladly and willingly, so happy was I to be done with my tainted Tatnall name.)

And that's when it happened, in an instant. I lost my temper. I had turned away, but then I turned back toward Andy and took a step forward, swinging my shoulder bag at him in frustration and anger, and some embarrassment. He ducked, and I missed, but my bag, which was weighted with makeup; a thick, dog-eared paperback of *The Moonstone* by Wilkie Collins; my wallet and keys; the loaded water pistol; and a hardcover copy of *Slaughterhouse-Five* (from the New Haven Public Library, which many months later began to send me a series of importuning letters about this overdue book until finally, without telling me, Howard very gallantly went there one autumn day and paid for the lost book in order to stop the letters), flew off my shoulder and out of my grasp. It hit the barbecue grill, which tipped over in a shower of sparks, scattering white-hot coals and all those hot dogs on the flagstones, and then there was an enormous *whomp* of an explosion.

In an instant, the side of the Livingstons' house was a blue sheet of flames. Was this a nightmare? Time stopped and started again, and then everyone was shouting in the yard, and someone started screaming inside the house, and the sheet of flame grew and spread, the front line of inexorable flame advancing on a tide of curling, blackening, burning, melting vinyl siding. Wisps of lacy black smoke leaked along the edges of the siding in lengthening tendrils that curled together and knotted the air with a thickening haze. Now billows of poisonous black smoke poured from behind the siding, sifting through the seams, as another and another segment softened and smeared and then melted.

Smudgy plumes leaked around the edges of the kitchen window frame for a long moment before that, too, burst into flames as it was engulfed in the upward melting tide that advanced up the side of the house in a sheet of thin blue flame. Acrid black smoke was now pouring thickly from several places at once as the fire spread across the wall of the house and ate its way up toward the roof.

Everyone was screaming and shouting, and kids came pouring out of the house coughing and gagging and crying as the house filled with clouds of choking black smoke, and the flames spread unbelievably fast. And then the inside of the house was completely on fire, and windows were breaking, and the sound of the fire was ferocious as it roared and consumed everything; now the roof was on fire, and the scorching heat coming off the house was like an invisible wall that kept pushing everyone back, back, back.

Big black flakes wafted through the air, hideous confetti, some still glowing with a rill of toxic flame at their edges, and they floated up and down and up and down on the weirdly billowing hot air that surrounded us, before landing in the trees and on the parked cars with a festive glow, leaving faint scorch marks. Everyone standing there gaping and screaming and crying and shouting had to dodge and dance out of the way as these enormous glowing flakes of bitter ash rained down.

The police and the fire trucks arrived after what seemed like hours but was in fact nine and a half minutes from the first 911 call (not a great response time, really, now that I think about it as a tax-paying home owner), and I stood across the street with everyone watching the house burn while Beth Crabtree stared at me in horror, saying again and again, "Oh my God! What did you do? Oh my God, Alice! Your life is over! Oh my God!" until I told her to shut up, could she please just shut up, and she did. She left me and went to stand with the other kids, and then some parents began to arrive, and I was alone, and I could feel everyone looking at me.

3

FRIEDA OBVIOUSLY THOUGHT I was trouble from that very first day I walked in the door at Zip's Candies. She couldn't keep her beautiful son away from me; she couldn't even keep her unbeautiful husband from being charmed and amused by me right from the start. She recognized these defeats, but she never let me win her over completely, though she permitted numerous temporary small victories, which was, in its own subtle way, deceptive and controlling.

When Howard told his parents we wanted to get married at the end of that summer, they were having dinner at Kaysey's, their downtown favorite in those days (Frieda loved the big, high, red leatherette booths, which reminded her of sophisticated New York places like Sardi's, and Sam loved the potato pancakes with applesauce). Howard told me that Sam was elated, which irked Frieda considerably. "If you don't marry that girl, I will!" was probably not a good thing to say in Frieda's earshot, even if he didn't mean it literally.

Howard reported to me that his mother had sighed heavily and would only say she knew this was coming, knew it from her first glimpse of me in that ridiculous ice cream *shmatta,* when she should have recognized me as that scheming Arson Girl from the newspapers, a part of my résumé that I had failed to disclose to Sam, and perhaps I could fool everyone else, but not Frieda. She knew trouble when she saw it.

Although Frieda didn't want me to convert, as I have already mentioned (and how deeply strange is that, seriously?), I really tried to embrace the Ziplinskys and their beliefs. Which turned out to be my beliefs about their beliefs. I studied all aspects of the Jewish religion, all the rules and meanings. The more I learned, the more confusing it was, because nothing I could find in a book ever precisely matched the Ziplinsky methods for observing Jewish tradition. Were they Reform? Were they Reconstructionists? Howard was useless, because though he found my efforts touching, he would just laugh at my questions and say, "How the hell should I know?" even though he'd had a bar mitzvah, to please both his grandmothers.

Howard was much better versed in the quirky Malagasy *fady* taboos in some of the small villages on Madagascar, especially in the south. Even more nuanced than the Ziplinsky family definitions of kosher law, the *fady* beliefs varied from one village to the next. Here, it might be *fady* to touch chameleons, which could bring misfortune, there, it is *fady* to mention crocodiles. The prohibition of wearing red clothing was a common *fady*. All over the island there are certain *fady* rivers and streams in which one must never swim because they harbor evil spirits. There are *fady* days of the week on which one must never, ever, work, but those, too, varied from one village to the next. A deeply entrenched *fady* tradition the Madagascar government has been working to prohibit is the abandonment or separation of twins. When, during one of Howard's idyllic summers, the cat belonging to one of the kitchen workers on the vanilla plantation gave birth to just two perfectly matched kittens, one of them was killed instantly.

Howard admitted to me that he was such an indifferent Torah student that his bar mitzvah preparation was the quick and dirty kind, featuring a phonetic, easily retained Torah portion that would allow him to "read" while dragging the Torah pointer over random text. At his bar mitzvah, as Howard parroted his memorized Hebrew and performed this pantomime reading from the Torah, the crotchety rabbi had repeatedly grabbed the end of the pointer and slammed it down on the proper words on the scroll.

So Howard wasn't much of a Jew. I tried so hard, oh my God, for decades I tried to act like a good Jew myself. I was a parody of a good little Jewish wife, especially in those first years, when I went crazy memorizing all the rules, like the thirty-nine *melachot,* the categories of forbidden Sabbath activities. Do you know how hard it is for someone with my background even to pronounce a word like that? The "aacccchhh" does not come naturally to a Tatnall throat.

I probably did break many of the thirty-nine each Saturday, just the same (igniting a fire, extinguishing a fire, writing two or more letters, erasing, tying, untying, making two loops, transferring between domains), but as a member of the Ziplinsky tribe, I foolishly thought it was important to know the rules I was breaking. My favorite *melachot* among the thirty-nine? "Applying the finishing touch."

And the holidays! Ask me about Shavuot! Or how about that Tu Bishvat! I've got the scoop on Purim, the word on Haman and his tricorner hat, represented in those lead sinker cookies, hamantaschen, which I whip up in the Cuisinart, thanks to a Martha Stewart recipe.

Take Sukkot. There's a holiday. Ask me about the Lulav and the Etrog! The plural of Etrog, I happen to know, is Etrogim, not that I have ever been able to work that into a conversation, because you only need the one each year. *These Etrogim are so lovely it is hard for me to choose just one Etrog. Look, those Etrogim over there are even nicer.* I am sure Irene wouldn't know a Lulav from an Etrog from a Halloween pumpkin, but of course, that is what makes her a real Ziplinsky, her entitlement to her own indifference, the privilege of not noticing her own privilege.

THE FIRST TIME I hosted the Seder at our house was the year Sam died, when Passover was just a couple of weeks later. For some reason we thought it was too much for Frieda to manage the whole thing at her house so soon after Sam's death, so we decided to move the Seder to our house on Everit Street instead. Frieda resented this plan, but her resentment was in itself an activity that was very fulfilling for her. Logically, we should have gone to her that year, as always. She had that big, seldom-used dining room, and she had all that Waterford crystal she obsessed over (my failure to covet her damned crystal was yet another bone of contention between us), and she had those heirloom, gold-rimmed Pesach dishes that had once belonged to her aunt Pep in the Bronx. Frieda also maintained a fourth set of dishes, beyond the usual three for meat, dairy, and Pesach. This was a shelf of miscellaneous plates that were known as the trayfe dishes, which were reserved for pizza and other technically forbidden foods, a necessary accommodation when Irene and Howard were in high school.

I come from a family that believed one would never *buy* silver, because one simply *has* silver. My mother's second cousin Molly in Wilmington lays the table with her grandmother's service for twelve, which, she recalls fondly and frequently, was salvaged when Daddy's yacht sank off Nantucket in a squall in 1924. The loyal butler, Cope, had very nearly gone down with the ship. Family lore has it that he was thought to have drowned until he was seen staggering out of the surf, embracing the carved wooden chest containing this famous family silver. The family story does not include his first name, though the silver pattern, Sulgrave, is usually mentioned.

FRIEDA LOVED TO cook and bake and freeze. How many times did she confound my kids by inviting them over with a promise that she was baking her delicious walnut cookies, only to offer them semithawed, dried-out walnut cookies from the freezer? These they were expected to enjoy while sitting at the kitchen table breathing in the wafting aroma that lingered from the day's baking, while racks of soft, warm, fragrant walnut cookies cooled all over the kitchen in preparation for layering in wax paper and entombment in those plastic freezer boxes she cherished, as if they too were her legacy from Aunt Pep.

Frieda had three freezers in her basement. For most of the years I knew her, even when she was still working admirably long days at Zip's at a point when she would have been entitled to cut back her hours at the factory, she cooked and baked large quantities of food several times a week, preferring to freeze each sour-cream Bundt, each batch of mushroom soup, in appropriately segregated and labeled containers in these freezers, with meat in one, dairy in another, and whatever Seder foods she could prepare in advance, stashed in her Pesach Tupperware (I'm not kidding), in her Pesach freezer. What's especially impressive and odd about this was that she didn't exactly keep a kosher home, though she made a lot of inconsistent gestures in that direction. (The Ziplinsky style of kosherness was like some encrypted dress code so difficult to understand that it would make you yearn for uniforms.) Because she did so much cooking in advance, one of the hallmarks of big family meals at her house was the eerie spotlessness of her kitchen.

Three-Freezer Frieda (as Howard secretly called her at
times) vowed to give me all her Seder recipes. The day had
come, after twenty-two years. She told me she knew it was her
duty as a good Jewish woman to provide me, her only daughter-
in-law, with all the knowledge she had about how to make a
Seder, so that I could make a proper Jewish home for her son
and for her grandchildren. Though of course I could only fail,
she didn't say out loud, because a proper Jewish home for her
son and her grandchildren would not have had me in it.

She made a big production out of this, the handing over of
The Book of Frieda, as she dictated every single thing she could
think to tell me about this annual event that went by three inter-
changeable names so I always worried I was using the wrong
word, no matter which one it was: Seder, Pesach, Passover. (I
have come to believe that I can never get it right, because it is
like growing up a native French speaker, with the masculine
and feminine identity attached to each word as you learn it, so
you have a natural knowledge of gender, while the rest of the
world can never get it quite right. Intuition is insufficient for
French, a language in which a word for *penis* is feminine.) I
wrote it all down, word for word, in the same notebook I had
last used just a few weeks earlier for what turned out to be my
final lunch at Clark's with Sam, when he could barely eat a little
soup and I had to drive him there and help him into and out of
the car, and he nearly fell stepping off the curb when we were
getting back into the car after lunch. The last thing he said that I
wrote down was this: "A good person never falls into the trap of
loving things and using people—people should be loved, and
things should be used."

Now here it was just two weeks after Sam's death, and we sat
at Frieda's kitchen table, surrounded by the remains of various
eastern European carbohydrates of mourning that had been

brought by family, friends, and business associates calling on Frieda. She would soon banish them all, all the coffee cakes and strudels and rugelachs and kugels of sadness, even though the Seder would not be taking place in her house this year, in her great annual pre-Passover cleansing of the forbidden chometz. Paradoxically enough, Frieda's solution lay in giving them all to me in a few shopping bags when I left that day with my Pesach marching orders.

"Offer them to the employees, take them home, suit yourself," she said to me. This dovetailed nicely with her ongoing secret plan to tempt me at all times to eat calorie-laden foods so I would get fat. Also it was sending extra chometz into my house so as to sabotage any possibility that my Passover Seder could possibly be legitimate. And it was her way of handing off her chometz to a goy, part of her ritual that she thought I didn't understand, but I understood her perfectly.

And so I took a bite of a gummy raspberry rugelach I certainly didn't need, and I turned to a fresh page, and I wrote while Frieda dictated with great precision all of her extremely detailed bits of advice concerning the tiniest aspects of each recipe.

We began with the precious Ziplinsky family charoset recipe, which went well, though her charoset, an apple and walnut Ashkenazic formula, as she called it, was, in my annual experience, plausibly derived from the actual mortar used to build the pyramids when we were slaves to Pharaoh in Egypt. Year after year at the Ziplinsky family Seders, with various Bridgeport cousins and a couple of old Legion Avenue quasi relatives of Frieda's in attendance, as we got to that part of the group recitations, I would feel all the eyes around the table swivel my way in anticipation. Look, the shiksa wife is going to say it! Here it comes! There she goes! "*When we were slaves to*

Pharaoh in Egypt . . ." If I do say so, my own charoset, featuring raisins, dates, ginger, dried pears, walnuts, pignolis, and almonds, is far superior. Also? Forget the Manischewitz. A good grapey pinot noir is best.

For her matzo balls, Frieda revealed that the secret to their being so light and fluffy (and truly, they really were—that woman was a very competent cook at certain moments) was that she used seltzer in the dough. The little seltzer bubbles aerated the matzo balls, she said, before adding sharply that I shouldn't think of using Perrier; it had to be true seltzer water, from a siphon, like for an egg cream. (Do I look like someone who would put Perrier in matzo balls?) Our household, like hers, had a weekly seltzer delivery, a Ziplinsky family necessity, so I didn't even keep Perrier in the house, as she well knew, since Zip's Candies paid all the Castle Seltzer bills for all those years. Then she got to the ingredients and instructions for the chicken broth for the matzo ball soup.

"Take boneless chicken breasts," she said.

"How many?" I asked.

"Oh, whatever you think you need," she replied with uncharacteristic vagueness, which should have been the tip-off. "Five, or six, maybe."

"Boneless chicken breasts? Skinless?"

"It doesn't matter," she said. Let me repeat. She said, *It doesn't matter*. Those were her words.

"Are you sure?" I asked, pen poised on the page. "Boneless, skinless chicken breasts?"

"Do you think I wasn't making chicken soup for the Seder every year since I was a little girl growing up on Legion Avenue and my mother taught me her recipe, and now all of a sudden I don't know what I'm talking about?" she said tartly. "Okay, fine, you know better, you do whatever you think."

I wrote down the remaining ingredients for the soup as she enumerated them, the carrots, the onions, the garlic cloves, the celery stalk, the bay leaf, and we went on to other elements of the meal until I had everything she thought I needed to make the Seder.

She had the family Haggadahs stacked up on the table for me to take. She would bring along the gefilte fish and the freshly grated horseradish, because it was impossible for me to learn to make either of these things, Frieda had decided. Irene would be bringing fruit. Knock yourself out, Irene. When I was leaving, as I bent to take from her the last shopping bag of coffee cakes, to carry all the chometz out of her house and into mine, there on her doorstep, Frieda leaned over and kissed me on the forehead. This was uncharacteristically warm, but it was probably fueled by her ebullience over the chicken soup recipe she had just foisted on me.

Howard thought I should invite my parents up from Chapel Hill. He liked them, and didn't quite believe me that they were as cold and distant as I said they were. If you have had Frieda and Sam Ziplinsky for parents, you probably just cannot imagine the true coldness of Kay and Edwin Tatnall. You think you see something that isn't there. As a consequence of being loved sufficiently by your parents, you normalize, you fill in the blanks. For Howard, my parents were so Other that he mistook one kind of Other for another kind of Other. In his own way, feeling fond and unconflicted about my parents as he did, Howard has always denied me the right to my outrage at them for their minimal devotion to me.

I was dubious that Kay and Edwin Tatnall could possibly see themselves attending a Seder, even one populated by their only child and their only grandchildren, given their reluctance to attend any sort of family get-together. They were remarkably uninterested in Howard's family, and in fact I knew it wouldn't have occurred to either of them to write Frieda a condolence letter if I hadn't prompted them. It had been impossible to entice them to consider flying up for Grandparents' Day at the kids' school the previous autumn. Sam and Frieda, aka Grampa Sam and Nana, had been delighted to attend. (My mother never wanted our kids to call her anything but Kay.) I was relieved when they declined the invitation because it conflicted with an important bridge tournament.

"Would Daddy have to wear a *yar-nol-kee* on his head?" my mother had asked anxiously when I phoned with the invitation (phoning them like that was a deliberate ambush on my part), hedging her reply even before she remembered with obvious relief the conflicting bridge tournament schedule. I wondered if she would deny ever having told me, when I was about ten, that the reason Jews have big noses is because air is free. People are usually themselves, it turns out.

TWO DAYS BEFORE the Seder, I phoned Frieda to report that the big pot of chicken broth bubbling on my stove was sort of tasteless, nowhere near as good as hers, what was I doing wrong? Any suggestions? And she said, Tell me what you did, step-by-step, what did you do? So I read the ingredients to her—the bay leaf, the carrots, the flat parsley (not curly), the quartered onions, the whole onion studded with eight cloves, the celery stalk with leaves, the cloves of garlic smashed but not chopped, the boneless, skinless chicken breasts. And she said, "Oh, you used boneless chicken breasts? Skinless too? They don't have so much flavor."

And I said, "But Frieda, you told me to use boneless, skinless chicken breasts. I have it written right here."

And she said, "Well, I suppose if that's what you want to use, you can. But it's not as flavorful."

And I said, "You told me to use boneless, skinless chicken breasts."

And she said, "If that's what you want, I'm sure it will be good enough. You didn't know better."

"But Frieda, it's not good enough; this chicken soup is watery and insipid, nothing like yours."

"Ah! Why would it be? What do you expect when you used the boneless, skinless chicken breasts, dear? Without bones and skin, and flavorful dark meat, you don't get so much taste. Now you know. I always use a whole fowl. You have to skim, but there's much more flavor that way. A kosher butcher would tell you what to do. But I'm sure your soup will be fine. You can't expect to make such good chicken soup from scratch when it's not in your blood."

THERE WAS A wild current of attraction between Howard and me from that first moment. I am certain Frieda could feel it too—it was in the air—and she knew I was going to take her golden boy, her beautiful Howdy, the only one she had left. She knew I would take him away from her, and there was nothing she could do to stop it. She didn't know it quite yet, but I was the answer to her prayers. I would keep him from leaving, but she had to let me have him.

On my third day at work, at the end of that first week, Sam came and watched me on the Tigermelt line for a moment. I reached, shuffled, reached, shuffled those Tigermelts like a pro, as if I was a career Tigermelt-straightener, never missing a single bar, and as the expertly aligned bars clanked past us on their journey to the cooling tunnel and the wrapping machine,

Sam told me I was doing a very good job, and his son Howdy would presently give me a thorough walk-through on all three lines at Zip's, because I obviously had a good head on my shoulders, and cool hands, which was important, because hot hands smudged the finish on the chocolate, which was why women were traditionally employed on candy lines in positions requiring touching the pieces, because women have cooler hands than men. They should use me for more complex work than this, Sam said, and then he said to me, Kiddo, you're going to be good for Zip's, and Zip's is going to be good for you.

When the first lunch break came, during which time skeleton crews ran the lines slowly, in shifts (if they shut down completely something could harden, cool, or clog, so a few people on staggered shifts kept the tanks swirling, the belts moving, the panners tumbling), Howard beckoned to me, and I followed him. We had scarcely exchanged a word since our first meeting, but since then, several times while I was working I would feel his gaze on me, and I would look up and there he would be, somewhere on the floor, watching me, frankly staring.

Each time, when our eyes met, he would smile without looking away, and one of those times, when he was leaning over a railing up on a catwalk above the chocolate coating tanks, he had leaned over and pointed at me and mouthed, "You." I didn't know who the hell he thought he was. Gene Kelly in some cheesy musical number? Or who the hell he thought *I* was. The indifferent ingénue in her first role? I didn't know whether to be flattered or irritated.

The ten-year age difference between Howard and me has vanished with time, but it did signify then, I suppose, especially to some of his friends. At eighteen, I was still a teenager. Howard and I had grown up in slightly different times as well as worlds. When we first started spending time together, there were all sorts of gaps. I didn't know how to play golf and had never imagined that I would want to learn, any more than I would want to learn how to play bridge. Howard had never smoked pot, preferring beer or Dewar's White Label, the official beverages of DKE House, while I had never been drunk, but I had inhaled passed joints at a few concerts and parties, not that it ever did much for me. I listened to the Beatles; the Everly Brothers's "Wake Up, Little Susie" was Howard's favorite song.

Howard often referred to various girlfriends he had dated in high school and college. Until we met, I had only hung out in groups, but had never gone out with one specific person on an actual date. I had only ever kissed a boy during party games. The merciless teasing from Andy Ottenberg my senior year was the most attention I'd ever had from anyone, but it's hard to look back on his cruelty and see it as a flirtation, though maybe it was, for him. The truth is, when I met Howard, though I let him think otherwise when he made a remark about my previous high school boyfriends, I had only ever been with one man, and that wasn't a date.

ERIC HONIG WROTE to me two days after the fire. I had no idea how old he was, or where he lived, or why he was writing to me. My parents simply weren't curious about what came through the mail slot in our front door, beyond their anxiety about legal papers and money. Arson Girl received quite a number of hate letters in those days, which my mother left for me on the front hall table next to the bowl of keys and loose change. A lot of strangers were compelled to tell me they thought I should go to jail, starting the day after the fire, when there were so many crank phone calls we finally had to leave the phone off the hook.

The day Eric Honig's first letter came, there were several

other letters, including a really nasty one from someone who called herself "The Cat Lady of East Haven," telling me I deserved to die for what I had done to Debbie Livingston's cat. I felt horrible enough about poor old Homer as it was, and her letter had made me cry. I was grateful to read Eric's letter, because it wasn't like the others. It was a fan letter. His note was friendly and encouraging. He said I had a nice smile and he hoped I was getting some sleep because I looked tired.

After that, just about every day, right up to my last court appearance, I received a greeting card from Eric containing the most recent newspaper story on my case, clipped with pinking shears from the *New Haven Register* and festooned with his ballpoint-pen remarks, punctuated by multiple exclamation points cascading down the margins, about how unfair to me their coverage was. He mixed upper- and lowercase with abandon, and he drew smiley faces with word balloons saying things like, "ChEEr UP, SweET AliCe! YoUR're GReaT!"

There was never a return address on anything he mailed to me, so I had no way to reply, but as the days passed, his little notes and cards grew more intense and personal, as if we were corresponding. I looked him up in the New Haven phone book, but there was no Eric Honig listed, though his envelopes were all postmarked locally. He sent a greeting card with bluebirds sitting together in a nest, on the back of which he had scribbled "CAn'T WAiT Till Our SPECIAL Day!!!" The next week, though it was late June, a Valentine with lace trim arrived, signed, "Love you always, my sweetheart. Eric."

I never mentioned Eric Honig to my parents. Perhaps it sounds pathetic, but I was lonely, and whoever Eric Honig was, he was my friend, which was more than I could say for my former actual friends. (I never heard from any of my teachers, either, not even Miss Solomon.) The weekend after my regrettable guilty plea and sentence, on a hot, still Sunday afternoon, when I was home alone in front of the television, my parents having gone into New York for a bridge tournament, Eric Honig came to the door. I know I shouldn't have let him in, but it was hard not to, once he said he was Eric Honig. My first thought when I saw him was that he wanted to use our telephone because he had a flat tire. My second thought, when he said his name, was that I had been expecting just this moment, and I knew he had watched my parents drive away and leave me alone.

The next thing he said to me after identifying himself was that I was more beautiful in person than he had imagined, though I hadn't washed my hair in days and I was squinting through the screen door at him and wearing a frayed, blue button-down oxford shirt of my father's and cut-off jeans with denim shreds hanging down one leg, and I had a jar of Nutella in one hand and a spoon in the other.

As I opened the door, I realized that I was afraid of him (I wasn't an idiot), but how could I refuse him? This was Eric Honig, who liked me. And now he was inside the house, in the gloom of our front hall, and then we were on the couch together, while the 4:30 movie with which I had been wasting the afternoon, *Gidget Gets Married,* continued to flicker soundlessly on the television across the room, and then he was kissing me and telling me over and over how beautiful I was.

I can't remember what he looked like, other than in a general way. He was an ordinary middle-aged man. He wore a short-sleeved yellow shirt and khaki pants, and he had on bright new running shoes. I think his hair was wet. He smelled of cloves. He took a red and white tin of cloves from his pants pocket, and he put it on the coffee table in front of us as he sat down beside me, explaining that he was trying to quit smoking, and the strong taste of cloves helped him fight his cravings. He offered me a clove but I didn't want one, and then he started kissing me, and the clove taste on his thrusting tongue was as strange and inevitable as everything else about this moment.

He unbuttoned my shirt and rummaged for my breasts with one hand, while seizing my wrist with the other hand and pressing my palm down on the lengthening hardness trapped in his pants, sliding my hand rhythmically up and down on the hot lump under the thin khaki for a moment before shifting to unzip his pants while murmuring into my mouth, Oh yes, oh yes, babydoll, you light my fire, yes you do.

He really said that.

It wasn't rape, because I never asked him to stop. I never spoke at all. The clovey smell, the way he looked at me and spoke to me and touched me, the way he seemed to be reaching through me and speaking past me, that is what has lingered in my mind all these years, if I think about it at all, not the actual sensations, not what his face or his body looked like. (A week later, I wouldn't have known him on the street.) It must have hurt, but I have no memory of that either, though I spent half an hour scrubbing the bloodstain from the cushion of our faded chintz couch so when my parents returned they would notice nothing. The faint maroon wisp of the stain, twined through the vines and leaves of the pale green and pink floral pattern, was visible only to me, and then only when I looked for it, which I did from time to time when I was in need of a reality check.

What has stayed with me is the pounding, insistent weight of him as I sank into the soft, familiar cushions, pinned under his frenzied thrusting, my shorts bunched at my ankles. I grew more and more transparent until I was entirely invisible, doing everything I could to remove myself so he could penetrate to the core the exquisite object of his desire, which had nothing at all to do with me. It was over in a few minutes. He left in a hurry, his 1.25-ounce tin of Schilling whole cloves, packed in Baltimore, MD, USA, forgotten. I kept that tin in the back of my under-wear drawer for years, until the contents were nothing more than a jumble of tiny, knotted twigs with no discernable aroma. He never wrote to me again.

The lesson of the story? Have sex with your stalker if you want him to leave you alone forever.

So here I was, not quite a month later, the once and future Arson Girl, grateful to be dwelling in the new, sweet, fragrant world of Zip's Candies, with Howard Ziplinsky walking me through the lines, machine by machine. I was perplexed by how powerfully attracted to Howard I was. On the face of it, he wasn't my type, if someone in my circumstances could be said to have a type. There was something a little too polished yet incom-plete about him, even then, when he was still quite lean and had not yet developed that pampered, slumpy, too-tanned, executive-on-the-golf-course softness of recent years.

As I followed Howard across the factory floor, I stopped to glove up at the first dispenser we passed, and he waved in my direction impatiently for me to catch up. I noticed his beautiful hands for the first time. Howard's wrists are graceful and per-fectly proportioned. For years, before he started wearing that ridiculous fancy watch the size of a Reese's peanut butter cup, every glimpse of his wrists made me inexplicably happy. Howard has always possessed an astonishing number of mag-nificent shirts, more than Gatsby, and I was attracted to that, too (my father wore only blue or white oxford cloth button-downs), to Howard's confidence and pleasure in having those shirts to choose from every morning. On that third day of my Zip's employment, the sight of his blue-and-white-striped shirt cuffs grazing the thick dark hair sprouting from those elegant wrists was almost embarrassingly thrilling, like a foreshadowing glimpse of his naked torso under a bedsheet. He was utterly unself-conscious as I followed those beautiful hands. I was mesmerized by each gesture as he pointed at the various Tigermelt wrapping machinery components and explained their functions.

As we approached the Mumbo Jumbo line, Howard put a hand on my arm to steer me across a treacherous spill of red licorice goo, and then he left it there as we stood at the side of the churning machinery watching rows of fragrant red discs tumble out, slide down the sorting chute, and land one by one by one before chugging by on the belt. The heat of his hand was shockingly intimate through the thin sleeve of the simple white cotton button-down shirt I was wearing over loose white cotton pants, an outfit that met the requirements of the factory floor for summer so I didn't have to wear a hot factory coat. I admit I knew my shirt was very snug and contrasted nicely with my tan, plus I never wore a bra in those days.

I asked as many questions as I could think to ask, as we stood there, but I wasn't listening to Howard's answers about the moguls and the cornstarch molds and the politics of red food coloring (Zip's had recently switched from cochineal extract, which is made from crushed insect carcasses, to Red Number Three, erythrosine, which enhanced shelf stability, plus was not made from insects), and from there he went into an exegesis on the history of the balky molding machine. I was leaning into the pleasant buzz of his voice over the clacking, chugging, and clanking all around us, all the while acutely aware of the radiating warmth of that hand.

"So are the red ones Mumbos and the black ones Jumbos, or are the black ones Mumbos and the red ones Jumbos, or are they red Mumbo Jumbos and black Mumbo Jumbos?" I babbled, truly curious about the answer, but also wanting to prolong the moment, feeling semimesmerized by the ceaseless flow of candy, candy, candy all around me; I had yet to develop immunity to the chronic thrillingness of that. An infinity of jittering red Mumbo Jumbos slid by. Or were they Mumbos? Or Jumbos? I wasn't listening. I felt light-headed, having left the house without breakfast. Nobody was near us, and we were momentarily alone in the middle of this candy hive.

Wordlessly, Howard steered me toward the Little Sammies panning area, and we stood over a deep bin filled with penultimate, uncoated Little Sammies awaiting their shiny hard-shell chocolate bath. He leaned over and reached into the bin with both hands and lifted them, letting the Little Sammies sift through his fingers back into the bin (I knew this was not in accord with Zip's sanitary standards) as he continued to explain the principles of each stage along the line to me. I asked some detailed questions about various mechanisms and adjustment controls, even though I could hardly hear Howard's answers over the din of the incessant sugary clacking. He had stopped talking, and now he was leaning close and brushing my hair aside to speak into my ear. Any more questions? What? Questions! Sorry, I wasn't listening! You weren't what? Listening! His hot breath in my ear was suddenly intimate.

He reached out to touch my chin, to turn my face so he could wipe off the smallest drop of Little Sammies coating chocolate. Like a first raindrop, a single stray chocolate droplet had landed on my cheek, and he dabbed this driblet with his fingertip, and then he put his finger in his mouth, onto the tip of his tongue, without speaking. He just did this and looked at me.

We looked at each other, and we just stood there, so close between the machines. I shivered. I could feel my nipples tingle and harden under my white shirt, and although he didn't take his eyes from mine, I could see in his face that he noticed. Why did the man yell "Fire!" when he fell into the chocolate? Howard asked me suddenly. What? Why? Howard leaned in close, his hot breath in my ear again, changing solids to liquids, tempering something deep inside of me, and murmured, Because nobody would come if he yelled "Chocolate!"

Several line workers were drifting back from their brief lunch breaks, and I turned away from him then, feigning curiosity in all the wrapping machines, trying to recover from this vertiginous moment. Howard followed behind me, and a moment later I had accidentally led us into a sort of blind alley formed by a stack of palleted wrapping materials and the back end of the Tigermelt wrapping machine. It was very loud, making a *chug-chug-chug-chug-chug-chug-CHUNK, chug-chug-chug-chug-chug-chug-CHUNK* sound that corresponded to six finished Tigermelt bars at a time reaching the end of the line, where they were each sledded onto a cardboard tray and then sleeved in a wrapper, which was then heat-sealed at both ends.

Howard stood right behind me, close, close but not touching, and he explained into my ear the steps required by the Tigermelt wrapping process, which was fully automated, unlike the semi-automated Little Sammies wrapping process, which required certain manual stages (because there was not yet a machine on the line that could efficiently pack the three Little Sammies together onto the cardboard sleeve all heads up, faceup, with any reliability), while I asked nonsensical questions, all of which he answered very thoroughly. Howard was extremely knowledgeable about the quirks and twists of every machine on the floor.

He was dedicated in those days. I would never say otherwise. For many years, Howard Ziplinsky was as dedicated and loyal to the family business as could be. Everyone saw in him the ideal heir, the future of Zip's Candies. I didn't know then that he had not been born to this role, but when his older brother, Lewis, died in childhood, everything shifted, and Howard, not the heir but the spare, had been moved up the line of succession. The future of the family business had weighed on him from the day Lewis died at fourteen, when Howard was twelve.

Finally I ran out of questions, and I felt Howard moving closer to me, and then, standing right behind me, he put his hands on my breasts, very lightly. Something like an electrical current ran through me, from here to there, and I felt as if parts of me were lighting up. Does that sound completely absurd? It was the single most erotic experience of my life to that moment. Perhaps even to this moment. What does *this* button do, he murmured softly in my ear, mimicking my earlier stream of questions, but not unkindly, touching me gently, so gently.

I rinsed his faint chocolate handprints from my shirt when I saw them in my reflection over the sink in the women's bathroom a little while later. I had finally detached myself from that intoxicating fermata, thinking I should make some kind of an effort to pull myself together. Had anyone noticed the smudges on my shirt as I emerged from behind the Tigermelt wrapping machine and skibbled to the ladies' room? My dabbing at the handprints left big wet circular splotches that rendered my shirt almost transparent, so I put a white factory coat on over it until it dried, which it soon did, but with chocolate tide marks bordering the former wet spots. This gave Frieda something to comment on at the end of the day as I clocked out, when she reminded me sourly that I needed to pay stricter attention to the hygiene guidelines for wearing a clean white shirt onto the floor if I wanted to keep my job at Zip's Candies.

What else can I say about Howard? I am trying to be fair. He was, when I look back now through the *Had I But Known* lens, a bit too pretty (prettier than me), maybe a bit too casual, certainly careless (careless with me). He was reckless. Howard was, after all, not only ten years older than I was, he was also, in effect, my employer. What about him was so enticing to me? Everything. I had never met anyone remotely like him before. Howard enjoyed privilege, he enjoyed having money, and he radiated a kind of entitlement, an entitlement to do anything, including this, this homing in on me. But his was a generous entitlement, one that invited me along. He made me feel that anything was possible.

At the same time, there was something a little smirky about Howard, something of the obnoxious frat boy. When his DKE brother George W. Bush was elected president in 2000 (if you can call that an election), Howard wanted to send him a case of Little Sammies to celebrate the inauguration, but I objected. Howard insisted that George had been a good guy at college, a lively presence in DKE House on Lake Place, a true friend, all of which seemed like somewhat revised history, a Howard specialty.

"Seriously, Howard?" I was skeptical. Howard had told me about some of the casual nastiness and racism he had witnessed, if not experienced, at Yale. "W. wasn't one of the anti-Semites you told me about?"

Howard got a look on his face that I know well, a defensive sheepishness, as he tried to find the words to explain what he meant. He was especially proud of his DKE affiliation, and I had heard more than once that the DKE man was in equal proportions the scholar, the gentleman, and the jolly good fellow. "It depends on how you take his sense of humor," he said, finally. "Once there was a group of us hanging out at Bulldog Pizza after a hockey game, and someone was complaining about this annoying guy we all knew who never put enough money on the table for his share of our beers when the check came, and George said, 'What do you expect from a Jew?' So I said 'Hey, asshole,

I'm a Jew too,' and W. said, 'Howdy, you're different—you're a white Jew.'"

Howard thought this was funny. I didn't. I had no sense of humor at all about the election—in fact I was sick about it— and I probably focused all my wrath and disappointment on at least keeping those Little Sammies out of the White House. I really insisted that he not send them. I was belligerent and relentless about it. Finally, Howard agreed that he wouldn't send them, and the subject was dropped. But then about a month later an envelope from the White House arrived in the mail for Howard. It contained a glossy color photograph of George W. Bush smirking at his desk in the Oval Office, and it was signed in black Sharpie with a scrawled "Thanks, Howdy— Say, Dat's Tasty! GWB." That photograph is framed and hang- ing on the wall in Howard's office (which is now my office) at this moment. I keep meaning to take it down. I know it's petty of me, and insignificant in the larger scheme of things, but every time it catches my eye, I am indignant all over again. How could he?

DESPITE HOWARD'S EXTRAORDINARY self-regard and sense of entitlement, which has always made him capable of behaving so badly, there was for so many years something very gentle and loving about him that always redeemed him in my eyes. Some- thing genuinely sweet, too. I thought I saw in him more Sam's son than Frieda's. More kindness. I was mistaken. Like everyone else in this story, I have always seen only what I wanted to see. In 1975, our thrilling mutual attraction felt like a surprising yet inevitable part of my sudden immersion in Zip's Candies, my pleasurable slide into that warm chocolate vat.

We spent almost every night of the rest of that hot summer

together, and it was an exceptionally hot summer. Every evening after work we would drive around in Howard's old chocolate-brown Fiat Spider, making out at red lights, going for fried clams and lobster rolls at the beach in Madison. Top down, radio up! Sometimes we would cruise the Wooster Square neighborhood for a parking place so we could get a white clam pizza at Sally's. Often we would go to the last showing of a movie, it didn't matter what, for the air-conditioning. I loved freezing myself at the movies after baking myself at the beach.

Howard always lingered at the refreshment counter, scrutinizing the candy assortment with an appraising professional eye. He was genuinely annoyed with my fondness for Milk Duds to the point where I didn't dare choose them, opting instead for the safety of off-brand malted milk balls, even though they were inevitably stale, which pleased Howard. He would murmur a stream of candy talk in my ear while I chomped my way through the box as we waited for the lights to go down, feeling the heat of my sunburned skin glowing in the frigid air, my sunburned legs soothed by the worn velvet of the theater seats, knowing we would go back to his apartment and make love with all that frantic urgency we had for each other. It was a sweet time.

Whoppers, I learned, avid student that I was, started out being sold individually, two for a penny, but they were bigger than standard malted milk balls today, real gobstoppers, and when cellophane wrapping machines were introduced, a smaller-sized Whopper was packaged in "fivesomes," which sold for a penny a pack. I loved the way Howard cared so much about all this.

And it's a worthy passion, one the family has perpetuated. When the kids were growing up, we could talk all through dinner about candy bars of the past, and it was always fun to get

Howard started on candy-bar trivia. We would name any letter of the alphabet or any state in the country and Howard could name an obscure bar that started with that letter or was manufactured in that state, or he could bluff persuasively. The weirder the bar, the more certain we were that he was bluffing, but usually, such a bar had actually once existed and Howard not only knew its name, but he also knew the slogan for it and the makeup of the bar. When Jacob saw *Rain Man,* Dustin Hoffman's Raymond reminded him of Howard's encyclopedic candy-bar knowledge, and for a while that's what he called his father, Rain Man, whenever Howard started talking candy.

Jacob and Julie never tired of hearing about the Chicken Dinner bar (a pioneering concept, since it was in some ways one of the first protein bars, the succulent roast chicken on the wrapper suggesting as it did that one could have something equal to a nourishing dinner for a nickel, though it was an ordinary candy bar, and chicken was not an ingredient). First introduced in the 1920s by the Sperry Candy Company, possibly inspired by President Hoover's campaign promise of a chicken in every pot, the bar grew in popularity during the Depression, when many people couldn't afford a real chicken dinner.

Prohibition, which began in 1920 and ended thirteen years later, was great for the candy business, and it is not a coincidence that those dry years were the heyday for candy bars, a convenient and cheap replacement for a quick pick-me-up. Never before had candy been consumed in such quantities. Never before was candy so conveniently packaged and available, the candy bar offering an experience distinctly different from selecting a single morsel from a gift box of bonbons.

Candy bars were a playful gratification that could be enjoyed by men, women, and children equally. In 1927, Lucky Strike cigarettes aimed a daring campaign at women, encouraging them to smoke. Eating a lot of candy bars could lead to weight gain, and here was a healthful alternative: "Reach for a Lucky instead of a sweet." Sugar and nicotine were legal stimulating habits when alcohol wasn't, and even after the Volstead Act was repealed in 1933, America continued to smoke and eat candy as never before, though some of the stranger bars that had flourished in those golden years didn't survive past World War II.

Julie and Jacob could never hear enough about those ghostly candy bars such as Old Nick, Fat Emma, Whiz, Candy Salad, Chump, Big Dearo, Denver Sandwich, Zep, Vegetable Sandwich, Lindy, Roasty Toasty, Vanilla Jitney, Doctor's Orders, Baffle, Coconut Grove, Cherry Hump (tragically discontinued in the 1980s because of a chronic leakage problem), Pierce Arrow, Poor Prune, the Bolster bar, and let's not forget the Amos 'n' Andy bar, which had the slogan "Um-Um! Ain't Dat Sumpin!"

This bar came out several years after Little Sammies, and Zip's Candies actually contemplated legal action against the Williamson Candy Company over that slogan. Eli engaged in correspondence with a Philadelphia law firm specializing in copyrights and patents, which advised him that although he had several valid points, and they were sympathetic to his situation, they couldn't agree that he could prove a sufficient influence, given that the Amos 'n' Andy bar was a chocolate-covered, crisp-honeycomb-centered, two-piece product, and in any case they didn't think a court would find merit in Zip's Candies proprietary claim on the word "Dat" in a candy-bar slogan.

Jacob and Julie would make up bars, too, the sillier the better: the Mint Chipmunk Chunk bar ("Save One for Winter!"), the Thunder Thigh bar ("From Your Lips to Your Hips!"), and let us not forget their answer to the Mars bar, the Uranus bar ("The Protein Bar for Colonic Health!").

❀ ❀

THAT FIRST SUMMER, sometimes I didn't get home for three or four days at a time, spending most nights at Howard's Chapel Street apartment over the head shop called Group W Bench. The back stairs of the building always had a faint but persistent patchouli and marijuana vapor that seemed to float up from the shop, which was nicer than the building's top notes of litter box and frying.

Although Howard was twenty-eight when we met, and I was, in his words, barely legal (which definitely seemed to appeal to him), Sam told me years later that he had told Howard, soon after it had become evident that we were together (and in retrospect I am embarrassed at how transparent we must have been, rutting around the factory floor), that I might be the one who was too old. Sam observed a few times over the years that I had an old soul, which I took as a compliment, and I am inclined to agree. That's a perfect example of the kind of thing a Ziplinsky might say to you that no Tatnall would ever think to mention.

My parents had nothing to say to me about my new life, no questions, no opinions, though they must have noticed how absent I was that summer, and, when our paths did happen to cross, how inexplicably happy I must have seemed. Though it was my habit to feign indifference around them, if they were paying any kind of attention, you would think they might have wanted to check in with me. Also, my mother might have thought to offer a little chat about birth control. But she probably assumed I had taken care of all that on my own. (This was correct; my first experience at the Planned Parenthood clinic on Whitney Avenue, soon after I started working at Zip's Candies and long before I was to serve on the state board, was as a patient whose chart had a "Do Not Contact" sticker at the top.) It would have been a radical departure for her to get that personal. I might as well wish for her to have been more interested in my lonely independent life all along, more than she was interested in, say, her collection of vintage Nantucket Lightship Basket handbags. It wasn't in Kay's and Edwin Tatnall's natures to feel anything but relief that I was going, going, gone.

ONE DESULTORY SUNDAY afternoon that summer, on our way to dinner at Frieda and Sam's, perhaps the third time I had been there, Howard took me to the Jewish Home to meet his grandmother, Sam's mother, the legendary Lillian. For the first few weeks, even when I had begun to sort out the Ziplinsky family history a little bit, I hadn't realized she was still alive, because she had only been spoken of in the past tense whenever anyone mentioned her at Zip's.

But there she was, cheerfully demented and quite frail, and though she was only seventy-two, she seemed to me like someone in her nineties. (As it turned out, this was to be the only time I ever met her, because she died soon after that, on the last day of summer, in her sleep.) When we got to Lillian's room, she wasn't in it, but Howard knew where to look, and we found her down the corridor, in a wheelchair parked beside the piano in the dayroom, where a volunteer was earnestly plinking out "Willow, Weep for Me." The sour old spinet was missing some of the ivory veneers on certain keys and had a number of bad strings. There is a piano like this in every nursing-home dayroom.

Lillian smiled at us both in a warm and familiar way. Howard introduced me as if she could understand what he was saying. I loved how respectful and devoted he was to his grandmother. He said I was his girlfriend. Of course this is what I was by that time, but it hadn't ever been said before. She seemed delighted to hear it, and delighted to shake my hand, though she didn't speak, and then she seemed equally delighted to shake Howard's hand next, though he had called her Nana and told her he was Howdy as he kissed her hello only a minute earlier.

Howard told me that he was the only one in the family who still went to see her with any regularity, because it pained Sam too much that she no longer recognized him. Howard's sister, Irene, whom I had met only once at that point, was too busy to get there very often, though when she did show up, she tormented the staff by lecturing them on nutrition and the elderly, and she had apparently seriously offended the food service staff by demanding that they remove all aluminum pots from their kitchen. Frieda and Lillian had never really gotten along, each feeling crowded by the other for so many years. Howard told me that his mother's last visit, a definite disincentive for future visits, had concluded with Lillian's looking at Frieda with a sudden glimmer of recognition before she exclaimed, "Oh it's you! When did you get so fat?"

"The one thing Nana always seems to recognize is the Little Sammies jingle," Howard whispered to me, after I whispered to him about her obvious love of the labored piano music that was holding us captive. "You know the jingle? You must know it!" Howard was certain I knew it. How could anyone not know the Little Sammies jingle? He shook his head in mock exasperation. This was an example of the vast cultural gulf those ten years between us could suddenly open up at certain moments.

I didn't think I knew it at all, but I nodded that I did, feigning a sudden recollection, Oh yes, of course. Maybe it was one of those little riffs like "I'll fly to the moon for a Lorna Doone." In fact, when Howard sang it for Lillian (once the volunteer had finally concluded her self-important, community service–inflected performance and gotten up from the piano, releasing us from our respectful audience mode), it was familiar.

I had a fleeting recollection of the cartoony line drawings that went with the jingle for the television commercial for Little Sammies I must have seen in my earliest childhood, when the commercial was still running. Zip's sponsored a local children's television program on Saturday mornings from 1958 to 1962, so I would have been four, at most, when I saw it.

As Howard sang it again, and Lillian beamed and conducted with an age-spotted claw, I had a sudden, vivid, kinetic memory of sitting on the living room floor in front of our big console television, watching Larry, Barry, and Harry, three clown brothers who starred in the weird and creepy *Happy Playtime!* ("What time is it, kids? It's Happy Playtime! And who's here to play with you? Larry, Barry, and Harry! And what do they want Mom to give you for a treat? Their favorite Little Sammies! Be sure to ask Mom to get you some!")

So I hadn't told a lie after all. As Howard sang it a third time, I joined him, but I had only gotten to "One, two, three!" when Lillian cocked her head to one side with a troubled look, not sure she liked my harmony at all. She waved her hand in a correcting gesture in my direction, and I stopped, leaving Howard to finish, solo.

Little Sammies hit the spot
Just a nickel buys a lot!
They're the greatest, you'll agree,
You will eat them one, two, three!

Little Sammies are for you
Fudgy goodness through and through,
Don't be hasty, have another,

Don't be hasty, have another,
Don't be hasty, have another—

Say, Dat's Tasty!

Howard has a nice baritone. He sang the "Don't be hasty" lines in an increasingly sped-up and admirably unself-conscious sort of Mighty Mouse voice, before dropping down into a stagy basso profundo for the interrupting "Say, Dat's Tasty!" tagline.

"You know Jimmy Ray in shipping?" Howard asked me as we were pulling out of the Jewish Home parking lot. Lillian had been rolled into the dining room for her five o'clock evening meal, and though she accepted our hugs and kisses warmly, our departure had been of no consequence to her.

"Is he the old guy, the bald one who whistles?"

"That's Eddie Sohovik. No, Jimmy Ray, the black guy."

"Okay—"

"That was his voice. He's the 'Say, Dat's Tasty' guy," Howard said, blatantly running a red light at the corner of Winthrop Avenue as we traversed that desolate stretch of the abandoned urban renewal project that still bisects New Haven. This was the site of the old Jewish neighborhood, where Frieda grew up (though I didn't know it that day); it was destroyed in the early 1960s to make way for a new city plan that never materialized when funding vanished. The pointless destruction of their Legion Avenue home and the loss of that community was a bitter subject for Frieda in those years when I first knew her. The forced Oak Street diaspora had taken place the decade before, but she never got over her resentment, even though Sam told me her childhood block was in the heart of a slum that wasn't quite as golden as she now recalled it to have been, with rats the size of cats darting between parked cars on hot summer nights.

❀ ❀

THE SCATTERED LIEBASHEVSKYS have kept that proprietary blend of nostalgia and resentment simmering to this day. At Frieda's funeral, I overheard some of her cousins from Valley Stream and Great Neck criticizing the pastries from the Westville Bakery that I had obtained at the last minute for the post-funeral gathering, because Irene had promised to help with the food and then had changed her mind the night before. She had agreed only because she was under too much stress to refuse when we spoke about it, she told me, and her new therapist in Telluride had helped her to see that it was time she learned to stand in her Wise Adult and say No! to me, the competitive sister-in-law who has no right to steal her power, and so she stood in her Wise Adult and took her power back. The night before the funeral she phoned me just before midnight from Frieda's house, where she was presumably sifting through all the family treasures she was worried I might try to claim, to say, No, Alice! No! I cannot and will not help you with that! Further-more, this was going to be her answer from now on whenever I tried to control her or place unfair demands on her. Listen, America! Irene Ziplinsky Weiss has hereby declared that she will no longer accommodate the needs of others at the expense of her own integrity! So I had to get the damned pastries myself.

The Liebashevsky cousins were like-minded about the Westville Bakery schnecken; both the raspberry and the apricot were very ordinary, nothing to write home about. (But what do you expect, from *her*? Julie told me she heard one of the Great Neck gargoyles say, pointing at me while helping herself to another of the offending pastries.) But then they began arguing with bitter urgency about which had been the best in the old Legion Avenue neighborhood, the transcendent strudel from

Rosenberg's Bakery or the miraculous poppy-seed cake from Cohen's Bakery or the astonishing babka from Ticotsky's Bakery, as if a determination had to be made here and now, though all three of these establishments vanished some fifty years ago.

"WHAT DO YOU mean, that's his voice?" I asked Howard as we headed toward his parents' Westville neighborhood. Three ghetto kids on raggedy banana-seat bikes cut in front of us repeatedly, zigzagging for sport while we kept pace behind them for two blocks, before Howard gunned the motor to show he meant business and nosed past them.

"I mean my mom sang it for the commercial, and he went with her and sang that last line."

"Wait, you're kidding. Frieda sang it? That was *her* voice I heard in the commercial when I was little?"

"She wrote it, she played the piano, and she sang it."

"Wow." A whole side of Frieda I had not yet glimpsed, her glam secret inner Kitty Carlisle.

"Yeah, she was inspired by the Chock full o'Nuts lady, whose husband owned the company. So first Mom talked Dad into running a radio commercial, and when he agreed to that, she worked out a deal for Little Sammies to sponsor baseball games on local AM radio for a season. Then she wrote the jingle, and then she went to the radio station in Bridgeport to record it."

"And how did Jimmy Ray get involved?"

"There was this other black guy at Zip's when I was little, Dave Washington. He and Jimmy used to work together in shipping—maybe they were cousins or something—and I think my mom overheard them singing doo-wop harmonies together while they stacked boxes. When I was a kid, I thought they were the coolest guys in the world. Whenever I went to the factory, those guys were so happy back there, singing and jiving. Dad always ignored their craps games, because they got their jobs done. Jimmy Ray got a hundred dollars and he got the whole day off, too."

I wondered even then if Howard knew how he sounded when he said things like this, or if he really had no clue that there was a hint of Massa on the plantation loving the sound of the happy darkies singing their charming spirituals while totin' dat barge and liftin' dat bale.

DINNER THAT NIGHT with Frieda and Sam was startlingly lively. Frieda's cooking was downright exotic compared to my mother's, plus these Ziplinskys talked avidly about everything they ate, which was somehow just not done in my family. I loved gossiping about the delicious food, I loved the jokey conversation, and I loved them, even if Frieda was determined to remain uncharmed by me. (I even kind of loved that, when it was still new, still a challenge I thought I could meet.) After dinner we watched *Maude* on television (Frieda was excited that Maude was so clearly Jewish) while Sam nodded off in his chair and Frieda kept jumping up during commercials to wash dishes.

Howard and I went back to his airless apartment on Chapel Street, where we lay naked in his bed and talked and laughed until very late, listening to the obscene shouts of the transvestite prostitutes who used to frequent his corner, clustering every night in their bulging hot pants in front of the regrettably named Gag Junior's Lunchette, until it got so late that even they finally gave up and went home, as the sky was graying with dawn.

We fell silent. Something shifted. We turned to face each other and lay there under the tangled sheet, not speaking, just tracing each other's bodies with a light fingertip. Howard's touch made me feel safe. We looked into each other's eyes in the dim light from the window and then we each leaned toward the other until our foreheads just touched, as if this were a familiar ritual of intimacy. He looked into my eyes, and I felt so deeply seen and known. I will never be that seen and known again. I roamed freely over the hills and valleys of Howard's clavicle with grazing fingers, walking an itsy-bitsy spider across his furry obliques, and everything else was still, stiller, stillest, until suddenly he laughed and rolled on top of me. We were so tender with each other, everything was so clear and present, and we made love for what was then only the eighth time, and it was the first time Howard told me he loved me.

You see? I remember everything.

Say, Dat's Tasty!

Words and Music by
Frieda Ziplinsky

4

The day I first walked through those factory doors, about half the Little Sammies line and the entire Tigermelt line still ran on the original machinery Sam's father, Eli, had cobbled together to start his candy factory in 1924. Establishing Zip's Candies in New Haven was the fruition of Eli's American dream, the Zip's literature will tell you. He had a brainstorm and then he followed his passion to manufacture the three candies he was inspired to create after he happened to pick up a copy of *Little Black Sambo* that had been left on a table at the Ottendorfer Branch of the New York Public Library on Second Avenue.

And so the fate of Zip's Candies has twice depended on someone's happening to pick up and read something discarded by another. Of course, the influence of *Little Black Sambo* on our product line has been in, then out of, and is now back in the official Zip's Candies history. These days, the political incorrectness of Little Black Sambo, that huge headache in the sixties, has been trumped by the appeal of Little Sammies to nostalgic baby boomers who, like their parents, grew up with them. What is even more of a market for us these days is the next generation of ironic hipsters, who have discovered for themselves the retro coolness of Little Sammies.

"Say, Dat's Tasty!," dropped from the Little Sammies wrapper for twenty years, was added back in 1999 for what was intended only to be the seventy-fifth anniversary limited-edition wrapper, but then we kept that wrapper, minus the seventy-fifth anniversary designation, when "Say, Dat's Tasty!" became a hip catchphrase first used by the rapper Krazy Koon, along with his famous signature gesture, that one extended index finger twirled comically against his cheek. The phrase and gesture were perpetuated all over the place, on radio and on television talk shows (thank you, thank you, David Letterman), and then high school kids everywhere started using the phrase and gesture sarcastically. William Safire wrote a column about the etymology of the phrase "dat's tasty," with citations from minstrel shows and a particular radio episode of *Amos 'n' Andy* during which the Kingfish exclaims, "Mm, ain't dat tasty!" over a succulent piece of fried chicken. Now of course it's all over the Internet; there are countless "Dat's Tasty!" and "Say, Dat's Tasty!" tagged videos on YouTube, and those words pop up on all sorts of other blogs and websites (my daughter, Julie, who has the self-conferred title of Zip's Web mistress, keeps track of these things). Just now, when I Googled "Dat's Tasty!" it produced 547,862 results. Some of these are vulgar and therefore extremely problematic references, but Julie and Jacob have persuaded me that it's all good, as they say.

THE COMPANY IS proud to tell you that Eli Czaplinsky, a Hungarian Jew, an orphan who arrived at sixteen with his older brother, Morris, at Ellis Island in 1920, was a pushcart peddler with ambitions to do better with the rest of his life than sell caramels and boiled sweets on Orchard Street in all kinds of weather for two or three dollars a day. The company history certainly doesn't mention the third and youngest brother, Julius, left behind with cousins in Budapest at the last moment when the two older brothers realized they wouldn't have enough money for the three of them to travel to Danzig, book passage, and procure enough food to survive the ocean crossing in steerage on the SS *Karpinski,* the dilapidated vessel that brought them to America.

The company history doesn't explain that Eli liked to go to the Ottendorfer branch library near the rooming house on East Seventh Street where he and Morris shared a room (and a bed) quite often—in fact, nearly every day—not because of his love of books, but because it had a nice toilet in a warm room in the basement, which he preferred to the foul communal toilet in a shack in the courtyard behind their tenement. Owing to a peculiarity of its endowment, half of the library's collection was in German. Eli would from time to time take a book from the shelves and struggle through a few pages, trying to make the most of German's proximity to Yiddish. More appealing to him were the three Yiddish newspapers to which this library branch carried subscriptions. These were much nicer to read than all the German books with their formal language that had nothing to do with everyday New York life. Eli would visit the public library, the official story goes, to read these newspapers in a familiar language, and to take home a new children's book each week in order to teach himself better English so he could get ahead in America. (It was his casual perusal of *The Tale of Tom Kitten* that led to his lifelong use of the surprising phrase "I am affronted" if something offended him.)

Also not in the official Zip's Candies history are any details about what happened to Eli after Morris died in the diphtheria epidemic that swept New York in 1921 and Eli was left alone in the world to fend for himself at age seventeen. He became a tough street kid, still roving the Lower East Side hawking caramels, bull's-eyes, blackjacks, and root-beer barrels from his pushcart, but now also running errands for a bootlegger called

Little Augie. Eli was one of the Little Augies, as the street gang was called.

It was a way to be safe and to make some extra money, and nobody was suspicious of the sweet boy with the big smile selling candy from his pushcart, which made him a very useful errand boy, and who can say what else might have been in the bottom of that pushcart? Eli transported guns from here to there, and more often than not there were hefty bundles of cash as he made his rounds peddling sweets, collecting from Little Augie's customers along his route. Sam would tell me about these things, but then he would half take them back, always concluding with a remark to the effect that nobody really knew for sure what Eli did for Little Augie, and maybe he just left New York to get a fresh start and everything about the money and the guns was an exaggeration, and anyway, it was all a long time ago. I note with interest the relationship between the names "Little Sammies" and "Little Augies."

WHENEVER WE TALKED about Eli—Sam and I—he would always say the same thing, in the same way, with a rueful shake of his head: that Eli rarely told him any significant details about whatever it was he did to get by in New York. Once, though, Eli described to Sam how he bought his first good shirt at Wanamaker's department store, the kind of shirt a gentleman would wear, with money he and Morris had made all in one day, when they had the idea of hawking sweets in Union Square at a union rally commemorating the tenth anniversary of the Triangle Waist Company factory fire. Eli and Morris circulated through the crowd shouting out, Remember the victims! Buy a Triangle Toffee! Which perhaps misleadingly suggested that their proceeds would benefit a union fund of some kind.

It was a cold and blustery March afternoon, and Morris had a bad headache and a sore throat. By the end of the day, he was too hoarse to speak at all. The next morning, Morris was feverish and couldn't get out of bed, and within a week he was dead and Eli was wearing his new shirt from Wanamaker's to stand at his brother's grave and say a Kaddish. Sam said that Eli always wondered if Morris had caught the diphtheria germ in the Union Square crowd, or if he was already infected and had perhaps spread his germs among all those people, including the many children for whom their toffees had been purchased.

What is established fact, if not the sort of detail Zip's Candies has featured prominently in its literature over the years, is that Eli left New York in great haste at the end of August 1923, because he witnessed the murder, in front of the Essex Market Courthouse, of a gangster called Kid Dropper Kaplan, who was at the time in police custody. The Little Augies were implicated in the killing, and let's just say there is reason to assume that Eli may have been more than a witness and it was a good time to disappear. All the rest of his father's life, Sam told me, even long after Augie Orgen and Louis Kushner and Lepke Buchalter and all the rest of them were locked up in jail or safely dead and buried, Eli got nervous and changed the subject abruptly whenever anything about this time in his life before New Haven came up.

That August day in 1923, the day Kid Dropper was himself dropped by a bullet in the back, Eli went straight to Grand Central Terminal. Sam told me this story many times over the years, often over lunch at Clark's, where we would go for a quick grilled cheese and a shared order of French fries, just the two of us, to take a break from the din and tumult of the Zip's floor and, no question, to have a relaxed conversation unsupervised by Frieda. Sometimes we shared a chocolate milk shake, too.

Write this down! he would command me. You're the only smart one who's got an interest, kiddo, so you're the only one I'm telling this to. Am I telling it too fast? he would ask, without slowing down, as he recounted yet another bit of weird Ziplinsky family lore, or as he expounded on his philosophies of the candy business, or as he theorized about some nuance of nougat-making. And I would, I would write it all down, in one of the notebooks I always carried for just this purpose. I have those notebooks, all twenty-two of them, dated and numbered, on a shelf at home. We had lunch at Clark's once or twice a week for twenty-three years, until just before Sam died, when he wasn't really able to eat the kind of food they serve at Clark's, except for maybe a cup of soup. Their avgolemono soup is outstanding.

Sam loved his soup. He loved a lot of things. He loved life. I really miss that man. I have always had to deal with the way Frieda bore me so much inexplicable animus over the years, long before she had any specific reasons to dislike me. But her coldness was tempered for me by the genuine and deep connection I had with Sam, from that first day. Our mutual love really had nothing to do with Howard, strange as that sounds. Of course Sam was soon enough my father-in-law, and then my children's grandfather, but I really loved him for himself. And I know he loved me. And we all know there is concrete proof of this. He was of perfectly sound mind when he made his final decisions. He was an astute businessman and an astute judge of character, and so he anticipated the need to protect me as he did. He's been gone eleven years now, and I miss him every day.

SAM ALWAYS USED the same words, telling the story of Eli's flight from New York. Straight to Grand Central Terminal, straight from Essex Street, Sam would say, and then, invariably, he would pause to add, You know, kiddo, the right name for the train station is Terminal? You got that straight? Because Grand Central Station is a post office branch and all you could buy there for yourself is stamps, not a train ticket.

So Eli took himself from the Essex Market Courthouse straight to Grand Central Terminal, leaving his pushcart on the street, right there at the bottom of the courthouse steps, without even stopping at his rooming house to collect his few possessions, his habitual library book still in his jacket pocket, never to be returned. Straight from Essex and Delancey to Grand Central Terminal he went on a nickel train ride on the Brooklyn–Manhattan line, and there Eli bought a ticket for the last stop on the very next train to leave the station, and on the train he read and reread that little book he happened to have in his pocket, to pass the time, and to calm himself. It was a copy of Helen Bannerman's *Little Black Sambo,* which is how he got to the end of the line, New Haven, with an idea.

I AM PERFECTLY aware that a lot of this information about Zip's Candies and Ziplinsky family history and Eli Czaplinksy's flight from New York is not in dispute, and therefore some of this history could appear to be irrelevant to the matters that *are* in dispute, but in order to provide all the facts, I prefer to give the most complete context possible. The Ziplinsky family has tried to control the story of their business and their family history over all these years, which has made it especially necessary to tell this counterstory, to note the elements in the Zip's time lines and glossy official histories that have been shaded or obscured. Just as chocolate is tempered in order to achieve maximum gloss and snap, so has the Zip's Candies history been tempered. I have begun as I mean to go on; it is extremely important to me that these pages lay out with complete clarity every aspect of my knowledge and beliefs and experience with Zip's Candies and the Ziplinsky family. So this is a warning to any party reading this affidavit. If you get impatient and start to skim, believing either that you already know everything and there is nothing new here, or that the details I hereby provide so meticulously have no significance, you just might miss what is most interesting and important.

WHEN THE CURTAIN rises on Eli's next act, according to the official Zip's Candies time line, it is springtime of 1924, and he has been working in New Haven for Armenian cousins who make chocolate-covered coconut bars overnight in their basement kitchen when the air is cool so they can sell them door-to-door each morning before the day warms up and the Choclettos and Coconettos melt. So here is Eli once again walking the streets, selling candy from a pushcart, working for whatever he can make in a day. Is he restless? Is he convinced that he can do better? Of course he is. He is a married man now, with a pregnant bride, the former Lillian Rosenfeld, a pretty girl in her photos (though she thickened and aged very rapidly after the death of her second son). Lillian is a highly skilled dipper whose departure from the coconut bar line was a blow to the Armenians. She will soon give birth to their firstborn child, their son Sam, a robust eight-pound baby who will be born "two months premature."

Lillian had been their prize dipper, quick and precise, efficient and tidy. One day as Eli waited for his stock, she caught his eye. He was mesmerized by her quicksilver hands, enticed by her deft way with the lumps of shredded coconut, intoxicated by her speed and composure. He asked her to show him how she dipped the Coconettos so quickly and neatly. She giggled and showed him. He tried to imitate her movements, but he dripped melted chocolate all over the dipping table and down his shirt. Soon they were keeping company.

When Peter Paul Halajian and his brother-in-law Calvin Kazanjian, with backing from Shamlian, Hagopian, Kazanjian, and Chouljian cousins, decide to expand their operations and open a factory in Naugatuck (where they name the company after Halajian, and place their faith in their Mounds coconut bars), Eli is invited to stay with the business and move with them, but he sees a bargain and buys the old equipment from the Armenians for a few dollars. And with enough money to buy a building, money that may have something to do with his hasty exile from New York (who can say if he managed to take one of those bundles of money from his pushcart with him when he ran away from the Essex Street Courthouse? It was a long time ago, does it really matter? This is how Sam would always tell the story), he waves his hand in the air so frantically that nobody wants to bid against him and so he places the winning bid for the River Street building and its contents in the bankruptcy auction of a small machine shop.

The building has most recently been home to Peet Engineering, a young business driven into the ground by its hapless proprietors in less than two years. The Peet brothers are hell-bent on producing their single-minded invention, the One-Lock Adjustable Reamer, but they give no thought whatsoever to marketing and distribution. Milo and Alvy Peet pour all their funds into pursuing this dream, the perfection of the One-Lock Adjustable Reamer, but nobody knows about it, and so of course nobody buys it, and the day comes when they have no money left in the bank, no way to pay their workers or their creditors, and the bank won't give them any more credit, and that's that.

Perhaps even with brilliant marketing there would never have been sufficient demand for this innovative product to keep a factory going, but who can say? They didn't plan ahead, Sam would tell me his father would always say, with a rueful shake of the head. They had only one product, and they were undercapitalized, they didn't have the cash to get off the ground and stay off the ground long enough to find out if it was a good thing people would want. Bad break for them, lucky break for the Ziplinskys. Eli gets the building cheap.

There is a candy factory to be assembled from the welter of mechanical creations left behind by this failed venture, a cautionary tale in itself. Motor-driven assembly lines snake through a series of workstations, tool benches, lathes, packing tables. Wrenches lie where they were laid down on workbenches holding half-finished machined objects, blueprints beside them, by workers at the end of their shift who did not know when the whistle blew that they would never hear it again, that the doors would be padlocked by the bank before morning.

The assembly lines are adaptable, and Eli is an adapter. He makes a candy factory. He is a man with a plan. The factory itself is not hexed. He will not rely on just one product. Zip's Candies will diversify before it begins, and risk will be spread among Eli's three *Little Black Sambo*–inspired candy products.

Workers are hired. Factory machinists with experience and nerve and nothing to lose are employed to repurpose and retrofit and solve the giant puzzle of how to make the three candies Eli has in mind out of these machines and the wagonload of candy-making equipment the Armenians left behind when they decamped to Naugatuck to build their own factory. While Eli makes do with their castoffs, Peter Paul would churn out Mounds and Almond Joys (and, less successfully, Dream, Main Show, Almond Clusters, and the especially lamented Caravelle; when they acquired the York Cone Company, they made York Peppermint Patties, too) in their modern, streamlined factory, until the bleak November day in 2007 when the factory would go dark, the brand having been sold to Cadbury, which after a few years licensed it to Hershey's, who decided despite earlier assurances to the contrary to consolidate manufacturing operations by moving the Mounds and Almond Joy production to Virginia, putting two hundred and twenty loyal workers out of their jobs.

As a completist, I note in passing that Naugatuck has also been abandoned by the United States Rubber Company (as it was known until 1961, when it became Uniroyal), maker of automobile tires and the nearly eponymous Naugahyde, and Keds. Poor postindustrial Naugatuck, once proud home to so many industries churning out all-American products, but now just another very quiet, old-fashioned town built on an obsolete foundation, with only a few desultory small-town businesses dotting Rubber Avenue.

I don't know why, exactly, but Frieda used to characterize with her most withering disdain people or things that did not meet her standards as being "strictly from Naugatuck." Possibly this had to do in some way with her barely concealed jealousy about the immense success of Peter Paul compared to Zip's, which has always had a niche and held on to it, but certainly has never achieved a fraction of the market share of those ambitious Armenians and their coconut candies.

THE TIGERMELT IS a straightforward bar, distinguished by the tiger stripes of dark chocolate over the milk-chocolate coating, which enrobes a classic nougat and caramel peanut bar. It is inspired by the tigers in *Little Black Sambo*, who take all of Little Black Sambo's fine clothing, from his red coat to his blue trousers and his beautiful little purple shoes "with Crimson Soles and Crimson Linings"—they even take his beautiful green umbrella—only to get into an angry dispute about which of them is the grandest in his fine clothing.

"And at last they all got so angry that they jumped up and took off all the fine clothes, and began to tear each other with their claws, and bite each other with their great big white teeth . . . And they came, rolling and tumbling right to the foot of the very tree where Little Black Sambo was hiding, but he jumped quickly in behind the umbrella. And the Tigers all caught hold of each other's tails, as they wrangled and scrambled, and so they found themselves in a ring round the tree . . . And the Tigers were very, very angry, but still they would not let go of each other's tails. And they were so angry, that they ran round the tree, trying to eat each other up, and they ran faster and faster, till they were whirling round so fast that you couldn't see their legs at all. And they still ran faster and faster and faster, till they all just melted away, and there was nothing left but a great big pool of melted butter round the foot of the tree."

Mumbo Jumbos are two ridged discs of licorice candy, one black, one red, which fit together with a satisfying, yin-yang click, like two stacked contrasting checkers. They are named for Little Black Sambo's devoted parents, his mother, Black Mumbo, and his father, Black Jumbo. Mumbo Jumbos don't melt very easily. Every chocolate candy company should have a nonchocolate, warm temperature–stable candy option, like a seafood restaurant's having steak on the menu for that one person at the table who hates fish. It's smart business.

LITTLE SAMMIES, IN fact named for Little Black Sambo himself, are clearly the single confection to which Eli is most dedicated, having been profoundly influenced by his first American sweet, a Tootsie Roll given him by a kind guard while he waited for his medical inspection the day he arrived at Ellis Island. By the time Eli passed his trachoma inspection (the man in front of him, who was also from the Pest side of Budapest and had boasted to Eli and Morris about his cousin in Brooklyn who delivered ice and had a job waiting for him and said maybe he would help the Czaplinsky boys find work, failed the trachoma test, and his coat was chalked on the back with a humiliating *X* before he was led away), he was savoring on his tongue the last lingering, sweet morsel of that inaugural Tootsie Roll.

Little Sammies are by far the most complex of Zip's three products to fabricate. The inch-long chewy chocolate-toffee figures require precise molding, cooling, and coating. Hand-dipping is not entirely satisfactory for achieving the glossy chocolate coating shell Eli strives for, because in his mind's eye Little Sammie should shine, though the earliest Little Sammies are out of necessity hand-dipped, and soon enough the giant rotating kettle that had been used to hold the annealing bath for machined cogs and screws is converted into the Little Sammies panning drum and then, say, don't those Little Sammies shine as they tumble off the line!

ON NOVEMBER 12, 1924, a score of workers is poised. The power-supply lever is pulled, the first machines are switched on, and then the next machines are activated, all down the lines, and like new rides at a carnival, the mechanical contraptions that will make the three confections for which Zip's Candies will be known for decades to come, into the next century, all clank and whirr and hum to life. There is a photograph of this moment. We see a white-coated Eli, with a full head of dark hair, standing proudly with his hand on the lever like the captain at the helm of his ship, with his grinning paper-hatted crew at their places all along the lines. An unsmiling Lillian, in a flowered dress intended to conceal her postpregnancy bulk, can be seen off to the side, holding a swaddled bundle that is her infant son Sammy.

Moments after the photograph is taken, smoke pours out of the motor driving the head pulley on the Mumbo Jumbos belt, and it has to be shut down immediately. A month goes by before that line is running smoothly and true production of stock can commence, but the photograph reveals no herald of that temporary setback, and shows only the ignition of the Zip's Candies engine that would drive Eli just as Eli drove it, working perpetually to keep his dream of his beautiful sweet candies and the success and prosperity those candies bring moving forward, always moving forward. He kept the lines moving until the day he died at a regrettably young age of a massive heart attack only twenty-two years later, sitting alone in his office on a Friday night, reconciling order sheets to close out the week.

HERSHEY'S CHOCOLATE HAD contracts to supply the U.S. military with Ration D Bars and Tropical Bars, both created with an innovative formulation that kept them from melting, which made them stable in the North African desert, even if they did have the texture of chewy linoleum. In the course of the war, Hershey's produced more than three billion of these bars for consumption by American troops around the world. Eli admired the way Milton Hershey parlayed those contracts, because not only was this an extraordinary volume of business, but it also allowed Hershey's to expand production capabilities on the government's nickel. In 1939, Hershey's could produce a hundred thousand ration bars a day. By the time the war ended, Hershey's was cranking out twenty-four million ration bars a week. But Eli took more than a little satisfaction in the knowledge that even Milton Hershey was not immune to the stresses of war, which forced him to suspend production of Hershey's Kisses in 1942 because of a shortage of the foil used to wrap them (production would not resume until 1949).

Eli recognized a good marketing strategy when he saw one, and figuring that he had the advantage of offering his first line product, not some inferior-tasting, gritty, shelf-stable nutrition bar made to government specifications, he went after government contracts for Zip's, but his efforts failed. Instead, Eli went all out with significant Little Sammies donations to the Red Cross for food parcels in the final twelve months of the war and the first six months of occupation. It was a hardship, because commodities were expensive and unpredictably available. Lillian made numerous objections to giving their product away at a time like this. Perhaps he had gone too far. But Eli insisted, even though he was bitter about Milton Hershey's cleverness in finagling those contracts that eluded him. He recognized the genius that lay behind Hershey's investment in giving American soldiers a taste of home that would create a permanent atavistic association with America and the taste of Hershey's slightly sour milk chocolate.

By the end of 1946, the postwar sugar shortage had not quite ended, but the insatiable demand for Little Sammies by returning GIs was the payoff for all the Zip's Candies donations to the Red Cross. Sugar was very hard to come by from week to week. Milton Hershey had that angle covered as well, with his own Cuban sugar plantations, even his own railroad to carry the sugar across Cuba from his refineries to the port of Havana. Processed cacao supplies were irregular. Eli had taken to staying late at work in order to make call after call to chocolate processors and brokers who might have some new sources for him. There were rumors of small quantities of decent cacao beans coming out of Congo, Trinidad, Ghana. But now he had found the solution, a surprising source in Madagascar that would both ensure Zip's Candies a guaranteed supply of good cacao and also change the course of Ziplinsky family history. His body lay on the floor behind the desk, samples from the day's Mumbo Jumbos scattered around him, when young Sam, married just a few months to Frieda (who was by then pregnant with the first of their three children, the doomed Lewis), eager to claim his weekend off and irked by the disruption of his plan to take his pregnant bride to the movies (she adored Dana Andrews, and they were planning to see *The Best Years of Our Lives*), having been sent back to the factory by his mother that Friday evening when she became concerned that Eli hadn't come home for his dinner, found him.

THE TRADITIONAL MUMBO Jumbos pack has a very good reputation among licorice aficionados. The package is a graphic delight, one that has hardly changed from the original to the present moment. It features the Zip's green umbrella against a festival of contrasting stripes, which make reference to the colorful outfits worn by Little Black Sambo's mother and father.

The market for licorice has always been small but steady. Devotees are appreciative of a good, chewy, flavorful licorice disc, especially one modeled on the wheat-based Finnish licorice nibs Eli knew from his New York street peddling days, and not on the more elastic, corn-based products like those that had already been around for decades by then—Red Vines, made by the American Licorice Company in Chicago since 1914, and, even older, the various licorice candies made by Young & Smylie since 1845 (Young & Smylie became part of the National Licorice Company in 1902, which in turn renamed itself Y&S Candies in 1968), those red and black twisted vines that over the years mutated into the nearly plastic Twizzlers, which dominates the licorice market share today and which since 1977 has been owned by Hershey's (that insatiable devourer of small candy brands, from Good & Plenty to Heath Bars to Jolly Ranchers to Reese's to Dagoba to Scharffen Berger). I am partial to Red Vines, which are best eaten when slightly stale. They can be toughened up in a few hours by deliberate exposure to air.

TIGERMELTS DO WELL from the beginning, with plentiful orders—it's a familiar combination bar, the dark-chocolate tiger stripes are a pleasant gimmick, the wrapper features a row of tigers chasing one another in a circle, and there is a charming slogan on the original wrapper, too: "Plain Hungry? Or Tigermelt Hungry?" (We had to drop that slogan when we redesigned the wrapper to accommodate nutritional information, once that became a legal requirement.)

But it's the Little Sammies that are a tremendous success, once they are finally perfected by the middle of 1925 and are tumbling off the line with the glossy finish exactly right, exactly the way Eli dreamed up his Little Sammies, his true confections. The public loves them from the start. Originally, they are packaged in twos, in that waxy yellow wrapper with the Zip's signature green umbrella emblazoned with the words "Say, Dat's Tasty!" The innovation of adding the third Little Sammie comes in 1932 as a way to offer the penny-pinched consumer more value for the same nickel, and Little Sammies have stayed three to a pack ever since. (Because this is a bit crowded, Little Sammies may get stuck together in the package; we recommend that you open the package and expose them to the air before you eat them.)

Little Sammies have always been fresh, I would like to point out, unless you let them grow stale after purchase. We make them, we ship them, they sell. I can only laugh at the genius who dreamed up the Hershey's marketing campaign for "Fresh From the Factory" opportunities, one select line at a time, on their website. All of our candy is always fresh from the factory! It's true that any limited availability can create an artificial surge in demand for product, the same way a limited-edition brand extension does, whether it is a variation that swaps dark chocolate for milk, or uses almonds instead of peanuts, or adds a mint or a caramel option, to name the four most obvious limited-edition variations.

Last year Jacob and I sent away for some "Fresh From the Factory" Twizzlers in order to see firsthand what Hershey's was actually selling. The product was impressively fresh, to be sure. One of those F From the F Twizzlers will droop if held balanced on your index finger. In contrast, an off-the-rack Twizzler from the Stop & Shop is darker and so much stiffer that holding it in the same way is like balancing a pencil. The not-so-fresh Twizzler was also noticeably tougher, bite for bite. Jacob admitted that he preferred it to the droopy Twizzler, which was like an edible lanyard. Jacob can be perverse that way. If "Fresh From the Factory" is billed by Hershey's as the optimal, premium taste and texture experience, isn't that a rather risky strategy, cultivating in consumers an awareness of the staleness and inferiority of all the rest of your retail stock?

❉   ❉

THE FIRST LITTLE Sammies sell out in New Haven and then they sell out again; production is increased, and they sell out all over New York. Soon national retailers are clamoring to place orders, and then the New Haven Railroad wants to sell them on all the passenger trains that run through New Haven, and then the Boston & Maine Railroad wants Little Sammies as well, and three chains of movie theaters start stocking Little Sammies. Within months Little Sammies have slots in grocery stores and gas stations across America. And canny Eli requires that for every case of Little Sammies ordered, a certain number of boxes of Tigermelts and Mumbo Jumbos must be ordered as well, thereby ensuring growth and steady business for the other two Zip's lines.

And so former Little Augie errand boy with a pushcart Eli Czaplinsky becomes Eli Ziplinsky, the beloved, innovative, industrious, hardworking, visionary founder and proprietor of Zip's Candies, maker of one of America's most beloved childhood treats, Little Sammies. The lines are in perpetual motion forever after, these crazy aggregations of thriftily appropriated machinery mixing and blending and forming and extruding a never-ending flow of Tigermelts, Mumbo Jumbos, and Little Sammies.

5

Sam, obviously, felt that I was family. He chose to reward my loyalty and devotion to the family and the business. That is the only explanation for his decision to leave me, as he did, 25 percent ownership of the Ziplinsky Family Limited Partnership, which is to say, Zip's Candies. Whether or not all family members agree with his choices, whether or not all family members respect his choices, surely the time has come to accept them. For God's sake, it's been eleven years now. The last will and testament of Samuel Ziplinsky has been honored by every court. The estate is settled. The distributions have been made. The identities of the Ziplinsky Family Trust beneficiaries are in dispute, but there is really nothing left to haggle over in Sam's estate. As the only living child of Eli and Lillian Ziplinsky, Sam had total ownership of Zip's Candies, having inherited the business from his mother, Lillian (to whom ownership had passed when Eli died without a will in 1946), when she died in 1975, just a few weeks after I walked in the door at Zip's. I am glad I met Lillian that one time, as it connects me to every generation of the family business.

I should add here, in the interest of delineating every branch of this bonsai of a family tree, that Sam's younger brother, Milton, died just months before the end of World War II, in his first week of basic training, at age nineteen, when he was accidentally shot in the face on the rifle range at Camp Jackson. Fortunately, he had no children—none that have been identified, anyway. I

should know better than to assume anything about the repro-
ductive habits of the Ziplinskys, but if Milton's children exist,
they have badly missed the boat on stepping forward with their
hands out, and given how useful their existence could have been
to swing the majority vote in order to force a sale of the business,
and how nightmarish that revelation would have been for me, I
am pretty sure any issue of the late Milton Ziplinsky would have
been truffled out by now.

So Milton doesn't play any part in this history or the present set of conflicts, though as the unofficial family historian/
counterhistorian, I note with interest that he does take his hal-
lowed place among the missing in this peculiar family, Milton
being his generation's golden boy who dies a tragic early death
and leaves the family out of balance, with a cascade of shifting
roles.

Howard and Irene's older brother, Lewis, is another piece of
the strange pattern. Frieda's golden boy, Lewis—her firstborn,
the clear heir apparent to the business even as a child, by all
accounts a wonderful, charming, smart, handsome boy—died at
age fourteen when he was struck by lightning in Madagascar. I
know how outlandish that sounds, like a perverse joke. He and
Howard were there together that summer. Howard was twelve.
They had been working among the vanilla orchids, doing a lot
of tedious hand pollinating, and then the two of them had skived
off with Andry, a local boy apparently their age who was nomi-
nally in charge of them, for a swim in the river. (They had been
warned to keep a watch for crocodiles, believe it or not. How
could anyone have thought this was a safe place for these tender
boys to spend their summers? Especially cautious Jews?)

Black thunderheads rolled in, the wind shifted, and fat drops
of heavy rain were suddenly pelting down on them. Tropical
rainstorms can be sudden, and they can end just as suddenly. As

the boys horsed around in the water, the rain seemed to let up, but then it intensified all over again and there was a rumble of thunder. Andry and Lewis very responsibly swam to the water's edge and started to hoist themselves out onto the sandy river-bank. Howard was still bobbing around in the middle of the river, his head tilted back with his mouth wide open to catch the raindrops, when lightning struck the wet boys as they clambered out. Andry, who was touching Lewis's arm when the lightning strike occurred, was severely burned, but he lived, though today he walks with a limp and is thought to be a bit simple. (He is still employed by the Czaplinsky family, as a gardener with few gen-uine responsibilities.)

Lewis had been struck directly, and he died instantly. Howard told me this story when we went out to dinner that first time. He narrated in a careful and remote way, with little emo-tion beyond a small sad smile that wasn't really a smile, pulling his mouth down at one corner, and I really thought at first that he was making it up. He described these events to me the way he might have been telling me about a disturbing movie he had seen a long time ago. When I look back now on the way I fell into that inexplicably intense relationship with Howard, I believe Lewis is in the story. His tragic death, the way each Ziplinsky carried that sorrow—it attracted me. I know it did. I was moved by the unbearable sadness that surrounded the story of the short life of the older brother, which added meaning and context to Howard's glibness and clowning, but at the same time, Lewis's absence made me feel that there could be a place for me in this family.

Morris, Milton, Lewis: all those missing sons. Irene would tell you it is Kennedyesque, the way those first sons were struck down. This pattern has obviously been broken in the next generation, though I say that with just a little bit of a sense of whistling in the dark. My two kids are healthy, as is their cousin Ethan. But who can guarantee anything? (And of course there are the cousins in Madagascar. I know I brought them up, but Newton and Edison Czaplinsky don't come into the story quite yet, though of course they will have been there all along.)

I suppose you could count Irene's high school abortion as technically having fulfilled the peculiar Ziplinsky destiny of doom for the firstborn child. Please don't misunderstand me; I served two terms on the state board of Planned Parenthood of Connecticut twenty years ago, and I was tireless in my efforts to keep abortion safe and legal and available to girls like Irene. The offices were in those years located above the New Haven clinic on Whitney Avenue, and some afternoons, on my way out after committee meetings, I would see high school girls in the waiting room, many of them in the plaid skirt and green sweater that was the uniform of St. Mary's two blocks away. I was the youngest member of the board at that time, and I knew that many of the older board members were motivated by their fond dedication to a lifted-pinky and benevolent sort of eugenics. These dowagers in Lilly Pulitzer dresses and Mother's pearls worked like busy little bees providing birth control to the lower order, poor people and "minorities." Until 1965, all birth control was technically illegal in Connecticut. In its way, it was admirable if misguided work. Sometimes people do the right things for the wrong reasons.

Anyway, Irene had an abortion three years before *Roe v. Wade* made abortion legal in Connecticut. Howard only told me about his sister's abortion when she was pregnant with Ethan. She had just begun eleventh grade at the Day Prospect Hill School, and Howard was a sophomore at Yale. Apparently her boyfriend (or boyfriends, who knows) had no awareness of her pregnancy. Howard even paid for Irene's abortion. (I find that creepy, the way it suited her to have him take the responsibility as if he was the father.) He set it up with a doctor he found because one of his Yale freshman-year roommates had been through it with his Smith College girlfriend. Never let it be said that the chief benefit of a Yale degree is being a Yale alumnus. Those Ivy League educations really prepare you!

Howard drove Irene to Springfield on the appointed day. He left her off at a certain intersection, as instructed, and watched her get into the green Buick that pulled up a moment later, and then he waited on that corner six hours later for her to be dropped off. In the intervening time Howard took himself to a German restaurant festooned with hideous beer steins hanging down from the ceiling like Prussian stalactites. It was October, and they were having a game festival, with partridge and elk and bear on the menu, so he ordered a bear steak and a mug of sudsy lager, but a group of people at the bar were singing drinking songs in German, and when his food came, he couldn't eat it. Was he the only person in the restaurant who wasn't there for the monthly meeting of the Springfield branch of the Baader-Meinhof Gang?

With a great deal of time to kill, Howard then went to visit the site of the apparently historic first Indian Motorcycle factory. (He had always wanted to own an Indian 101 Scout, and when I bought him one, a beautiful, cherry red, restored 1930 101 Scout, for his thirty-fifth birthday, despite my very reasonable fears about head injuries, I did so with the hope that this would satisfy Howard's chronic adolescent need to flirt with danger.) It began to drizzle, and it got dark, and Howard sat with an unread history text in a donut shop near the appointed intersection, and there he waited and waited for Irene to reappear.

She was almost two hours late, and he had begun to imagine that she was dead and he would be blamed. How could he face Frieda and Sam and tell them they had lost another child because of the carelessness and stupidity of their only remaining child, the dumb one? Irene threw up in his car on the drive back to New Haven, Howard went to a party that night, where he drank until he passed out, and they never, ever spoke of that day again.

If Irene is outraged that I have just provided these private details in this account of family history, then I can only suggest that she review her own choices, which have led to the necessity for the whole truth of this document.

SAM TOLD ME more than once, usually in the context of memories of the family's anxious vigil when the draft lottery numbers were announced in those Vietnam years (Howard got lucky each time, with very high numbers in the years when he had no deferment), that he felt terribly guilty about his younger brother's death, which he always believed contributed to Eli's fatal heart attack not so long after. Sam had been ineligible for military service, being nearly entirely blind in one eye, a trait he inherited from Eli.

Howard did not have this familial refractive amblyopia, which would have kept him from military service even with a low draft number, but Irene did. She says this is why she has never worn eye makeup, because she can't see with her blind eye when her good eye is closed, so it's very difficult to apply makeup, but she has also said at other times that she never wears eye makeup because of animal testing, and there was a year at Brown when she was militantly opposed to makeup since it represented the tyranny of the male fantasy of woman as whore, because cosmetics are designed to enhance and exaggerate the secondary sex characteristics of the female, and lipstick in particular is used because it makes women's lips look labial. That was the same year she stopped shaving her legs and under her arms. All that ended when she started going out with Arthur. As is so often the case with Irene, who can say what the truth is?

IN ANY CASE, Sam was the only heir to the Zip's Candies empire. What he made of it was his legacy to the family. Given how he was forced to take on the huge responsibility of running the business when he was twenty-two, when his father died so unexpectedly, Sam's stewardship of Zip's Candies was almost not a second-generation passing of the torch so much as it was in many ways simply the continuation of everything Eli had started. There was much more of a next-generation feeling when Howard took over in 1998.

Running a candy company was probably not what Sam would have really wanted to do with his life had he not been born into it. But Sam never had a chance to have any other kind of vision for himself. His life's work was simply to do everything he could to honor his father's vision and ambition, and to support his mother. Keeping Zip's healthy, making Zip's bigger and better, little by little—that was the only thing he know how to do, the only thing he could do, after Eli died.

I asked Sam once, over one of our hundreds of grilled cheese sandwiches, if he had ever thought of not going into the family business at all. After a moment's reflection he admitted that he would have loved teaching, and perhaps coaching high school baseball, but then he interrupted himself to declare that he really couldn't remember even imagining any other life. He was proud to have been so successful with Zip's that he could offer that freedom he never had to his children and grandchildren, whom he claimed were welcome to go anywhere and do anything they wanted to do, with his blessing.

That said, and said sincerely, and often, I do think he would have been devastated if in his lifetime there were no heirs apparent named Ziplinsky, whether by blood or by marriage. "Candy makes people happy," Sam used to say as a way of summing up and moving the conversation past a challenging moment, "and I make candy. So my business is to make people happy. Who could ask for anything better?"

Zip's Candies might make people happy, but it doesn't make the Ziplinskys happy. I take peculiar solace in finding myself part of a great American tradition of troubled candy families. At an awards dinner during a candy and snack show in Atlanta last year, an inebriated vendor told me fascinating details of two Mars family divorces, which make my situation seem like a piece of cake. And let us reflect for a moment on Hart Crane's suicidal leap into the sea from a ship sailing between Havana and Florida at age thirty-three, in 1932. His father, Clarence, had invented Life Savers candy twenty years before, inspired by the recent innovation of round floatation lifesaving rings on ships.

When he sold it in 1909, Clarence Crane's Ohio maple-sugar business was the largest maple-sugar producer in the world. He started the Queen Victoria Chocolate Company after that, and he went on to develop hard peppermint candies for the summer season, when business slowed because chocolate melted in the heat. Crane was inspired to create a new round shape for his peppermint candies by a glimpse of a hand-operated pill-making machine at the Cleveland pharmacy where he bought his flavoring extracts. He formed his round, flat peppermints on a machine adapted for the purpose. The finishing touch was a small hole punched in the middle of each one to create Crane's Pep-O-Mint Life Savers, packaged in cardboard tubes depicting a sailor tossing a life preserver to a pretty girl, "For That Stormy Breath."

But the Crane family hardly profited from this innovation, as the rights to Life Savers were soon sold for only $2,900 in 1913 (doesn't every family have at least one mythic lost family fortune?), and Clarence Crane went back to chocolate, which did not interest his poet son one bit.

As Hart Crane removed his topcoat and in his pajamas climbed over the railing of the SS *Orizaba,* "tilting there momently, shrill shirt ballooning," did he note the irony? He was last seen swimming toward the horizon. His body was never found.

It's a good thing Sam never lived to see the family at war this way. Though of course it was his death that set the crisis in motion. Howard must have known, if he thought it through, that everything would come to light sooner or later, but Howard has not exactly made a name for himself as the man who thinks things through.

I should explain why I am the only member of the family who doesn't call Howard by his nickname, Howdy. Actually, I am the only person in his life who doesn't call him Howdy. It's like the way Beaver Cleaver's mother was the only one to call him Theodore. Everyone knows Howard as Howdy. It's printed on his Zip's Candies business cards. I have been Mrs. Howard Ziplinsky for more than thirty years now, but you wouldn't know it. If I identify myself that way when charging something, or phoning in an order, there is always a puzzled silence, followed by a correction: Oh, you mean *Howdy* Ziplinsky. Okay, thanks, Mrs. Ziplinsky! Have a nice day!

When Howard and his older brother, Lewis, were little, they loved to watch *Howdy Doody* on television on Saturday mornings, and Sam started calling them Buffalo Bob and Howdy Doody. I don't know if Lewis was called Buffalo Bob for very long, or if it was ever shortened to Buff, or Bob. I wonder now if Sam realized that he was assigning Lewis the part of the responsible adult while Howard was designated the unserious puppet. Nobody talks easily about Lewis. Because he died the way he did at fourteen, every memory of him seems to be encoded with that inevitability, as if he lived his short life hurtling toward his death, and so the fact of his death retrospectively colors every fact of his life.

In his childhood, Howard was called Howdy until it caused some bullying in seventh grade and he made everyone drop it. He signed his name with a very serious "Howard M. Ziplinsky" all through junior high and high school. But when Howard went to Yale and his DKE frat brother George W. Bush started calling him Howdy, though it may have been intended as a putdown, Howard went with it, and soon everyone, even his professors, was calling him Howdy.

It's a friendly name, I admit, an openhanded, slap-you-on-the-back, pleased-to-meet-ya! kind of name, but it doesn't work for me. I tried to call him Howdy when we met, but it's not really a very respectful name, and then, soon enough, it didn't feel like a very romantic or sexy name either, and I just never could say it and mean it. If I called him Howdy it came out with a forced casualness. (And as a name, it's a bizarre one for an adult Jewish man from New Haven, isn't it? Wouldn't you expect it to be the nickname for a broncobuster from Oklahoma, at least?) Long before Howard started being a little too eager to tell people that his nickname had been conferred at Yale by that incompetent who occupied the White House for those eight long years (which of course isn't quite true), I had ceased calling him anything but Howard.

"Howdy" suggests goofiness to me, jerkiness, clowning. And as a child, the few times I happened to see it in reruns, I was genuinely frightened by the *Howdy Doody* show. It seemed sinister to me, the idiotic Howdy puppet itself, with those cruel freckles, and the supporting cast was unspeakably creepy, from the Flub-a-Dub thing (which had a duck's bill, cat's whiskers, a giraffe's neck, and spaniel ears, on a dachshund's body, with seal's flippers, and a pig's tail, plus an elephant's memory), to that big-headed Princess Summerfall Winterspring. Clearly, the show's writers had a weird obsession with blending and hybridizing, and it gave me the willies. But then, I was a child who didn't want my vegetables touching on my plate. My mother used to be irritated with me when I told her I didn't like food with ingredients. I have never liked things that begin and end and begin again. I have always liked clearly defined borders and boundaries, lots of space between one thing and another thing. I hated the pushmi-pullyu in *Dr. Doolittle*. I traded with Beth Crabtree in seventh grade to avoid doing a report on the Minotaur, opting instead to take her far more manageable assigned topic, Daedalus and Icarus. Even now, I don't like ligatures in type, and I don't care for succotash. When Jacob went through a grade school Transformers obsession, I managed to tolerate them, but it was a huge relief when he lost interest and we could donate his collection to a homeless shelter.

But really, there was nothing to like about the *Howdy Doody* cast of characters. I hated them all: Clarabell the Clown, Chief

Thunderthud, Phineas T. Bluster, Dilly Dally, and let's not forget the obscure sister, Heidi Doody. (I admit that at times my secret nickname for Irene has been Heidi Doody.) And they all lived in Doodyville, which was a name that frankly embarrassed me, growing up as I did in a household where we didn't speak baby talk but called things done in the bathroom by their proper names, urination and defecation. (In elementary school I was horrified to discover all the pee pee poo poo talk that went on in my friends' households. Barbara Roth's family called it wizzy and push, for God's sake.) And another creepy thing about *Howdy Doody* was the frantic laughter from the Peanut Gallery, which was like the sound of a fever dream.

And so I have always called Howard, Howard, and I am the only one to do so. He even wanted Jacob and Julie to call him Howdy, instead of Dad, but both of them called him Daddy when they were little, and these days they call him Pop, or, when they are speaking to me, sometimes they simply refer to him as "my father," or "your ex-husband."

Therefore, Howard, his actual given name, is, in effect, my private nickname for him, since nobody else uses it. Dr. Gibraltar said that this impulse of mine, this refusal to call Howard by the name he wants me to use, my too-rigid insistence on addressing my husband with a formal adult name instead of a childlike nickname, was a way of avoiding my own id-driven desire to regress to that child I was who was so frightened by everything about the *Howdy Doody* show. Ellie Quest-Greenspan helped me see that I have spent all these years fruitlessly addressing Howard's inner adult in the hopes that he would respond as Howard the grown-up instead of Howdy the child. She said that when she looked at Howard she could clearly see his ungoverned and endlessly needy wounded inner child, the Howdy who was splashing in that river with his big brother that terrible day when he witnessed Lewis's death, a stuck, wise-cracking Peter Pan with car keys and a credit card and a fractured heart.

So MUCH HAS now changed in the family, in our situations and circumstances. But I want to be clear about something. I really had no clue for nearly thirty years that mine was not a happy and contented marriage with the mutual intention to grow old together, the best is yet to be. I didn't know that those were the best years of my life. And those years with Howard were happy years, with a comfortable intimacy between us, a good work relationship, and an endless variety of ordinary, pleasant family activities.

We took a family trip to Vermont every summer, just before Labor Day, staying at the same farm, where the kids could gather eggs and watch the milking and help roll out piecrusts with the farmer's wife (she used canned pie filling, but in its way, that, too, was part of the authentic experience). We spent happy days at the beach in the summer, we drove down to the Bronx to go to Yankees games, we went skiing at Butternut in the winter. Howard is a graceful skier, and he taught the kids to ski with infinite patience and humor. We laughed together all the time. For so many years, there was always that eye to catch at those moments of mutual recognition, especially in our shared pleasure in our children, as for example the time we were driving home from an entirely rainy and muddy Vermont trip and the whole family had become irritable, and then we overheard this from Julie and Jacob as they squabbled in the back seat:

"You're ovnoxious," said Julie self-righteously.

"It's not *ovnoxious,* it's *ibnoxious,*" Jacob retorted with all the superiority and confidence in the world.

❀ ❀

ZIP'S CANDIES HAS been in a state of flux for too long. It is only thanks to my loyalty and hard work that stability has been maintained while the internecine battles have raged. Not that I am waiting for anyone other than my own children to send any gratitude my way. But nobody in the family can claim to have been impoverished by the outcome of Howard's and my divorce settlement or the way the courts have denied the challenges to Sam's estate. Meanwhile, all the attorneys have certainly prospered.

I do resent the continuing insinuations about the nature of my relationship with Sam. He was my father-in-law. He was my children's grandfather. Our relationship was one of mutual love and respect. He recognized my aptitude for the business. He appreciated the spirit and energy I brought to Zip's. Surely my tireless efforts over the years to make Zip's Candies grow and prosper are not the usual hallmarks of a gold digger. Surely a gold digger would be first in line to cash out and would hardly go to so much trouble to preserve the family business. How could any reasonable person deem my actions "irresponsible" or "dangerous," let alone "duplicitous" and "manipulative"? (Not to mention the outrageous statement that I'm the one with the "vicious temper.") I have been a more loyal Ziplinsky than anyone.

It is inevitable, I suppose, in Irene Ziplinsky's world, when viewed through her lenses of jealousy and suspicion; a sexual connection between Sam and me would seem like the obvious explanation for his favoring me so generously. I suppose, too, it is a mark of my outsiderness that I see this assumption as perverted and offensive, insulting to me and insulting to the memory of Sam Ziplinsky, rather than logical. I have nothing more to say about these vile assertions.

No, actually, I do have one more thing to say about these vile assertions. Shame, shame, shame on you, Irene Ziplinsky Weiss, sitting there smugly in your $7 million log cabin in Telluride with your fond belief that you have, in your words, "stepped outside the economic factor" with your solar energy and your composting toilet, spouting your virtuous fair trade, sustainable, organic, free-range, antibiotic- and hormone-free, handwoven, sanctimonious crap. He always loved you like a daughter, because you *were* his daughter, as hostile and rejecting and critical as you were. Sam was a devoted father.

He loved both you and Howard, and he came to love me—his son's wife, his daughter-in-law—for good and honorable reasons. I don't know why this is so unbearable for you, but I recognize that it is, and I am sorry you feel so diminished and threatened by something that has never been about you at all. Sam's bequests weren't final report cards. It's time to stop acting as if I cheated and got an undeserved A, while you dutifully turned in all your homework on time yet somehow failed.

I AM CERTAIN that Sam's decisions were very considered. His longtime lawyer and adviser, Ben Gottesfeld, won't take my calls and hasn't been very helpful to any side in this situation, preferring to step back and leave all his options open. I'm disappointed in Ben, who used to be more of a mensch, and I do think Sam misjudged him. But I am certain that Ben wouldn't have let him make mistakes in the execution of his intentions. Especially given the way Sam and his mother were left to deal with the consequences of Eli's not having had a will, Sam was clearly focused on taking care of his family and seeing his legacy passed down just the way he wanted it.

By leaving 25 percent of the Ziplinsky Family Limited

Partnership (which owns Zip's Candies) to Howard, Sam obviously thought he was protecting the legacy of the family business, handing stewardship and prosperity down the line to the next generation. He often said to me, Blood is thicker than water, but business is business. I have certainly wondered if Sam was somehow assuming that Howard and I would stay together and our interests would therefore continue to be one and the same. He knew what Howard had done. I have proof of that, or I did, anyway, before the fire. Maybe Sam hoped, like Howard, that I wouldn't figure it out for a long, long time. Or maybe he intended to provide me with an independent source of wealth and security, come what may. After all, he could have simply left Howard half ownership of the Family Partnership. Or he could have named us as joint owners of a half interest, with right of survivorship. But he didn't do either of those things. He broke his agreement with Howard, to reward him with the business if he stayed long enough. Sam knew the score, and I believe this was his way of trying to offer me some compensation and balance. It was a gesture of gratitude.

Either way, in our divorce settlement, given community-property laws in Connecticut, and given our history, and given the terms of the divorce (Howard's position was *vacuus a crur subsisto in*, according to Charlie, in other words, without a leg to stand on), whether or not any portion of the business was already in my name had no bearing, and I was entitled to half of Howard's interest in Zip's.

Howard claimed at the time of Sam's death that his father had promised to leave him a controlling interest in the company. Howard said that he and Sam had a deal they had made at the time of our wedding. Whether or not this is true, and I have reason to believe that it is, though of course I never said a word about that during our divorce proceedings, it simply doesn't signify, since it wasn't in any of the provisions in Sam's or Frieda's estate. Apparently, Howard didn't know that his father had actually drawn up a contract for this agreement. Sam himself said to me more than once that a verbal agreement isn't worth the paper it's written on. It is certainly worth no more or less than a draft of an unsigned contract.

Owing to some tricky math of the kind they do in Superior Court, our settlement agreement when we divorced awarded me a little less than half of Howard's 25 percent of the business— as we all know, in addition to the house and an equitable portion of our other assets, I was given two fifths of his share of the partnership, in other words, 10 percent of Zip's. Which is why today I am the largest single shareholder of the Ziplinsky Family Limited Partnership.

I am really, truly not some destructive, power-hungry monster who has invaded the precious family in order to seize control of the business, notwithstanding Irene's hilarious remark to me outside the courtroom last time we appeared for a hearing, when she muttered at me, "Ours was a decent family before you entered it." I'll say it again: Sam chose to leave me 25 percent of the business. That's the way the cookie crumbles. I have only been a Ziplinsky for three fifths of my life, unlike all natural-born Ziplinskys, but now I own two fifths of the Ziplinsky Family Limited Partnership, which is to say two fifths of Zip's Candies, and unlike most natural-born Ziplinskys, I have earned it.

MAYBE I NEED to explain the outrageousness of Irene's claims more clearly. Sam left Irene a portfolio of stocks and bonds worth almost half the paper value of Zip's Candies, which was, as he made clear in very precise language, compensation for not giving her any ownership of the family business. However, her only child, Ethan, as a grandchild, has a share in the Ziplinsky Family Trust, which now, with Frieda's death, goes to the beneficiaries. The trust owns half of Zip's Candies. Under the terms of the trust, the CEO of Zip's Candies is one of the three trustees of the trust, and I maintain that with Howard's departure, I have been functioning in that capacity ever since, which means that I am, by definition, one of the three trustees of the Ziplinsky Family Trust.

Irene's son, Ethan, being a beneficiary of the trust, owns a share of the family business. And so despite the dispute about who exactly are the beneficiaries of the trust, which is at the heart of this mess, no matter what else Irene might claim, there is simply no validity to Irene's belief that she has been unfairly treated. And meanwhile, irony of ironies, all the discovery documents make evident that Irene is the richest of us all, despite her poor-mouth campaign. Why choose to be pathetic and victimy and undignified? Why the determination to be seen as someone who has been cheated and disinherited?

Frieda's death also ended the regrettable tradition at Zip's of distributing big, unearned quarterly checks to Howard and Irene equally. Not exactly the definition of sound management practice. Howard has always drawn a good salary with benefits, and there were all kinds of over- and under-the-table benefits, but until he left, he worked hard for the business. He put in his hours, and he was kind and fair to his employees; it could be said that those quarterly payments were a reasonable bonus.

But Irene was just a parasite with a no-show job on the so-called Zip's "board," which "met" once a year at Passover. You would think she would have some pride. She's fifty-six years old! Surely the time has come for her to stop thinking of Zip's Candies as her personal Xanadu, from which she has been inexplicably exiled.

Now she is an angry baby denied her bottle. No more having

our bookkeeper pay her credit-card bills, no more having our accountant do her tax returns for her, no more sending imperious holiday emailed lists to the office with names and addresses of people to whom we must send gift boxes of Zip's Candies "from" Irene. She has been tempered and molded and enrobed and drizzled and cooled and wrapped and extruded right off the end of the line. And I canceled her company ExxonMobil Speedpass, too.

IRENE'S ENTIRE OTIOSE connection to the business was really only ever about her own status and prosperity. She has used her money over the years to fund a wide variety of half-baked do-good, feel-good enterprises of the moment. The sad truth is that Irene could have done anything in the world if she'd had the motivation. But Irene never gets traction on anything for very long, and she has never had any singular abiding passion. She's never been hungry enough to succeed at anything that required persistence. I know I can be like a dog with a bone, but my God, she has the attention span of a gnat. She's too self-involved to be reliable in ordinary ways, which is why she has never had a real job, though she allegedly worked in the office at Zip's each summer while she was in high school, before I came along.

Irene has always been satisfied just coasting. In every part of her life, really. She got good grades at Brown, which she manages to mention very, very often, because it is one of her only achievements that wasn't entirely bought and paid for. She met Arthur Weiss in their junior year; they married right after graduation, and they divorced after eleven years together, when Ethan was five. Arthur is now a successful anesthesiologist (how often those two words go together!) living in Princeton with his second wife (his former office manager) and their children.

Irene has made a career out of discovering herself since the divorce. She is always totally obsessed with her projects of the moment, and even now when we are barely speaking I still get email bulletins about her sensitive responses to world disasters and her deep personal awareness of global warming and the need for worldwide sustainability. I find her very silly. I suspect Ethan does too.

It's a miracle he has turned out to be as decent as he is, with those parents. He was a monstrous child, "self-regulating," rather than disciplined in any way whatsoever, so he was always cranky and sleep-deprived, always whining, always eating sugary things right before meals, always having tantrums, always demanding the next thing and the next thing. And Irene's attempts to civilize him were always situational, with no underlying consistency or ethic.

"Stop smearing your cupcake on the sofa, Ethan, sweetie," she would say, only after I was clearly reaching the end of my tether, though under ordinary circumstances I was reasonably patient with most kids. "Your aunt Alice doesn't like it when you do that." I felt guilty disliking that child as much as I did. One shouldn't loathe toddlers, should one? But he was a disaster.

To his credit, Ethan would clearly prefer to stay the hell away from both of his parents as much as he possibly can these days, and he's turned into a reasonable adult. Neither of my kids is especially close to him, their one and only American first cousin.

This brings me to the Madagascar cousins. Darwin and Miriam have no children. Darwin's sister, Huxley, had a baby a few months after Howard and I were married. I remember hearing about it from Frieda, who mentioned it several times, in a rather conspicuous way, in retrospect. Was she testing me, to see what I knew? Newton (don't those Czaplinskys have the craziest names? Where's Copernicus Czaplinsky?) was an only child for a long while, until his younger brother, Edison, was born, soon after I had Jacob.

Because Newton was five years older, Jacob never really got to know him the way he became close to Edison during those summers they worked and played together on the plantations. Jacob and Edison, though both born in 1982, were not technically of the same generation, since Newton and Edison were actually Howard's second cousins, making them second cousins once removed to my kids.

I know that parsing who is a first cousin once removed as opposed to who is a second cousin is excruciating for most people, who couldn't care less. It's a particular skill you develop at an early age in a family like mine. To be a Tatnall is to have an anxious desire to have precise knowledge about your degree of relatedness to Benedict Arnold's wife. But it's important to understand these Ziplinsky relationships with clarity, given the situation we're in now. The obsessive scrutiny and analysis of the family tree with which I was raised turns out to be a somewhat more useful skill than, say, scrimshaw, after all.

I NEVER WENT to Madagascar. I always meant to, and most people who know a little bit about our family story—Eli's amazing reconnection with his long-lost brother, who settled in Madagascar during the war, the fortuitous way the families found each other just before Eli died because a cacao broker with whom they both did business happened to notice and comment on their similar names—assume quite naturally that I have been there. People who heard about the Madagascar family would tell me they envied me the exotic trips they assumed I had made, and I would usually gloss over it and change the subject,

unless pressed, when I would have to say with some awkwardness that it had never worked out for me to go there, though
everyone else in the family has spent time on the family cacao
and vanilla plantations.

That's not quite true. It is more accurate (and painful) to
admit now that I allowed myself to be kept away. The human
heart has an amazing capacity to know and not know at the
same time.

In the first years of our marriage, Howard would travel to
Madagascar once or twice a year, often during the rainy season,
which can be dangerous, with mudslides and flooding. It is certainly not a brilliant time for tourism, he pointed out on each
occasion when the possibility of my accompanying him arose.
He always told me I should go in another season, for sure, maybe
in the fall, maybe in the spring, and we spoke of making such a
trip together, but the years kept passing. His photographs
were beautiful. The immense baobab trees lining the road lead-
ing to one of the cacao estates looked as if they grew in a Delvaux
landscape.

Then I had babies, and they were too young to travel to a
place like that, a malaria zone, and also too young to leave for
more than a few days, not that there was anyone I would have
trusted to take care of them. With whom would I have left Julie
and Jacob when they were growing up? Irene? Frieda and Sam,
so Frieda could brainwash my children to regard me, the one
non–blood Ziplinsky, as an outsider the way she did? Now
that would be evidence of irresponsibility! It might have been
different if I'd ever had any close friends, the sort of people who
very naturally love your children and are eager to take care of
them so you can travel, but I have never cultivated or maintained friendships.

And then as the kids grew older there was always something urgent and unmissable of theirs on the schedule, and when Howard would go, it never seemed like the right time to leave our kids, or to leave Zip's, where I was very much a cog in the machinery, especially with Howard away. And it never felt right for me to consider making a trip on my own to go to this difficult, remote place to stay with these relatives I didn't know, beyond the one strange encounter at our wedding.

Over the years, Julie and Jacob and I enjoyed the times when Howard was in Madagascar, where he went every six or seven months. His absence was relaxing, because I had fewer domestic requirements for daily living without him. I suppose it is a cliché, the way I was a contented and unsuspicious wife who used to enjoy the luxury of my temporary solitude when Howard was on those Madagascar trips. I became indulgent about letting the kids stay up late on school nights, a secret violation of one of Howard's most serious theories of parenting. It was always clear to me anyway that his motives for maintaining strict bedtimes were based on his preference for the end of the evening to be unencumbered by the needs of children, not about any true philosophy of child development. It was a break for me when I didn't have to honor Howard's food preferences, which ordinarily had me preparing elaborate meals most nights of the week. When he was away, the three of us would depend on take-out Chinese food or pizza, in rotation with another Daddy's-away tradition of ours, which was what the kids happily called "breakfast-dinners."

On those nights we would have scrambled eggs and bacon, or French toast and sausages, or pancakes with sautéed apples and bananas swimming in maple syrup. Although Howard didn't manifestly endorse Frieda's belief that women who served their children scrambled eggs or French toast for dinner were all alcoholic Protestants, my doing this made him uneasy. What's more, the three of us would change into pajamas and robes and slippers before we ate our breakfast-dinner. This would not have suited Howard at all.

WHEN EDISON WAS twelve, he came to stay with us in Connecticut during a school break in the monsoon season. He was a beautiful boy, with an almost angelic look to him. I had never met his mother (and I never will—why would I want to meet the sperm embezzler who has taken away the life I deserved, the life I worked so hard for, the life I earned?), but I imagined her to look as fiercely exotic as her brother, Darwin. The fuzzy snapshot of her that Edison kept under his pillow (I found it when I made his bed) confirmed that. Those half-Czaplinsky, half-Malagasy offspring are remarkable genetic upgrades, I have to admit.

Edison was paler and more Caucasian in his features than I remembered his uncle Darwin being, but he had those startling blue eyes that run in the family, and that same fierce island look about him, like a young warrior who is coddled in his youth but will one day be challenged and hardened to face the responsibilities of manhood. He definitely didn't look Caucasian (I realize I am dwelling on his appearance), especially in February, in New Haven, Connecticut, where he seemed to glow with a tropical radiance against the New England grayness. He was amazed and horrified by the snow and ice, and he was miserable in the cold.

Edison was a sweet boy, polite, eager to pitch in, undemanding (though he didn't like a lot of our food and was happiest at any meal with a banana and a big bowl of rice), but he was very timid around me. He would always cast his eyes down when I spoke to him. I couldn't decide if this was a cultural imperative or something specific to his awkwardness around me. He was more relaxed around Jacob and Julie, whom he was meeting for the first time, since Jacob was also twelve and would make his first Madagascar trip the following summer, and Julie was then only ten.

It was difficult to get anywhere with him conversationally, because he was so shy with me. One morning while I watched him tuck into his banana and rice, I asked him if he had any brothers and sisters, and he replied, "Newton," in a whisper. That was the name of his older brother. Howard explained to me that Newton, who was some six years older than Edison, was beginning to take on some of the administrative tasks of the Czaplinsky cacao plantations, working for his uncle Darwin.

Edison was almost clingy with Howard, in a babyish way for his age, though what did I know about how a twelve-year-old Malagasy boy should comport himself? Whenever I tried to hug him he stiffened up and tolerated me politely, but it was like hugging a cooperative chicken. I wondered if it was considered unmanly to accept a woman's affection if she isn't your mother, let alone if she's a strange white woman, whether or not you have been told she is in your family. I asked Howard what his cousin Huxley was like, wondering if Newton and Edison's mother was very undemonstrative. I realized I had never heard a word about her in all these years. I cannot stress enough how out of focus the Madagascar family was always kept. Howard was very vague in his reply. Perhaps, too, there was residual resentment among the Czaplinskys over Julius's having been left behind? And about Eli's failure to find him over all those years in Budapest? I asked Howard about both of these issues more than once, but he told me dismissively that I was looking for trouble, and that most people don't carry grudges the way I think they do.

A few times in the course of those weeks, I heard Edison call Howard "Baba." When I asked Howard why, Howard told me it was just a nickname he had with the Czaplinsky boys, because when Newton was a baby, he hadn't been able to say "Howdy," and had used baby babble when he greeted Howard: "Babababa." And then it just stuck all these years, so it was natural for Edison to call him that as well, since that was what he grew up hearing Howard called by his older brother. While true, that was an incomplete answer.

And so the years passed, and Jacob began to go to Madagascar each summer. Julie never wanted to go that far away from us, plus she had developed a terrible fear of lightning on Madagascar, having heard the story of Lewis's death. Julie was an anxious child with a number of phobias, not only a fear of thunder and lightning (Astraphobia, murmured Dr. Gibraltar) but also a fear of lightning bugs and any other bioluminescent creatures that might light up anywhere near her; after his first Madagascar trip, Jacob had described seeing on the dock in Antsiranana harbor some bizarre glow-in-the-dark sea creatures from the deep that been inadvertently landed, entangled in a fisherman's nets.

Julie also had some significant allergies and easily triggered asthma, which at times made Howard impatient, because he thought she brought it on herself with her unnecessary anxieties. He felt that it would be unwise for her to go to that potentially difficult and primitive place, when something could go really wrong, as the family knew so well. And so the women in the family didn't go to Madagascar, just the men.

With Jacob on Madagascar for those two months each summer, having his independent time among his cousins, a summer visit for me became problematic, because, and Howard felt strongly about this, I would have been crowding Jacob. It would be unfair, a real Jewish mother thing, like something Mrs. Portnoy would do, for me to follow him there. Even Frieda had given Howard that freedom. The first time Jacob went to Madagascar, the summer he had just turned thirteen (having dropped out of Hebrew school after deciding against a bar mitzvah, a choice we let him make, which gave Frieda immense, grim satisfaction), Howard flew there with him and got him settled in, returning to Connecticut two weeks later, while Jacob stayed all through the summer and made the journey back on his own, just before school started, very pleased with his independence. After that, Jacob went on his own every summer as soon as he finished school, changing planes in Paris, returning over Labor Day weekend most years, until college, when his American life started looming larger, with friends, girlfriends, and internships breaking the pattern.

Was there a moment when I figured it out? There were so many moments, and yet I kept not knowing, and not knowing, over three decades. Did everyone in the family know the truth except for me? Did Irene know? She only went to Madagascar herself that one time when she was a kid. And she has always been remarkably uncurious about other people's lives unless they had a direct effect on her. Maybe she didn't. I can't believe she wouldn't have wanted to lord it over me in some way if she did. The Ziplinskys are notoriously bad at keeping secrets, though this was one Howard managed to hold on to for a very long time. Sam knew. Irene's argument that he didn't know, and so his intentions for the trust could not possibly have been meant to include Newton and Edison, is shamefully meretricious. Of course he knew. That's why he made the deal with Howard, promising him the business if he married me and stayed in New Haven and worked at Zip's. Ironically, given the lengths to which everyone went to conceal the truth from me at the time, I believe that had I known, I would have agreed to marry Howard just the same. I would have helped Frieda and Sam keep Howard. I would have been willing to go along with it. They didn't have to use me.

Frieda had to have known, maybe not in the beginning, but I am sure she figured it out or Sam told her at some point. She probably hated owing me for keeping her precious son tethered to the family and the business, but my being in the dark all those years must have given her huge satisfaction. Jacob knew for at least three years before I could stop denying the truth to myself. He told Julie a couple of years in, but he couldn't face confronting me with it.

And so Howard's betrayal effectively partitioned me off from the people in the world I loved and trusted the most—my kids, Sam. And I could always feel it, just below the surface, but I just wasn't ready to face the truth. Of course it was always there. Why was I in such denial? I could have dealt with it. I would have been reasonable about Newton. I know I would have been. It happened before Howard and I met. It's not even clear that he knew about Newton when we decided to get married.

But how am I to forgive Howard for Edison?

When I married Howard, I wrote a note in my journal, "I am being taken in by this wonderful family." How true was that?

Malagasy for "Thank you very much" is *Misaotra betsaka tompoko.*
Malagasy for "You are welcome" is *Tsy misy fisaorana.*
Malagasy for "I love you" is *Tiako ianao.*
Malagasy for "Daddy" is *Baba.*

Julie keeps her distance from Newton and Edison. She regards them as problematic strangers who have caused our family much unhappiness. But Jacob, having spent so much time on Madagascar, has a warm and close relationship with his half brothers, who are also his second cousins once removed. I try not to begrudge him it.

When Jacob came back from Madagascar at the end of the summer he was fifteen, he was transformed from a weedy teenage boy into something more masculine. He had turned into the man he is now, though I could still catch a glimpse of his baby face if I peeked in on him when he was sleeping. That autumn, he had a slightly different, somewhat pungent and very pleasant aroma about him for weeks after he returned. He would sense me sniffing his neck and say, Cut that out, Ma! and push me away, but I couldn't get enough of it.

Yes, I had missed him, but frankly I just loved this new smell. Vanilla, plus something earthy and raw. Was it an oil, a product, something in his diet? He had subsisted mostly on *mofo gasy*, a pancakey bread, and *koba akondro,* a sweet he would buy at the side of the road from old ladies with food stalls who spent their days wrapping a batter of ground peanuts, mashed bananas, honey, and corn flour in banana leaves, which they steamed until the batter formed a small cake. His other favorite from the roadside stalls was *caca pigeon*, literally, "pigeon droppings," a snack of deep-fried salted dough and steamed manioc over which they poured sweetened condensed milk.

When his Malagasy aroma started to fade, I tried to duplicate these dishes for Jacob in the secret hope that if he ate enough of these foods his spicy odor would return, but he was only slightly polite about my attempts to duplicate the food of rural Madagascar with ingredients from the Stop & Shop, and I gave up.

Jacob kept detailed journals during those summers before he

went to college, and while I would like to say he showed them to me (because I would like to think I am the kind of mother whose son would want to share all of his experiences), he didn't. But the journals weren't hidden, either. I never would have read them if he had hidden them out of sight. But Jacob kept them on the shelf over his desk, and so in the course of tidying his room I would always read his latest entries. I have such admiration for his vivid and sensitive writing skills. Reading his journals, I felt as if I had been there with him.

Jacob and Edison worked side by side through those summers, cutting cacao pods, pollinating vanilla orchids, preparing the fragrant and rare Porcelana cacao beans for drying in the sun. "Dancing the cocoa," they called it, the shuffling of the fermenting beans with their bare feet, turning the beans, kicking and dragging their feet in big sweeping circles. Jacob and Edison would exhaust themselves, slamming together in wild and athletic dances on the flat drying roofs of the cacao-bean sheds.

Now of course they are both involved in the production of the Zip's Bao-Bar, and that binds them in some new ways, but theirs is an incredibly complex connection, one they will be sorting out together for many years. Newton is also a partner with Jacob and Edison in the Bao-Bar venture, as is Zip's Candies (in a cashless exchange for the contract manufacturing on our premises; since the Bao-Bar runs on the Tigermelt line, Zip's has a 25 percent stake in the Madagascar Bao-Bar Company), and he is the main grower and supplier of the dried baobab pulp that makes this bar so different from all the other energy bars on the market. Dried baobab pulp, which is rich in fiber, has antioxidant properties to beat the band, is loaded with B1, B2, and C vitamins, and also has a stunning amount of calcium. And the

Bao-Bar is the only energy bar on the national market with Madagascar (or any other kind of) baobab.

One of the significant ingredients in the Bao-Bar is the tiny sprinkle of crushed cacao nibs in the core. These nibs are supplied to Zip's from the special Czaplinsky production of an exceptionally rare cacao, which otherwise is sold to just three chocolatiers, all of them in France, all of them willing to pay sig-, nificantly more for these nibs, ounce for ounce, than the going rate for the finest Beluga caviar. Julius was cultivating this unusual cacao at the time of his death. (The time he spent under the mother trees in the humid, insect-infested, tropical environment required for cacao to pollinate and fruit exposed him to the mosquitoes carrying the malaria that killed him.) It's genetically related to the Porcelana and the Criollo cacao varieties. Julius's name for the variety in his notes (which he kept in Yiddish) was "Gewurzik Geshmak," which translates literally to Spicy Tasty. Edison honors this, and calls the cacao Gewurzik. Surely it is the only Yiddish appellation for any cacao production growing today in the fifteen countries in the equatorial belt around the world that grow 98 percent of the world's cacao. The Gewurzik is a slow-growing and unproductive variety, which limits the commercial possibilities, but the limited yield of cacao from the unusually small and rounded cacao pods is simply exquisite.

Jacob samples each small batch of roasted beans as it arrives, and his intensity gladdens my heart as he sits at his worktable, hunched over his bean guillotine making notes about nice fissuring and deep, even color. Every parent wants her child to find his passion. Not only is the flavor of the cacao nibs spicy and tasty indeed, but they also have an unusually sky-high level of flavonoids and other polyphenols, which have a proven antioxidant, anti-inflammatory effect on the human body, especially the heart. Further, the Gewurzik has loads of anandamide and tryptophan, both potent brain stimulators, and theobromine, which stimulates the nervous system.

There are lots of technical explanations for how these chemicals affect us, but the simplest way of talking about it is simply to say that the smallest nibble of Gewurzik cacao makes you feel really good. I am opposed to marketing the Bao-Bar as a "neutraceutical bar." I don't like the word. But my preference did not prevail, and I have to admit the success of the bar in these first months has been far beyond any of our most optimistic projections.

I know that Howard has taken charge of the Gewurzik project these days, even though it has never been acknowledged to me, with Jacob, Edison, and Newton running interference so I have no direct dealings with him. I hope it makes him happy. Maybe he imagines he is back in his boyhood, frolicking with his brother, Lewis, under the tangled canopy of the mother trees shading his precious cacao plantings. I am sure he is the Grandest Tiger in the Jungle, with his beautiful family at his side. Presumably he is taking his antimalaria medication.

Between the unusual texture from the dried baobab pulp and the presence of the Gewurzik nibs, the Bao-Bar is a pure and simple bar like no other. It is also chewy and delicious, with just a hint of Czaplinsky Pure Madagascar Vanilla, with neither the cardboardy, fiber-is-good-for-you texture nor the cloying virtuous sweetness of too many energy and protein bars.

Newton is impressively altruistic, a trait he surely inherited from his Malagasy grandmother, Julius's common-law wife, Lalao, and not from any Czaplinsky or Ziplinsky genes. His choices in life are truly admirable, and it isn't hard for me to say that. He is dedicated to running a baobab cooperative project in several remote villages on Madagascar, and he is keenly interested in helping the poorest Malagasy people learn how to utilize every part of the huge, ancient upside-down trees that have loomed over the dry deciduous forests for hundred of years.

The fresh fruit is sweet and chewy, while the white, powdery pulp of the fruit can be mixed into porridge. The leaves can be made into nourishing soups and stews, and the seeds can be pounded and pressed to yield a useful if odd-tasting cooking oil. Even the bark fibers can be woven into ropes and cloth. Jacob has shown me some of his literature, and it's impressively thoughtful. Utilizing the baobab trees in these ways offers an incentive to these tiny villages to preserve these trees and thus help maintain the soil structure and the whole fragile ecosystem instead of recklessly clear-cutting in order to plant transient cash crops, a chronic temptation. I'm actually quite proud to be associated with Newton, strange as that may sound.

THE FIRST PASSOVER after Jacob was born, I was so anxious to do everything right, to fit in with these people who had become my people, when we were all together around the table at Sam and Frieda's house on Marvel Road in Westville, the house where Howard and Irene grew up, the house where Howard and I were married. Ethan was born two years ahead of Jacob (and so he was at the table whining and threatening harm to Frieda's precious Pesach dishes), and I didn't like the way Irene was so triumphant about pointing that out repetitively, as if she had won a competition I didn't know we were having.

I was holding infant Jacob on my lap, and he was squirming and hungry, but I was worried that nursing him at the table, no matter how discreetly I did it, could be a conflict with the rules because it was a meat meal. I know this sounds really stupid, but at the time it was a serious worry for me. How was I to know how to make sense of these rules? Nobody could ever really explain any of the kosher laws to me very clearly, let alone how this family did and did not choose to follow them. There seemed to be no such thing as information, only interpretation. Three Ziplinskys, five opinions.

Whenever I asked questions at moments like this they would all start giving me conflicting answers, and then they would argue with one another, and then the disagreements and corrections would begin (I know this is a clichéd outsider's perception of Jews, but there it is) and there would be escalation until sometimes somebody would withdraw in aggrieved silence, or even storm out in a huff, and somebody else would have taken umbrage. For a while I believed *umbrage* must be a Yiddish word, having never heard it used before I met these umbrageous people. Meanwhile I could never get a straight answer to my questions about things like why shellfish is forbidden in the home but it is permissible to order Kung Pao shrimp at the House of Chao on Whalley Avenue, or the House of Chaos as we always call it, ever since Julie misread their sign when she was little and a precocious reader.

Sam was carving the standing rib roast Frieda had just brought to the table, but I couldn't catch Howard's eye to check with him about the breast-feeding question, because he was having a testy conversation with his mother about whether or not Princess Diana was an idiot. They both thought she was, so I have no idea what they found to argue about, but their perpetual mutual belligerence, their need to trump each other with superior credentials for holding shared opinions, this was a ritual of Ziplinsky family occasions as traditional as the lighting of the Sabbath candles.

The things Howard and Frieda found to agree about while arguing in this way! That evening alone, following the Princess Diana idiocy analysis, came the designated hitter rule and whether it did or did not ruin baseball (it did), the spelling of the word *ketchup* (they agreed that only the insane prefer *catsup*), the way most people don't use the term "hoi polloi" correctly (the hoi polloi themselves being the biggest abusers), and whether or not what John F. Kennedy said in 1962 when he was awarded his honorary degree—"It might be said now that I have the best of both worlds, a Harvard education and a Yale degree"—was a deliberate insult to Yale (it was, but in a good way).

The prayers, the narration about the symbols, and all the singing had occurred, and the Haggadahs had been put aside. Arthur, with whom I had a superficial sort of alliance in those early years simply because we were the two non–blood family members at the table, having silently watched the Ziplinskys being Ziplinskys with his slightly contemptuous gaze, leaned over and told me apropos of nothing that he had decided to specialize in anesthesiology because he preferred patients who were mostly unconscious so he would hardly ever have to talk to them. He was in a cardiology rotation at the time, which he complained about. He couldn't wait to get away from the needy patients who always wanted reassurance from him with each encounter.

"Then you might consider psychoanalysis, where you also would never speak and would be dealing mostly with the unconscious," I replied, and everyone around the table looked at me blankly. It was not the time to announce to the collective Ziplinskys that I had embarked on my analysis just a few months before, when I was pregnant with Jacob, although Dr. Gibraltar had warned me that it was a highly dubious time to begin an analysis, when the analysand is pregnant, and previously repressed female castration fantasies and phallic defenses might emerge. (He really talked like that, when he spoke at all. It was always very dry, but at the same time it made me feel like a respected colleague.)

It seemed to me like an outstanding time to begin analysis, if all that stuff might bubble up so easily, without my having to strain. Isn't that what analysis hopes for, previously repressed defenses emerging? I wanted to start right away, the sooner the better. I couldn't wait to throw myself down on his couch and begin the ambulatory brain surgery.

When not so long after that Irene found out about my analysis from Howard, who, typically, despite his promise, forgot to not tell anyone in his family about it, she was scornful ("Freudian?") and jealous ("You go four days a week? It costs how much?"), and soon enough she had embarked on her own short-lived analysis, with Andy Seckel, a very nonstandard practitioner with nonstandard credentials. He deemed the analytic couch infantilizing, and so they lay together on an inflatable mattress on the floor in his office over a grocery store on Orange Street. All the real analysts in town had their offices on Trumbull Street or Bradley Street, not to mention that they all sat in comfortable chairs as they presided over their couches with the requisite fresh paper towel laid out each hour for the next neurotic head.

I used to see Andy Seckel around New Haven long after Irene had divorced Arthur and moved to Telluride. Like so many New Haven analysts he had a white beard (I say this from personal observation, since for decades many of them, including Dr. Gibraltar, who had his own white beard, have congregated for their fifty-minute lunch hours at the Clark's Dairy counter, where there is an unspoken tradition that at lunchtime the doctors go to the right and the patients go to the left), but he often wore a pajama top and a cowboy hat, so he was easy to distinguish. When he died a couple of years ago, I read in the newspaper that he left his entire estate to Thunderbolt, a carved horse on the carousel at Lighthouse Point Park. Talk about estate nightmares.

On the rare occasions when we are forced together with the rebarbative Irene and her poor son, Ethan—the last time being at Frieda's funeral a year ago—the cousins have been able to be guardedly friendly with one another without acknowledging the family crisis. Not that it's relevant, but I think Ethan might be gay. Nature or nurture? Julie came out to us when she was in her junior year at Wesleyan, living in Womanist House, and at that point it didn't surprise me, but Howard was really thrown. He was more bothered and disappointed by this revelation than was reasonable, and I think he secretly blamed me for it, as if having a lesbian for a daughter was somehow a failure on my part.

Arthur Weiss doesn't seem like a man who would be thrilled to have a gay son. Well, I suppose not even the most enlightened man is overjoyed to have a homosexual son. I know Arthur has a successful practice and is well regarded, but there is something deeply wrong with that man. He's phlegmatic and bloodless, the opposite of Irene and her flighty enthusiasms. And why would any sane, normal man marry Irene? As Julie would say, what was up with that?

HOWARD HAS TOLD me for years that I could afford to cut Irene some slack. The hell with that! She has been cutting herself miles and miles of slack for years. She has been unstinting in her efforts to provide herself with every possible healing opportunity and alternative treatment, and since her move to Telluride she has become a real process junkie, always on her way to the next retreat or ashram, always flinging herself, checkbook in hand, at one or another guru of the moment.

Sam gave her enough. More than enough. Dayenu! To quote from that wonderful Passover song which everyone in the Ziplinsky family should probably have studied more carefully, because despite the rollicking annual renditions at Seder after Seder, there is no evidence that the meaning of the song has ever really been taken to heart.

As we all know, in his last will and testament, Sam created the Ziplinsky Family Trust, with Frieda as the sole lifetime beneficiary. The trust was funded with several million dollars in equities and bond funds, along with its biggest asset, half ownership of Zip's Candies. The trustees (Howard, as CEO of Zip's Candies, Ben Gottesfeld, and Carly August, a peppy banker who was always incredibly patient with Frieda, who made it very clear that she would never have the time of day for goyim), were given a lot of latitude to make distributions to Frieda, but the trust's interest in the business could not be sold or altered or deeded in any way. Sam's will named Howard to succeed him as CEO of Zip's Candies. These are all facts beyond dispute.

By making these plans and provisions as he did, Sam was of course ensuring family loyalty to the business into the next generation. But here is where it gets tricky. His intention regarding the generation after that, his grandchildren, should be just as clear, except that Irene insists it isn't clear at all.

And so here we are. At Frieda's death last year, the Ziplinsky Family Trust, in its entirety, with all those cannily invested millions (which have grown nicely despite the roller-coaster market, and despite the endless generous distributions), plus the half interest in Zip's Candies, became the property of the remainder Beneficiaries, per stirpes and not per capita, to be shared equally among them, with all administrative decisions concerning distributions of principle as well as income, up to and including the sale or division of any and all assets of the trust, including dissolution of the trust itself, to be determined by a simple majority vote among the beneficiaries. And in his will Sam identified the beneficiaries of the Ziplinsky Family Trust with this language: "my grandchildren who survive me, the issue of my son Howard and my daughter, Irene."

And there it is—that one simple, seemingly straightforward phrase that has put us in the soup.

6

As a naturalized Ziplinsky, I probably know and understand far more Ziplinsky family lore than anyone else alive. Unlike any natural-born Ziplinsky (my own two children excepted), I am completely interested in the inner workings and unique sensibilities of the family, and have been from that first hot afternoon when I crossed the threshold of Zip's Candies. I would also like to point out my clear and objective ability to put all of these facts into this narrative. I have been accused of exaggeration, of embellishment, of adding and subtracting meaning, but it should be abundantly clear that I am in fact a very reliable and coherent source of valuable insight. My memory is flawless.

I have always been a quick study, too. During my two-week home stay with a rural family in Burgundy, the summer I was fifteen, I picked up more French than anyone else in my group (we were assigned to families scattered throughout the village), despite, or perhaps because of, the unpleasantness of my host family, who were not at all interested in me, and were unabashed about being in the home stay student hosting business entirely for the money. Contrary to all the clichés about the French, *la famille* Lagache, who had a dry cleaning establishment in the village, were unattractively lumpen, unstylish, and very dependent on frozen food. I quickly learned how best to feign incomprehension while deciphering their mumbled, insulting, unkind observations about me (*Même le chien ne l'aime pas!*—Even the dog doesn't like her!) as we ate our depressingly identical portions of freezer-burned *dinde à la crème* in the flickering glow of Eurosport News.

Immersion in a culture helps you learn a language quickly, and I certainly had a Ziplinsky immersion that first summer working on the Tigermelt line, packing Little Sammies into boxes, cleaning the vibrator mechanism and the pre-extruder on the Tigermelt line, cleaning whatever else anybody told me to clean, simply learning by personal experience the intricate entropy of all three lines.

On that first afternoon, I pitched myself with headlong velocity into the Zip's machine, into a lonely exile from my own sad family. I was desperate to escape my Arson Girl fate, and I was captivated by every aspect of this stirring, sugary world of Zip's Candies and these lively, exotic Ziplinskys. I loved the roar and din of mechanical productivity. I inhaled that sugary, life-giving air with gratitude every morning when I walked through those factory doors, filling myself up with it, letting it sweeten and soothe every corner of my scorched, empty self.

I fell instantly into a rhythm with the routine at Zip's, and with my sense of having a place in that routine, my feeling of being a useful cog among many other cogs turning the gears of this vast machine devoted to simple pleasure, to the making of true confections. I was enthralled, utterly dazzled, to discover that every minute of every hour of every working day, the vast mechanism of Zip's Candies was chugging away, churning out row after row, box after box, stacked pallet after stacked pallet, hundreds and thousands of chewy, salty, sugary, nutty contributions to that quintessentially American privilege, the pursuit of happiness at the candy counter.

There was an old national distribution map of the forty-eight states, stuck with color-coded pushpins representing sales of Little Sammies, Tigermelts, and Mumbo Jumbos, which hung for many years on the side wall in Sam's office. This map was actually a bit grandiose, because until the resurgent interest in Little Sammies, sparked in 1999 with the "Say, Dat's Tasty!" phenomenon (and then bolstered by all the expanding sales opportunities with online candy sellers like OldTimeCandy .com, SweetNostalgia.com, CandyWarehouse.com, and Groovy Candies.com, to name just a few of our best vendors), Zip's penetration west of the Rockies was actually very small. Zip's has always really been a regional brand more than it could be called a true national brand, with most sales clustered on the East Coast, from Florida to Maine. But I have always loved the Zip's sales map and all the optimism it represented. The business of America is business! And the territory of Zip's is America! That map offered me an America that felt far more vivid and authentic than did the desiccated world of the Pilgrim Fathers and Original Signers and all those Patriots of the American Revolution from whom my family proudly descended on both sides.

Today, after all these years as a Ziplinsky, I feel quite disconnected from my family of origin, as Ellie Quest-Greenspan insisted on calling my parents whenever they came up, which was generally only when she brought them up. (Dr. Gibraltar brought up issues of billing and scheduling but otherwise initiated topics very rarely.) Yet of course I am not a *true* Ziplinsky, and so my Ziplinsky credential is deemed insufficient on the one hand and irrelevant on the other by those eager to discredit my standing. But I have pretty much left behind all my Tatnall and Dorr loyalties. So who am I?

"Family of origin" is such an odd sort of biological concept. "Origin" is a term used by the snobbiest of those self-important dark-chocolate connoisseurs, those irritating bean-to-bar obsessives for whom no dark chocolate is dark enough, the ones who carry their own little supplies for after-dinner duels of I'll see your 70 percent Ecuadorian Trinitario and raise you fifteen, as they deal out their precious little 85 percent, five-gram tasting squares of Indonesian Criollo, woody yet floral, with a heady nose and a long finish on the palate. Not that many of them would know in a blind test the difference between a decent Trinitario from Tobago and a square of that shoe polish Godiva calls chocolate.

The truth of the matter is, the percentage doesn't tell the whole story—what *does* ever tell the whole story?—and the question they usually don't know to ask is what percentage of cocoa butter and what percentage of chocolate liquor make up that precious little square. It's all about the balance and the mouthfeel, not just the straight numbers. Most of the boutique chocolatiers have started to cater to those so-called connoisseurs, forced to oblige them with ever higher numbers in order to stay competitive. But to preserve mouthfeel they are adding in more cocoa butter proportionately, otherwise the result of an 85 or 90 percent cacao chocolate would be about as appealing as dirt on your tongue. Seventy can be the perfect balance for a really good dark chocolate, and I see no reason to aim higher simply for the sake of number snobbery. But foodies (and my God, how much do I despise that twee term "chocoholic"?) love to follow trends, even as they love to deny that they do. Just ask the merlot people how they feel about the movie *Sideways*.

I think I have more than sufficiently explained how my years among the Ziplinskys have left me feeling untethered from the polite and chilly WASPy dynamic of my family of origin. Thirty years among door-slamming confrontational Jews will do that. Not that I am a door-slammer. I dwell in a kind of no-man's-land these days. Only my Jewish relatives think I am Protestant, and only my Protestant relatives think I am Jewish. I know the correct way to light the candles on the menorah for all the nights of Chanukah, and I know how to wrap a string of Christmas lights on a fragrant balsam fir in such a way as to get the lights to nestle deep in the innermost branches so the wires don't show and the lights aren't just flung haphazardly around the tips of the branches.

I am certainly the first Ziplinsky eligible for membership in the Daughters of the American Revolution. Julie is as well, given that she too has the requisite "direct lineal blood line descent from an ancestor who aided in achieving American independence." Though I can just imagine a chapter admissions committee casting its collective milky blue DAR gaze upon Julie Ziplinsky. At a glance, surely all they would see are the manifestations of those hardscrabble, entrepreneurial Ziplinsky and Liebashevsky genes. Next to the pale, prim, politely Episcopal, tiny-nosed Tatnalls and Dorrs, Ziplinskys look like gypsies. (The fur-selling Liebashevskys, who hail from Pinsk, tend toward potatohead shtetl faces; they all wear an invisible babushka. Let's just say they are also far from classic DAR material.)

Julie has her father's beaky nose and his dark, kinky hair (yes, all the clichés, but what should I do, pretend this is not so?), which she wears in what she persists in calling a Jewfro, just as she calls herself a Jewnitarian, while her girlfriend (her lover, her "primary dyadic partner," as they call each other, as if each is the other's case study for some ongoing anthropological research), the somewhat worrisome Kelly Harper, calls herself a Lesbyterian. They are affiliated with a group of people who call themselves "polyamory," and they claim to be comfortable having "multiple intimate, nonexclusive sexual and emotional relationships" (I'm quoting from the polyamory website they asked me to "visit," a term that in itself reveals such a disconnect between our generations, since they meant me to read some text on a screen while sitting at my own desk, and they were not actually inviting me to go anywhere).

It seems to me to be a rather limited and almost fetishistic way for them to define themselves, even though they claim their lives are more open and free than those of us monogamously inclined heterosexuals, who may be less open and free but who at least don't have to spend so much time codifying the nuances of our relationships with our various sexual partners. Frankly, when Julie and Kelly start explaining to me all over again about poly this and poly that, I just want to say to them, Polly put the kettle on, and we'll *all* have tea!

In other words, Julie is hardly living a life of DAR rectitude. And she does have all those facial piercings (and some others I don't want to know about), which always make me feel a little faint if I look at them too closely, though when I catch myself casting sidelong, sliding glances at Julie and Kelly, I feel guilty and inadequate and cowardly. Surely a mother should be able to gaze lovingly at her own child. What has become of my sweet little girl, who cried when I read *Are You My Mother?* to her at bedtime (it is, admittedly, a tearjerker), and later lovingly nurtured a pair of long-lived frogs (she named them Herbert and Cumulus), who dwelled in a tank in her room for eleven years? Julie used to be a kid for whom it seemed the world would be her oyster. She and Kelly are very devoted to each other, but I regret the way each seems to support the other's sense of being wronged by the world.

I am certain the ranks of the DAR have been filled over the years by numerous spinsters in Boston marriages, but nobody talked about it. Every time the Revolutionary War came up in my studies, my mother would stress with a certain pride that our heritage made us eligible for DAR membership, though to give my mother her due, and my father too, it should also be said that at our dinner table the DAR was mostly mocked and ridiculed and held up as the enemy, because they wouldn't let Marian Anderson sing at Constitution Hall in 1939. So we wouldn't have dreamed of joining, my mother and I, not in a million years—but we were eligible! The satisfaction in that! It was a bond of disdain that Frieda Ziplinsky surely would have understood.

The Ziplinsky family has an uneasy relationship with the heritage of ambition and success handed down not so long ago by that entrepreneurial goniff, Eli Czaplinsky. I think they should embrace it, the whole thing. The shadiest person in my family's history, the darkest sheep (until me), would be Margaret Shippen—Peggy, as we call her, as if she had been over for dinner just last week and not dead in her Tory grave since 1804—good old cousin Peggy, my first cousin six times removed, who married Benedict Arnold. Family lore has it that Peggy Shippen was poor, naive Benedict Arnold's downfall, her greed for status and her ceaseless desire for pretty things being what drove him to his treasonous betrayal. I suppose it is reckless of me to provide such obvious material about my background under these circumstances when questions of loyalty and betrayal are so prominent, but this is the fact of my heritage, which is not to say that sometimes the apple rolls quite far from the tree.

THE STORY OF Eli Czaplinsky coming to America and making his fortune is so much more real to me than the textbook history lessons that are my heritage. Everything about him has always intrigued me—his arrival at Ellis Island, the whispered connection to the murder of Kid Dropper Kaplan and his hasty exodus to New Haven, the touchingly naive if hugely misguided inspiration of *Little Black Sambo* for his three candy lines. But what about the undocumented interlude in Eli's life, when he first arrived in New Haven? How did he survive when he stepped off the train here in August 1923?

The official Zip's Candies history refers to his employment by the Armenians selling their chocolate-covered coconut patties. But before that he found work doing odd jobs for a pair of elderly spinster sisters, Emma and Dora Hodgson, who presided over a sweet shop on Chapel Street that was locally famous for chocolate-covered cherries and their unusual chunks of chewy nougat brittle, which they called Peanut Charms. They let Eli sleep in the back room for four months, and he learned from them all sorts of useful skills, from tempering chocolate to making fondant fillings for bonbons and mastering the alchemy required for cooking up delectable batches of caramel kisses from sugar, molasses, milk, butter, and salt.

All the Zip's Candies dead files have languished for years in a welter of sagging cardboard boxes in a corner of the factory basement. You can learn a lot, reading through the old files of a family business that has been documenting itself for better or worse since 1924. The Hodgson files, for example, had a folder devoted to a settlement agreement made in 1956, when Sam had to pay twenty thousand dollars to their only heir, the son of their brother who had married and moved to Ipswich. The Hodgson nephew, prompted by the growing success of Zip's Candies, had brought a suit alleging that the original formulation for the Tigermelt center was derived from the secret recipe stolen by Eli for those long-gone Hodgson Peanut Charms.

Sam told me about this claim over lunch one day so long ago the kids were still in elementary school and it would be years before they would have to decide if they wanted to work in the business. But he had brought it up, the question of the next generation, as he did from time to time. I never wanted to make

Jacob or Julie feel that they were expected to work for Zip's Candies, but from the time they could walk they both loved going to visit the factory, and as they grew older, they appreciated the social value of being in a candy-making family. For every school fund-raiser, for every auction benefit, New Haven Country Day could count on Zip's Candies for generous support. One year, we donated the top raffle prize, a Zip's Golden Ticket, which granted the winner free candy from Zip's every day for a year, up to ten pieces each day. Howard loved being admired for our support of all those school events. We were good citizens of New Haven Country Day, despite my many skirmishes over the years with various faculty and other parents over a range of small issues.

When the kids were little, I thought I might have a second chance in life to develop some friendships among the parents of their friends and classmates. But from nursery school on, I would feel drawn to people, their kids would get along well with my kids, we would start out with nice exchanges, playdates, outings, a few sleepovers, but then sooner or later the adult relationship would go off the tracks.

I have come to recognize that many people are both hypersensitive and judgmental. Apparently I can be too much for a lot of unimaginative people. I have always been very responsible for children in my care. But my altruism can be misunderstood, whether it takes the form of serving perfectly wholesome beef stew to a malnourished little second grader friend of Jacob's whose vegan parents were practically starving him, or giving a much-needed haircut to a kindergarten classmate of Julie's who was over for a playdate. That pixie cut really did improve the little girl's appearance. She had looked like Cousin It. I have no idea why her silly mother cried like that. It was just hair.

Howard usually shrugged off these minor dramas when he

heard about them, but he was quite irked with me when the kids were in the upper school and the parents association got involved with a Halloween campaign to post "No Candy Here" signs on the doors of known sex offenders living in New Haven neighborhoods conducive to trick-or-treating. Although I had certainly not volunteered for this, it was somehow assumed that as candy makers we would want to be involved in this ridiculous enterprise. I thought it was a terrible idea, one that seemed like harassment to me, and was possibly not even legal. And in any case, I didn't like the smugness of this virtuous shaming one bit.

The week before Halloween, I received in the mail a large envelope containing a list of fourteen names and a map of the Whitneyville section of New Haven, with fourteen marked addresses and fourteen "No Candy Here" signs to distribute accordingly. On Halloween night, children who were drawn to the "Candy Here" signs displayed at those fourteen addresses were rewarded with generous quantities of Little Sammies, Tigermelts, and Mumbo Jumbos. The signs were recognized, however, and later that night a group of perhaps a dozen indignant vigilante parents came to our door to pick a fight. Julie and Jacob weren't home yet, having been given permission to go to parties, it being a Saturday night (the second best night of the week for Halloween candy sales), and the trick-or-treating had subsided.

Howard answered the door with a bowl of Zip's candies, and instead of the almost-too-old final goblins of the night, he was confronted by this angry posse eager to tell him exactly what outrageous thing I had done with that list and those signs. People can be ridiculously judgmental and small-minded.

❄   ❄

WHEN SHE WAS in high school and had spent three summers working at Zip's, Julie told me I had hurt her feelings when I suggested, in response to a great seventh-grade report card, that with her powers of observation and her wonderful writing skills she might consider journalism. She admitted that for a long while after that she felt rejected by me, because this must have meant I didn't want her working at Zip's, that I was trying to keep her out with this diversionary suggestion, as if she was unsuitable for and unworthy of the family business. I was, of course, very sorry that I had given her that impression. As a parent I have always wanted my children to know how interested I am in their lives. It's what I wished for and never had. But of course each generation compensates for early deprivations by imposing new, different ones on our children.

THIS TALK WITH Sam about the next generation coming into Zip's Candies led to a chat about Eli's earliest days in New Haven, and the Hodgson sisters, and the subsequent claim. Sam told me where to look for the files on the settlement agreement if I was interested. Of course I was interested, as he knew I would be. This is why he told me things he never told anyone else. He also told me (I have my scribbled notes from that day right in front of me, in notebook #19, because I certainly did not burn my notebooks, and I can quote what he said) that while there was never any admission on the part of Zip's Candies when they paid off the nephew with this go-away money that bought a nondisclosure agreement, he believed that Eli did copy the recipe for those Peanut Charms.

"Eli was hungry," Sam said to me. "Hungry people don't always do the right thing. We're doing well, so we're not that hungry, so we can afford to do the right thing. The problem comes when people are well-fed for so long that they forget what hunger feels like, and then they also can start to forget what the right thing is. So the trick of it," he told me, picking up the check and studying it, having now eaten all our shared French fries while I was taking his words down in my notebook (I noted this too, in the margin—"S ate most of the ff again"), "the trick of it is to find the balance between being too hungry and not being hungry enough. And a rich man has to work very hard to find a way to make sure his children are just a little hungry."

He stopped my writing hand, wrapping it in his big knuckley paw, which was a strangely intimate gesture between us. Though he didn't smoke his cigar at Clark's, he always had that soggy, half-smoked unlit cigar in his mouth or in his hand, and so for the rest of that day my hand smelled strongly of his perpetual cigar, that corky odor I wasn't crazy about in his lifetime. Sam's office had a unique miasma, a blended aroma of the sweet candy-factory air and that sour cigar smoke, which I continued to taste for a long time whenever I had been in there for something. Sometimes it lasted into the evening hours, as if molecules of cigar smoke and chocolate and burnt sugar had lodged up my nose and in the back of my throat and on my soft palate.

Sam's own taste buds had been numbed by his years of cigar smoking, which sometimes led to arguments, especially when he sampled the Tigermelt center blends, since he always thought we needed to salt the fried peanuts more heavily. ("Everybody likes salt," he used to argue if he happened along as a batch of Tigermelt nougat filling was being blended. "Even if they say they don't. If two candies are very similar, and one tastes a little saltier, people will prefer that one. Always put in a little more salt.") Now that he is gone I miss that cigar smoke very much. I have more than once followed down the street a prosperous stranger puffing on a Macanudo, just to have a few stolen moments of breathing in that familiar aroma.

So I looked up when he stopped me from writing, and he said gently, "Alice, kiddo, you're the best thing to happen to this family. Howdy doesn't know how lucky he is. He thinks he makes his luck, but he has never been hungry enough to make his own luck. We gave him everything, after we lost his brother, and that was a mistake, because nothing was a struggle for him, everything came to him too easily. Frieda wouldn't hear me for many years, and I couldn't fight with her. She just wanted her Howdy to have what he wanted, when he wanted it. There was so much pain about Lewis. Howdy never learned how to make a plan to get what he wanted on his own, or how to do without. He never learned to wait, he never had to earn anything he got. He grew up believing that this was how life works, and he didn't realize that for other people there is much more struggle, much more conflict. Now maybe Frieda regrets this, because she sees what kind of man he is, but she doesn't say. He'll never be Lewis."

Sam was rarely disloyal to family members, unlike the subsequent generation, and though he seemed to be on the verge of saying something more to me after this soliloquy, he didn't. He still had my hand, as if to keep me from writing anything more (I made notes later, in my car before going back to work), so I closed the notebook. And then he said one more thing to me, which I also wrote down right away, so this is definitely accurate.

He said, "I'm not going to live forever, and I need to plan. One thing I didn't plan so well is that this family is small. If you want to keep a family business going, the smartest thing you can do is have a lot of brothers and sisters and a lot of children. That way you never have to scrape the barrel. You shouldn't have anyone doing a job in a family business if you wouldn't ever think of hiring that person if he wasn't family. In a big family, you find more qualified employees, you have family members who can find the right job in the business that suits them, and you can have good partnerships and plan your successions."

He looked at me then, and then he looked away and squeezed my hand very hard, and I could see him fighting tears. In retrospect this was probably as close as he could come to telling me what he knew and I didn't, but he breathed a long sigh instead, and then he just had one more thing to say:

"I'm counting on you to bring up Jakie and Julie so they know how to work for a living. It's the most important thing, and I know you won't let me down. It's up to you to keep our family going, even if things get complicated. If they know how to work for a living, they'll always land on their feet."

Mary the waitress came to clear our plates and drop the check on our table then. God, I miss everything about those lunches at Clark's with Sam. Ordering BLT's and grilled cheese sandwiches without a thought about cholesterol. The "plate of ice cream" on the menu. The creamy buzz of the milk-shake machines. Never once in all those years did Mary or Barbara ever ask us if we were "still working on that."

7

TELL PEOPLE YOUR FAMILY has a candy business, and soon enough *Charlie and the Chocolate Factory* comes into the conversation, the original Roald Dahl book and both movies based on the book, all of which are blended together in most people's minds as one delightful excursion to a fantasy chocolate factory, maybe one a lot like Zip's Candies.

Jacob and Julie each received multiple copies of the book when they were born, and subsequently not a birthday has ever passed without another copy turning up, as well as various videos or DVDs of both films over the years. We have probably had fifty copies of various editions of the book pass through this house. I can't throw them away fast enough. Sometimes I find mysterious copies of *Charlie and the Chocolate Factory* on a bookshelf, or a videotape of the 1971 movie, *Willy Wonka & the Chocolate Factory* (apparently the name "Charlie" had to be avoided in the Vietnam years because that was what we called the Vietcong, Victor Charlie) in with other old tapes. Twice, for no apparent reason, a DVD of the 2005 Johnny Depp film, *Charlie and the Chocolate Factory*, has arrived erroneously in our Netflix mailer. Sooner or later, no matter what I do, another version of *Charlie and the Chocolate Factory* will appear again somewhere in the house like a recurring fungus.

If Howard was more energetic and imaginative, I would suspect him of an elaborate plot to gaslight me. He always found my horror of all things *Charlie and the Chocolate Factory* amusing. He was not an attentive reader, and even when I elaborated on the reason for my loathing of this story, he always said it just didn't bother him. That in itself bothered me.

I regard each manifestation of *Charlie and the Chocolate Factory* with a white-hot, passionate hatred. I was given a copy of the book when it was first published in 1964, for my sixth birthday. My father read it aloud to me at bedtime, three nights in a row, until we reached the end. It was the only time he ever read to me, and I will never know how it was determined that this was the book for our one and only father-daughter bedtime bonding experience. I was utterly terrified, and hardly dared to go to sleep those nights, so fearful did the story make me.

Why did anyone think this was a suitable bedtime read for a child? (And why did my parents not take my terror seriously, instead of finding it funny?) The gratuitous cruelties, the violence, the casual viciousness—how did this book worm its way into our culture? How did it find its way so quickly to the beloved classics shelf, nestled between *Charlotte's Web* and *Little Women* in every children's library in the Western world? I hated it, and yet I couldn't resist it, and as I became a more proficient reader I would return to it again and again throughout my childhood and adolescence. I was like someone who despises black licorice but keeps coming back for just one more licorice allsort in order to savor her own disgust at the loathed flavor each time.

The world of *Charlie and the Chocolate Factory* is one in which all children are assumed to be greedy and obsessed with candy, while there is universal admiration for the sadomasochistic proprietor of the Wonka Candy Company. The cooked-up pathos of the poverty in which Charlie Bucket lives with his family as the book begins has always felt to me like a vicious mockery. Consider for comparison the genuinely wrenching penury of *A Little Princess* or *Oliver Twist*. Dahl is heartless. He is contemptuous of children; Veruca Salt's first name is the synonym for a kind of wart. There is an underlying contempt for all humanity, really, and an almost obsessive hatred for the innocent joys of childhood, as if all pleasure-seeking is a form of gluttony for which people must be shamed and punished. It's one big pleasure trap.

There is something obscene about the book, and I really mean that—this tasteless, horrible book feels to me much more like covert S and M pornography than children's literature. It is a wonder that I wasn't so scarred by my early exposure to this material that I didn't have an aversion to Zip's Candies, though when I got to this very issue in my analysis, Dr. Gibraltar suggested that my love for and attraction to a candy factory— and consequently, the way I have spent my life in the candy businesss—might well be a reaction formation. The blocking of desire by its opposite.

Meanwhile, everyone who has read *Charlie and the Chocolate Factory* or seen either movie version believes he knows something about the inner workings of a candy factory. Which brings me to the Oompa-Loompa problem. No, we do not have Oompa-Loompas working at Zip's Candies. And how very original of you to ask. How amusing is this notion of slave labor, this fun fantasy of workers who never leave the factory? What could be more pleasing than an army of small brown people who don't require wages working tirelessly in the production of cheap chocolate for the greedy public?

My copy of the book was the original first American edition. In it, the Oompa-Loompas are described as "black pygmies from the very deepest and darkest part of the African jungle, where no white man had been before." Later editions were revised in text and illustration, because of reactions to the blatant racism, so the Oompa-Loompas mutated into "dwarves" with "golden-brown hair" and "rosy white skin" who come from Loompa-land, a region of Loompa, a small isolated island in the Pacific Ocean. (In the 1971 movie, for which Dahl wrote an early version of the screenplay, they have orange skin and green hair, as if they have now mutated one step further into a tribe of enslaved laborers who match the Irish flag, surely another familiar and very British colonialist fantasy.)

But no matter how complected, we all know what Oompa-Loompas really are, don't we? Fun, guilt-free slaves! It's like diet candy, with zero calories! What cultural blindness makes it possible for people to cherish and adore Oompa-Loompas, while simultaneously recognizing the evils of child slavery in certain cacao-producing nations of Africa? How about if instead of a colony of pygmies dwelling in the chocolate factory, these tireless captive workers were diminutive Jews from a remote shtetl in deepest Siberia? Would that be just as charming and fun?

IRENE HAS NEVER shown any curiosity about the actual workings of Zip's, the day-to-day operations, how the raw materials are sourced, how the candy is manufactured and all we do for quality control, the concerns of marketing and sales, not to mention the issues of our hiring and benefit policies, which are so far removed from the employment practices of Willy Wonka. For years, her idea of involvement with the family business was the effort she put into generating an incessant barrage of newspaper clippings and sanctimonious emails.

These communications were always urgent, unrealistic demands related to the cause of the moment, usually a sudden inspiration that Zip's Candies should only use special biodegradable wrappers made of rice husks and printed with soy ink, or that we should immediately start using only organic ingredients, or that we should run our machines on used cooking oil instead of electricity, or that we should hire a bunch of displaced Katrina victims right away.

Then there was the unforgettable time she phoned me from her car, sounding desperate, asking me to meet her for coffee at Starbucks on Chapel Street right then, please! I postponed a meeting with a supplier and hopped in my car, worried that she had a health scare, or that there was some equivalently dire crisis that she needed to tell me about. Why me and not Howard? We had never met for coffee before.

I should have known. After I circled the block twice looking for a parking space, which were especially scarce because some recent heavy snows had left ugly scraped piles of dirty snow and ice along the narrow side streets around the Yale campus, I gave up and parked in a loading zone on Chapel Street (for which I got a parking ticket). Irene was at the front of the line, so I joined her and we gave our orders. I asked for a tall red-eye, and Irene ordered one of those narcissistic coffee drinks requiring modifications and extra shots of this and that, and the foam this way and not that way in relation to the caramel, and a venti cup for a grande drink. I could tell by the look on the face of the barista, a distracted high school girl who clearly hated everyone that afternoon as she listened to Irene's order, that she was going to give Irene real espresso despite the emphatic instruction about the three decaffeinated espresso shots.

When we had settled at a table, Irene pulled out a book from one of her many virtuous tote bags from do-good organizations and held it to her bosom before placing it reverently on the table between us. This system of understanding personalities would change everything at Zip's, she explained. It was the key to our future success. We needed to find out every employee's type right away so as to assign them to the tasks best suited to their personalities. We?

"You're a One, and I'm a Two," she said, "and this is why we haven't always gotten along very well." She seemed to think she was speaking rationally. I saw that the book was an introduction to Enneagrams. This was the emergency? "Twos are helpers," she explained. "Helpers are nurturers, focused on giving and receiving love."

I lost my temper, I admit. I told Irene that Zip's wasn't going to embark on a damned Enneagram management policy now or ever. And anyway, why not bring this to Howard if she thought it was so essential? Did she know I had canceled a meeting to rush here, because she had made it sound as if she had a personal emergency? What was *wrong* with her?

"Maybe you're not a One." She frowned, taking her book off the table and thrusting it protectively into a National Wildlife Federation tote. "Maybe you're an Eight. Ones are reformers and ideal-seekers, but maybe you're really more of an aggressive power-seeker than I had realized."

MOST URGENTLY, AND most repetitively and problematically, Irene was always badgering Howard and me with variations on the obviousness of the necessity for us to agree immediately to source all our chocolate from suppliers who guarantee that they only do business with cacao dealers who only do business with fair trade cacao buyers who only do business with organic cacao plantations. First of all, I think it is worth pointing out that the only thing the words "Fair Trade" on the label can ever really guarantee with certainty is that earnest crunchy people will pay a lot of money for any product so labeled. Fair trade is a nice idea, but the fact is that if you seek the best cacao beans and the best coffee beans, they are simply not going to be fair trade. And it's a system that has the potential to cheat farmers and workers, because it locks in buyer and seller relationships, but at the same time the prices can drop and the seller is closed out of the free market, while the buyer doesn't lose anything.

Second, organic shmorganic. I just don't see an adulteration problem with cacao and sugar, our two biggest ingredients. (But, by the way, do I get any credit at all for resisting the pressure from our brokers in recent years to buy cheap Chinese imports, from nuts to flavorings to condensed milk solids to enrobing chocolate? I have always had concerns about quality control, and I had several fights with Howard about this, the last one just a few weeks before the shocking news of melamine-tainted pet food broke. Only because of my caution did the worldwide melamine crisis of 2008 have no effect on us. Cadbury had to pull eleven different types of melamine-tainted chocolate made in their Beijing plant for the Hong Kong, Taiwan, and Australian markets. And tainted White Rabbit Creamy Candy from China was on shelves right here in Connecticut and across the country. But Zip's Candies were safe.)

I do worry a great deal about aflatoxins, which could be catastrophic in our peanut supplies, and so we really cannot risk sourcing organic peanuts. This means there is no point in sourcing any other organics at this time, because we wouldn't be able to capitalize on it; we wouldn't be able to put a designation on the label, since there is little value in a "Somewhat Organic" label, and if we can't profit from the extra expense by appealing to the crunchy upscale people, then it's a pure loss.

Anyway, lots of organic chocolate, perhaps most organic chocolate, has uneven quality control and can be unpleasantly musty, with a muddy mouthfeel and a moldy taste. That said, if Zip's Candies were to make a calculated decision to commit to

fair trade and organic ingredients, we would have to charge
north of three dollars for a pack of Little Sammies or a Tigermelt bar, instead of a worrisome enough retail price that has
finally gone over the one dollar line for the first time. That's not
going to happen, especially not now, with the economy the way
it is. This is no time to start making premium chocolates for the
prosperous. Except for the Bao-Bar, the best strategy for Zip's
Candies is to keep making cheap candy for working stiffs. I'm
counting on this depression to create another golden era for the
candy bar.

IRENE IS INCREDIBLY naive. I recognize that her heart is in the
right place (about most things that aren't directly connected to
me). I don't even disagree with her about these goals, in the best
of all possible worlds. But one of the many differences between
us is that unlike her, I was not born a princess, and I live in the
real world. And meanwhile, since I have touched on fair trade
and other problematic issues of cacao production, let us not forget that whole fiasco just six years ago, when Irene embarked on
a campaign to end child slave labor on African cacao plantations,
feeling, as she claimed, a personal responsibility, having "blood
on her hands," she actually said more than once in interviews,
because of her family's chocolate candy business.

I have always refrained from suggesting that there was any
impropriety in Irene's relationship with Abu Nkongo, who was
both younger than her own son, Ethan, and also extraordinarily
attractive and charming in a very sensuous, almost animalistic
way, in those months when she had him living with her and they
did all that traveling around together. Perhaps others thought
there was something going on between them. It's not my place to
speculate.

Am I the only member of the family who has not forgotten about this episode, when Irene toured for months lecturing people on the shameful origins of their cheap chocolate? It was potentially very harmful to Zip's Candies, it was certainly embarrassing in candy-manufacturing circles, and it forced us to take a position. Julie, who was already remarkably adept at website management and all things Internet even then, created a page on our site for a bland statement about our views on the fair trade issue and our hopes for more future involvement, stating that meanwhile of course we support the efforts being made to improve the quality of life for all cacao workers in Africa. It's so much more complex than that, of course. But Irene pushed us to the wall. She forced us to say something about this so we would look good instead of bad, when we would have preferred to remain silent.

This issue of child slavery on cacao plantations in Africa became Irene's raison d'être. It ended in embarrassment, if not humiliation. The randomness of her lighting on this issue in the first place is actually funny. Irene didn't discover the plight of the African cacao workers because of her guilty conscience about living off a chocolate candy company. And she didn't discover her destiny as a spokesperson for the cacao slaves because of inner soul work with any of her rent-a-gurus, either. Hardly. It all came about only because she went to Paris for a meditation workshop she never even attended.

On her first morning there, Irene went out to do her daily requisite twenty-four Tai Chi forms in the little leafy park across from her Left Bank hotel. It was very early, and she was quite pleased with herself, being a fit American doing her Tai Chi in a park in Paris, feeling superior to the indolent, smoking Parisians, loving her own sophistication about being in Paris by herself, especially smug because she was staying in a cozy Left

Bank hotel instead of going back to the very grand Right Bank hotel where she stayed the only other time she had been in Paris, with Arthur, when they were first married. As she went into White Crane Spreading Its Wings, her favorite Tai Chi position, the one she most liked to catch a glimpse of herself doing in the mirror during her Tai Chi classes, she saw a huddled form shivering on a bench.

This was Abu Nkongo, a charming teenage boy who admitted to her, in answer to her questions, which she asked boldly and a little breathlessly while doing her stretches, using the bench on which he had spent the night for support, that he was hungry. She took him to a café for breakfast, feeling utterly thrilled and delighted with herself for doing this, and he told her his story, all about how he was from a small village in Côte d'Ivoire, how he had nothing, knew nobody in France, and had been sleeping in parks for many days, since arriving in the back of a vegetable truck full of tomatoes from Holland. How did he get into that truck? He sneaked aboard on a loading dock in Rotterdam. He had stowed away on a bulk container cargo ship in Abidjan three weeks earlier as it was loaded with cacao beans en route to a Dutch cocoa processor.

Droste? Irene wondered, naming the only Dutch chocolate company she knew, and Abu nodded. She was moved to tears by her sense of her own empathy welling in her chest for this sweet boy.

He was a Cameroonian citizen because his mother was from Cameroon, Abu explained to her as they walked back through the park, though his mother had arrived in Côte d'Ivoire before he was born, and so he had never seen Cameroon himself. Irene was able to get him a passport, working with a corrupt official at the Cameroonian embassy. I have no idea how, but apparently Irene, ditsy as she seems, knows how to find the people who know people who know how to make things happen (perhaps this skill is a by-product of her passing involvement in a druggy underworld), and she can certainly always come up with the cash.

Irene took Abu for photographs and had them delivered to the official, and then two days later she met the buyable Cameroonian embassy worker in a café, where they exchanged envelopes folded inside copies of *Libération*. He got up and walked away a moment later, and she sat there with her coffee for five more minutes, as instructed, peeking at Abu's new passport inside the folded newspaper. I am sure she thought she was Lillian Hellman in *Julia*.

Irene had meanwhile talked Howard into having Zip's Candies sponsor a work visa for Abu, some nonsense about cacao harvesting and consulting on chocolate candy manufacturing, and incredibly enough, after three dramatic weeks, during which time she fed him and paid for a hotel room for him, she was able to fly him back with her to New York. She brought him to New Haven for a week (they stayed with Frieda), where his consulting consisted of a tour of the factory and a prodigious consumption of Little Sammies and Tigermelts fresh off the lines. Howard took him along for a round of golf and lunch at his club, and reported afterward that Abu had been polite but quiet and had enjoyed driving the golf cart, and that if he was pushed off his set pieces, his fluency in English deteriorated markedly.

Julie and Jacob, who were both in college at the time (Julie had just started at Wesleyan, Jacob was in his last year at Kenyon), came home that weekend and found Abu strange and unlikeable. Julie thought there was something not quite right about him, but she couldn't really say why she got this vibe (she is a very good observer of people), and meanwhile, we were of course all contorting ourselves to find things to like about him and ways to make him feel welcome.

After it came apart, Julie accused the whole family of being naive limousine liberals like the people in *Six Degrees of Separation*. We had been so eager to embrace Abu as this heroic victim who made us feel better about our own white privilege, she said. She had a point. Would Irene have taken him under her wing if he were white and homely instead of an exquisitely beautiful African boy?

Irene took Abu home with her to Telluride. She dressed him in a lot of Patagonia fleece, which he liked very much. She began to write letters to newspapers on the plight of the cacao child slaves in Africa. They were invited to speak at a Telluride school, at a church in Montrose, and then on a radio station in Durango, and then, with Irene growing more and more passionate about the issues, and more and more delighted with herself for her noblesse oblige, they embarked on a lecture tour together, which she bankrolled. She hired a publicist, who was able to get them invitations to speak at churches and schools mostly, and they got good press coverage wherever they went.

Over and over, for the next three months, Abu told his heartrending story about having run away from a brutal cacao plantation where young boys were held captive and forced to labor under the scorching sun, harvesting cacao pods fourteen hours a day in exchange for prisonlike accommodations and scant meals of corn paste and boiled bananas, at risk of being beaten by guards if they failed to work quickly or efficiently enough.

It was quite moving, their show (Julie and I saw them at Wesleyan, early in their East Coast run), with Irene working the PowerPoint, with photos and graphs and charts and bullet-pointed phrases, while Abu explained in his halting English that he has learned that it takes four hundred beans to make a pound of pure chocolate, and each pod contains some forty beans, and all of these beans are harvested by hungry, scrawny boys who have never tasted chocolate. Abu himself first tasted chocolate in Paris, when Irene bought him a *pain au chocolat* for breakfast in the café that first morning, and he thought it was the sweetest taste in his mouth, like something surely from heaven, not something from the earth, and he was amazed that those dirty, gritty beans could produce such richness.

Irene told me proudly that he would always stop to say this, always using those words. His already moved audiences were rapt as he went on to describe how the boys would labor every day on the plantation, with dangerous snakes underfoot and stinging insects circling their heads. The boys, wearing little more than shorts and flip-flops, would just work and work, lifting the heavy machetes high to cut the ripest heavy pods from the trees—the bosses would be angry when some of the cacao pods were useless because they were blackened with disease from rot or bird damage—and then with their machetes they would slice each pod all the way around and then pull the two halves apart to get the placenta, the gooey brainlike mass of precious beans in the core.

The boys would scoop out the beans and spread them on woven mats or on banana leaves, and cover them with more banana leaves so they would ferment properly. Every day they would cut the pods and split the pods and spread the wet beans on mats for fermenting, and each batch, after a few days, once the sweet milky fruit surrounding the beans had fermented and begun to dry on the beans, would then be uncovered and the beans would be dried in the sun for a few days, perhaps a week, depending on the weather. Once dry, the beans would be shoveled into large burlap bags, each bag weighing some sixty-eight kilos, and the boys would carry these big sacks of dried beans weighing nearly twice their own weight to a collection point, and there they would load the bags onto the trucks that came.

Abu said he had been lured to the plantation from a bus stop outside the town of Daloa, when he was traveling from his rural village to visit his grandmother. He had been promised money, $150 for a year's labor, and a new bicycle. He was sixteen at the time, and small for his age, and the man who approached him had thought he was younger. Many of the boys on the plantation were only nine or ten. Abu was taken hundreds of miles in a truck with some other boys who had also been picked up that day, to the plantation. He didn't really know where it was, this cacao plantation where he spent more than two years in captivity. Abu never found out the name of the townland and he never saw any nearby villages. He never got his money or his bicycle.

Details of Abu's escape were murky, and he would always hesitate and then drop his eyes and lower his voice and say he could not tell all the truth of the story because he could not name the people who helped him without endangering them even now, from the person who helped him climb in with the sacks of cacao beans as they were loaded into a truck, to the driver who smuggled him with the cacao as the sacks were loaded into the hold of a cargo ship that sailed from Abidjan. He felt responsible for the other two boys who had run away with him, Malik and Jumo, both younger than Abu, who died when the bulk container of cacao beans was fumigated a few days before the ship arrived in the Dutch port. Abu didn't die only because he had crawled out of the container in search of water, and was in another part of the ship's cargo area during the fumigation. He was found by a member of the crew, who heard his anguished cries when he returned to the container with water for his friends.

Although he was being held for the Dutch authorities, a sympathetic sailor who was supposed to be watching him (Abu thought the boat and crew were from Singapore) turned him loose on the dock, he said, before the police arrived. Abu would always emphasize that the details of his personal story were unimportant, and what mattered was that everyone should know about the boys who had not escaped, all the hundreds and perhaps thousands of children who were wielding those rusty machetes to cut the cacao pods, all those children who were captive to this labor, living on corn paste and boiled bananas, living in fear of the guards who could beat them or even kill them if they didn't work hard enough, so the world could have its chocolate.

THIS COMPELLING TALK was given probably thirty times in various locations, with Irene making all the arrangements and covering all travel expenses. They raised more than two hundred thousand dollars for Common Dreams and the International Labor Rights Foundation. I am sure everyone who heard one of these talks was shocked and moved and shamed by these revelations about where our chocolate comes from. Just as we are all shocked and moved and shamed each time we are reminded where our clothing comes from. It's always uncomfortable to stop and imagine for a moment exactly what the origins of the chocolate in your M&M's might be, and to consider who has labored in what way, under what conditions, in order to provide that sweet melting-in-your-mouth moment. It is also difficult to consider the life of the child in Bangladesh who was paid pennies to make your Old Navy T-shirt. So I want to say again, Irene's dedication was impressive, and even though the inspiration for her involvement turned out to be a fraud, that doesn't undo her accomplishments in getting attention and raising money for a worthy cause.

Irene was in talks with a literary agent about collaborating on a book about Abu's experiences when their interview on *All Things Considered* aired on National Public Radio. Within days of the broadcast, it all began to unravel. Numerous listeners phoned or wrote to say there were many details that didn't add up in Abu's story, starting with the way his accent was all wrong for Côte d'Ivoire. This was correct; Abu was actually from Cameroon. Everything else was wrong, too: dates, places, the story of the bulk container of cacao in the Dutch port and his two dead friends, his journey to Paris in a truckload of tomatoes. None of it added up.

Abu was, of course, a fraud. All the parts of his story that didn't add up were always right there in plain sight. His compelling story was true, in a sense. It just wasn't his story. It was a blend of several stories he had heard about or read in newspapers. An athletic boy from a family of cacao farmers on the edge of Mount Cameroon (his two younger brothers, Malik and Jumo, were alive and well), Abu, who did in fact spend time working on his family's small cacao farm, was the star of his school's soccer team. He had been recruited by a soccer scout to try out for the French national team. His family had given all their meager savings plus some borrowed money to pay his way for this opportunity.

And so Abu was brought to France, to the soccer training camp in Vichy, where he had been housed and fed, and he had drilled and played long hours every day with the French team for three weeks. But he wasn't good enough. Very few of the African recruits ever were, though they were useful practice fodder, and every now and then someone with star quality actually did make the team. And so at the end of the three-week tryout (that he had only ever been offered a three-week tryout was news to Abu), he had been put on a train to Paris with fifty euros. Ashamed and frightened, Abu didn't know what to do when he arrived at the Gare de Lyon.

A sympathetic Senegalese taxi driver gave him a free ride to the Cameroonian embassy in the sixteenth arrondissement, but there was a long line outside, and he was discouraged. Abu found a very cheap and not very clean hotel room near noisy train tracks in the Little Africa neighborhood the cabdriver had told him about, La Goutte d'Or in the eighteenth arrondissement, and in a café on rue Doudeauville he listened to two Cameroonians at an adjacent table talking about three men from Ghana who had been found dead in a container ship in New York City, poisoned by the fumigation of cacao beans in the container in which they had stowed away.

When he awoke the next morning, his money and his passport were gone. The man at the front desk shrugged and turned away. Abu found his way back to the Cameroonian embassy and got on the end of the line, but at noon everyone on the street was told that the embassy was only open a half day on Fridays and they should all come back on Monday. He spent the day walking aimlessly through the streets. The next morning, Abu woke from a fitful doze on a park bench to see a rich American in her black running tights and her red fleece and her puffy white sneakers going through her Tai Chi poses in front of him. He never dreamed that Irene would believe his story, he admitted in his official statement to the American immigration authorities (from which I have gathered all this information) before he was deported to Cameroon, and he had really only meant to get a free meal and maybe a little money from her.

Abu's story brought out the best in Irene. I have certainly never seen her happier. Was her compassion any less real, was the issue any less true, when it turned out he was a fraud? But the outrage over his deception and her unwitting part in it was hugely humiliating for her. She went into a depression. She didn't return calls from agents and editors clamoring for her to write a book about her experience with Abu, and after a while the calls stopped and everyone lost interest. The story got pushed down the page, and then finally it was off the page.

Irene had been so moved by her own virtue, by her compassion for Abu. As were all the people in their audiences who gave generously to help change the system of child labor on cacao plantations in Africa. Was harm done, in the end? (Other than the bruises to Irene's sense of her own certainties about the world?) The money they raised didn't enrich Abu; it went to agencies set up to assist the child slave workers on the cacao plantations in Africa. Abu lived well for a few months and dined out on his appropriated story for a while, but he ended up right back where he started, with a wardrobe of Patagonia fleece and polypropylene underwear he would never wear in Cameroon.

He hasn't been heard from since. I can't imagine why some enterprising editor hasn't tracked him down with an offer of a ghostwritten memoir deal. It wouldn't be the first time such a book has been published. Maybe Irene bought his silence. Maybe in his own way he has some dignity and integrity. Maybe he came to feel that *she* had taken advantage of *him*.

Do I believe Irene's repeated claims that she never suspected Abu of any deception, that she never once questioned his story at any point in those months, from their first conversation in the park in Paris to the unraveling that followed their Public Radio interview? She defended him in the beginning, when the holes in his story first came to light, but then once the irrefutable facts just couldn't be explained away, she never made any public statement reversing her belief in him. She just withdrew. She completely dropped all her involvements with the various organizations working to end child slavery in cacao production in Africa. When I asked her a few months after the whole Abu crisis had died down if she no longer felt concern about the child slaves in Côte d'Ivoire, she was irritated, and snapped something at me about how that issue had become toxic for her and she had refocused her positive energy on global warming instead.

Fortunately, Howard had listened to me at the outset, when I enumerated all the reasons Zip's Candies should make no official statement of any kind about Abu or about Irene's campaign, given all the obvious conflicts and problems that association could have ignited, so when it came apart we didn't have to do any embarrassing backtracking. We dodged a bullet, not that anyone thanked me for my judgment. The sad truth is, we use chocolate that has been made from processed cacao beans that have probably been harvested by children living in deplorable conditions. We use this chocolate every day to make our candy. We make Little Sammies and Tigermelts, and we make Mumbo Jumbos. We source the best ingredients we can, for the right price. Zip's Candies is a business. We are not the UN.

I DO BELIEVE Irene. Despite how irrationally suspicious Irene can be about people who don't match her distorted expectations—like me—I think she believed Abu's story with all her heart. As I said, it wouldn't be my place to suggest that sexual obsession blinded her to the truth. Perhaps she was made especially gullible by her desire to see herself in such a noble light.

Lady Bountiful solving the world's problems. Because sponsoring Abu, doing all she did to rescue him and help him tell his story, that worked for her. It suited her needs perfectly. In the end, that kind of naiveté is actually a form of entitled arrogance, isn't it?

8

I<small>N</small> 1920, E<small>LI</small> <small>AND</small> Morris left their little brother, Julius, in Budapest with some cousins. There is nothing in any Zip's Candies record or family story about what provisions, if any, they made for him. Did they feel guilty about Julius, abandoned at the last moment with the Fischer family, barely known second cousins on their mother's side? Or did they put him out of their minds completely as they sailed away, leaving him behind along with everything else that was familiar? He was fourteen years old. Their parents had died just a few months earlier in an influenza epidemic (first one, then the other), and the brothers had promised their mother they would stay together. Now his two older brothers had foisted Julius on strangers who lived over a shop in a strange, bustling city, nothing like the small village, two days' walking distance from Budapest, where the Czaplinskys had been rooted for generations, selling live poultry in the market square.

Did Eli and Morris miss him, as they began their new lives in America? Did they think of him and wonder how he was managing, as they ate their meals, as they tried to get used to the bland American flavors he might have enjoyed, or despised? Did they wonder if that sour-looking aunt Borbála ever gave their little Julesy any sweet treats, a kiss good night, if she ever cracked that *ferbissenah punim* to give him so much as a smile? Was he in school, or had the Fischers put him straight to work in their dry goods business? Surely Eli and Morris had made promises to send for him when they could. Did they try to write to Julius, to Aunt Borbála? Did they think of sending money?

If Morris hadn't died in the 1921 diphtheria epidemic that swept New York, perhaps the brothers would have saved up enough money for Julius's passage. What then? The joyful arrival of young Julius after those terrible but mercifully few years of separation, and after that, perhaps the three reunited brothers would have gone into business together. And who can say, Czaplinsky Brothers Candy might have been very successful, even without *Little Black Sambo* for inspiration, and their sweets could have been delightfully appealing to young and old, and their business might have flourished, not only rivaling the likes of the now-vanished D. Auerbach & Sons, Peaks Mason Mints, or W. P. Chase in those halcyon years of candy manufacturing in New York City, but perhaps even outlasting them, swallowing them up, growing bigger and bigger. Who can say if the synergistic energy of the three brothers might have made Czaplinsky a household name, maybe the third big name in American candy, after Hershey and Mars.

But of course, that never happened.

HERE'S WHAT I imagine did happen. Yes, these are my perceptions. These are necessarily my interpretations of events. Does anyone have a more authentic or plausible version of this story? If so, let's hear it!

Julius was grudgingly taken into the Fischer family, and as time passed he became more and more content with his life in Budapest, the so-called "Paris of the East," as his aunt Borbála liked to say as she unfurled an array of the latest yard goods from France across the worn wooden counter of Fischer's on

Dohány Street while persuading a prosperous customer that her social status required the more expensive Jacquard-loomed damask drapery materials favored in the most fashionable salons on La Rive Droite.

Julius finished school and went on to university, where he was a methodical but uninspired student, though he enjoyed the café life that surrounded the university. He wrote several letters to his brothers in America, but he could only address them to Morris and Eli Czaplinsky, care of General Delivery, New York City. He didn't know that Morris was dead or that Eli had moved to New Haven, Connecticut, where he had become a Ziplinsky. The name change made for simpler spelling and less confusion. Zip's Candies was such a good American brand name. And surely the change was also inspired by Eli's desire to make himself unfindable either by New York City detectives who could have wanted to discuss his presence at the Essex Market Courthouse the day Kid Dropper Kaplan was murdered, or by anyone nosing around on behalf of Little Augie, who no doubt wanted his money back, with interest.

Ziplinsky was, anyway, a little bit more of an American kind of name than Czaplinsky, Eli thought, and it was a nice zippy, peppy, zingy name at that. Changing it more would have signified shame about his heritage (he considered Zipple, but even with his beginner's English he recognized that it was an undignified name, too much like the word *nipple*), and he looked down on all those eastern European Jews who chopped their names, those Whites and Whitemans who used to be Wiedermans, the Breitkopfs who became Brodheads. (Perhaps he was unaware of a certain Saxe-Coburg und Gotha family who simply became Windsors not long before then, in 1917.) By the time Eli became an American citizen in 1928, he was proudly signing his name with a big, flourishing Z, with the bottom serif of the Z underlining the rest of the name, a habit he maintained to the end of his life.

Julius had no way of knowing that Eli had written to him five times from New York, the last time to tell him the sad news about their Morris having succumbed to diphtheria. The letters were intercepted by Aunt Borbála each time, who opened them when they arrived from America. Finding no money or specific promises about any, she hid the letters away in a desk drawer, feeling justified in keeping Julius from getting his hopes up. Maybe she would give him the letters some day, but not now. In the future, when he would thank her for keeping him grateful for what he had, for all that the Fischers had given him, instead of dreaming about America. Julius was better off if he didn't think his brothers were going to send for him. These useless letters would keep him from forgetting his brothers. He needed to stop moping around so much, as if he was always waiting for something.

If they did send money for Julius, she told herself, the first priority would be to pay her back for the expense and bother of having added Julius to her household. It was too bad about Morris, because now it was even less likely that any money would ever come. Eli was just a boy himself, and probably he would forget about Julius. Soon there were no more letters, which proved her right. Her father always said those Czaplinskys were good for nothing.

When Julius never heard from his brothers he began to think they might both be dead, and even though Aunt Borbála never said anything, he tried on his own to make himself stop hoping for a letter. He didn't even know with any certainty that they had ever reached America. He continued to work behind the counter at Fischer's for several years, until he left to go into business with his cousin Péter, the least gloomy and conceited of the

Fischers, whose apprenticeship to an elderly baker in the old Jewish Quarter had given him skills and ambitions to open his own shop.

Fischer & Czaplinsky, a bakery with an adjoining coffee-house on Kazinczy Street in the heart of the bustling Jewish Quarter (on the flat, Pest side of the Danube), thrived immediately, and within a couple of years there were five employees working alongside Julius and Péter to keep the customers satisfied with their good strong coffee and all their buttery little cookies and *kiffles*, their *rigó jancsi*, their flakey strudels, and especially their signature *kürtöskalácsus*, a yeasty sweet dough wound around cylinders that slowly rotated over hot coals until the pastry was browned.

Julius, now a handsome and prosperous citizen of the neighborhood, had become something of a ladies' man, with a series of girlfriends, each one believing that she would be the one to claim this attractive and slightly melancholy loner, that she would be the one with whom he would want to settle down and raise a family. But sooner or later, each one would discover evidence of a growing indifference combined with hints of a new woman in his life. Each one would withdraw, defeated, with a slightly broken heart, to be replaced by the next one, and the next.

Then Szilvia Weisz came to work in the bakery at Fischer & Czaplinsky. She was a quiet little worker with a refulgent smile and the nimblest fingers when it came to wrapping the dough for the *kürtöskalácsus*, not too loose or it would fall onto the coals, but not too tight or it would crack apart as it sizzled and browned. Something shifted inside of Julius, some corner of his brittle heart began to soften whenever he saw her, but each time he asked her to go out with him, she told him she would not go out with a playboy, no matter how handsome or charming.

For six months she refused his advances until finally, when

he told her he loved her and had not been with another woman in all that time (which was very nearly the truth), she agreed to go to a chamber music concert with him. A few nights later they went to dinner, and shortly after that they were keeping company every evening, and then they were engaged to be married, and then they were married. The Weisz family, all of them hardworking diamond buyers and cutters, welcomed Julius, and made him feel truly part of a family for the first time since he was a child. Soon there was a baby girl, Matild, born in 1937, and after that a boy, Geza, born in early 1939.

The First Jewish Law, restricting to 20 percent the number of Jews who could have certain administrative positions or hold certain kinds of jobs, had been passed in 1938. Ten years before that, the entire extended Fischer family had converted en masse, all twenty-seven of them becoming churchgoing Lutherans at once, and so they did not think these laws applied to them. Two days after Geza was born, the Second Jewish Law reduced the "economic participation" of the Jews of Hungary to 5 percent, and soon after that the business dropped the Czaplinsky name.

Cash payments to certain officials who were friendly with other officials allowed the Fischer family to continue to avoid being named as Jews. While Julius kept working on the bakery side, he was no longer welcome in any Fischer home, and he was asked to refrain from claiming any blood connection to them. Restoring his name to the business was nothing to discuss at this time, perhaps in the future, if peace should ever break out.

More and more Jews were moving from all over the countryside to Pest, and Fischer's had never been busier. Julius and Péter added as many tables and chairs as they could cram in. Hungary's right-wing government was allied with Germany, and the quarter million Jews of Budapest, though increasingly constricted by the new rules in their daily lives, continued to go to work, conduct their business, marry, have babies, and raise their families, believing they were reasonably safe from further losses or restrictions. What more could happen?

SZILVIA'S YOUNGER SISTER, Ágnes, worked as a secretary at a prosperous law firm until she was forced to leave when the Second Jewish Law was passed. Her boss was very sorry to lose such a pleasant and efficient worker. She was really a very beautiful girl, nice to look at every day, and she had such a good knowledge of German and French. He really regretted that she had to go, especially for such a shameful reason (he himself had a Jewish grandmother, but thankfully nobody was aware of this blot on his record). When he encountered a government bureaucrat he had known since childhood when they both went out to smoke cigars during an intermission at the opera, he put in a good word for Ágnes and all of her desirable attributes.

Ágnes, who was fortunately possessed of blonde, wispy hair and dark blue eyes, was soon offered employment in the Budapest central government offices as a correspondence typist-translator, where her German skills were desperately needed. The job was hers provided that she promise to keep her mouth shut about her background.

It was an open secret that the employment laws were enforced haphazardly, though the increasing power of the right-wing Arrow Cross Party was making both the Jews and their sympathizers more paranoiac with every passing day. Szilvia was home with the children and no longer worked at the bakery, but Julius would often come in the door at night with upsetting reports about groups of Arrow Cross Party members swaggering into the coffeehouse and forcing Jewish customers to vacate the tables they wanted. One afternoon Péter quietly took Julius aside to warn him that he might not be able to keep working at Fischer's much longer, and it might be safer for them all if he were to try and find something else, for now.

On a hot August night, Ágnes came for dinner with Szilvia and Julius, and after the babies were asleep, she took off her shoe and unfolded some sheets of onionskin paper, illicit extra carbon copies of documents she had translated into Hungarian and typed that afternoon. There was a memo from the Reich Central Security Office in Berlin titled *Reichssicherheitshauptamt: Madagaskar Projekt*. The author of the memo was Obersturmbannführer Adolf Eichmann.

The Madagascar Plan called for the resettlement of all the Jews of Europe on Madagascar, a million a year, over a period of four years. This was so much more desirable and efficient than the piecemeal efforts at deportation of Jews into centralized holding centers as they were flushed out from every city and every town and every village of Europe. No Jews, none at all, would remain in Europe.

The accompanying memo by Franz Rademacher, the recently appointed head of the *Judenreferat III der Abteilung Deutschland* (the Jewish Department of the Ministry of Foreign Affairs), which Ágnes had also translated into Hungarian for distribution among the various government departments, included references to the stopping of construction of the Warsaw Ghetto and deportations of Jews into Poland, which had both been suspended on July 10. The Madagascar Plan would render unnecessary all that effort to transport Jews into Poland for temporary containment.

The Madagascar Plan memo went on to detail cost estimates for coordinating and commissioning sufficient fleets of seaworthy vessels for the massive transportation effort that would be necessary, which depended largely on strategies for using ships from the British fleet, the imminent availability of which was confidently anticipated. The SS would carry on the Jewish expulsion in Europe, before ultimately governing the Jewish settlement.

Madagascar would only be a Mandate; the Jews living there would not be entitled to German citizenship. Meanwhile, the Jews deported to Madagascar would lose their various European citizenships from the date of deportation. Having all the Jews of Europe residents of the Mandate of Madagascar would prevent the possible establishment by Jews in Palestine of a state of their own. It would also help prevent any opportunity for them to exploit the symbolic importance of Jerusalem. The Madagascar Plan would create a central European bank funded with seized Jewish assets; this money would pay for the evacuation and resettlement of all the Jews, and the bank would also play a permanent role as the only permitted institution for any transaction between the Jews on Madagascar and the outside world. Hermann Göring would oversee the administration of the plan's economics.

Most significantly, the Jews remaining under German control on Madagascar would function as a useful bargaining chip for the future good behavior of the members of their race in America. The generosity shown by Germany in permitting cultural, economic, administrative, and legal self-administration to the Jews on Madagascar would also be very useful for propaganda purposes. The administration and execution of the Madagascar Plan was assigned to various offices within the Third Reich: Foreign Minister Joachim von Ribbentrop's office would negotiate the French peace treaty necessary to the handing over of Madagascar to Germany, and it would help design any other treaties required to deal with Europe's Jews. The Information Department of the Foreign Affairs Ministry, along with

Joseph Goebbels in the Propaganda Ministry, would filter all worldwide information about the plan. Viktor Brack of the Führer Chancellory would oversee transportation. There was no mention of any consideration for the native population of Madagascar.

The three of them sat at the table studying the documents until after midnight, talking very little. Finally, Julius crumpled all the pages into a ball on a dinner plate and set them alight with his cigarette.

JULIUS LEFT FOR Madagascar three weeks later, with as many diamonds sewn into the linings of his coat and his best three-piece suit as he could safely carry without attracting attention. Péter had bought him out of the bakery and coffeehouse with cash, less than Julius thought was fair, but more than Péter had any obligation to provide, under the circumstances. Leaving only enough money for Szilvia to buy what she and the babies would need for a few months, all the rest of their savings had been converted to diamonds thanks to Szilvia's brother, who had gotten the highest possible prices for Szilvia's jewelry and her great-aunt Lena's upright piano, though the babies liked to hear Szilvia play it after dinner and Matild had cried when the men came to carry it down the stairs.

Julius promised Szilvia he would get word to her as quickly as he could. He vowed that he would be sending for them just as soon as possible, sooner than she could imagine. They would all be together again, and safe once and for all. Although he could hardly bear to leave his family, he set out, determined to find a way to make a new and better life for Szilvia, Matild, and little Geza. Ágnes, too, and the rest of the Weisz family. And Péter, if he had the sense to raise his hand as a Jew and leave with his family, early instead of late, rather than live in fear of discovery all the rest of his days in Jew-cleansed Budapest.

Did those stuck-up Fischers think they wouldn't be found out? With those noses? How much praying on those sturdy Fischer knees in a fashionable Lutheran church would it take to change Aunt Borbála into a gentile from Buda instead of the imperious Jewess from Pest she always had been? Did they really believe they would be able to keep their place in the world that was changing around them?

Julius's arduous journey to Madagascar took almost six months. It had been surprisingly easy to get a visa for Zanzibar, with the assistance of Ágnes's supervisor, who gladly swapped a furtive and efficient groping from Ágnes for rubber-stamped traveling papers for Julius that would allow him to cross borders as he worked his way south to the Greek coast. Julius took some trains, but mostly, he walked. From the Greek coast Julius sailed across to Egypt on a barge laden with barrels of olive oil. It was by then January 1941. Working his way down the east coast of Africa, Julius arrived in Madagascar on a freighter from Zanzibar.

OKAY, ACTUALLY I have no idea how Julius got from Budapest to Madagascar, or how long it took. I am at the limit of my imaginative ability for reconstructing the most likely scenarios. It doesn't matter. So let's just say that when we next see Julius, he has arrived in Madagascar from Zanzibar. It is the middle of March, the height of the hot, rainy season. Picture him in your mind's eye. We pick up the narrative thread here.

The Malagasy dockworkers think Julius Czaplinsky is a very funny sight indeed as he totters down the gangplank in his woolen three-piece suit, with his greatcoat folded over his arm, staggering slightly under the weight of his leather suitcase. As Julius traipses around the muddy, rutted lanes of the port town of Mahajanga, having spent most of the past month sweltering insanely in the heat so constantly that he thought he might die of heat suffocation, he finally feels it is safe enough to take off the jacket and vest of his suit and carry them over his arm with his overcoat. At last, he can wear his damp and grimy shirtsleeves rolled up to his elbows.

Julius has that Czaplinsky motivation and determination that has become so diluted in Howard. He has arrived in Madagascar to figure out the best claim to stake, and then he plans to stake it hard and deep, ahead of the four million Jews who will soon begin to pour out of ships at every port, each of them hoping (as displaced Jews always do) to find a toehold to start a new life in this alien place.

Julius is here to get established ahead of the competition. Should he buy buildings in towns, begin constructing simple housing on empty lots that he will be able to rent or sell at premium prices? Should he stake a strong position in shipping and import-export in one or more of the port towns? Should he buy arable land for agriculture? Where would it be most desirable for his family to live? In the central mountainous region or along one of the coasts? He has to find his way and think it all through, make the most of his advantage.

The Madagascar Plan had described the possibility of an all-Jewish administrative government that would be overseen by the SS. Perhaps he would qualify for consideration for some official position of authority, should that prove desirable, given his foresight about getting established early, without simply waiting to be one of four million souls rounded up and shipped to this strange island only 644 kilometers off the east coast of Africa, a world away from anything European Jews have ever known.

❊ ❊

THE MADAGASCAR THAT Julius discovered was sparsely inhab-
ited by a few Frenchmen here and there, but otherwise he was
intrigued by the curious specimens of humanity he encountered
everywhere he went. They didn't look like any people he had
ever seen before in his life. The Malagasy people had probably
never seen anyone who looked like him, either. Julius had those
piercing blue Czaplinsky eyes, that familial beak of a nose, and a
gaunt but somehow forceful bearing, though he couldn't have
stood more than five foot eight. His wild hair was jet black, and
it radiated out from his receding hairline, emphasizing his great
domed forehead. Though clean-shaven in Budapest, Julius had
a long dark beard by the time he arrived in Mahajanga on the
Zanzibar ferry (or whatever). His skin was of such a pale, pink,
nearly alabaster hue that he burned terribly after even a few
minutes in direct sun. In Madagascar, as the weeks passed, his
face and neck burned repeatedly and darkened to a leathery
brown, but Julius's body was otherwise still milky white, and
any inadvertent exposure of his usually covered flesh was a fasci-
nation for the Malagasy who happened to catch such a glimpse.
They called him *Vazaha,* white man, and they often gathered to
watch him eat, wherever he went, laughing with glee each time
he pulled his spoon out of his pocket to eat his *koba,* the pasty
mash of rice, banana, and peanuts that he had decided he could
live on safely (after a few disastrous encounters with wretched,
gristly bits of meat prepared with a stewy rice mixture studded
with muddy bits of vegetation). As he fed himself this mash each
day with his daintily deployed spoon, instead of scooping it from
the bowl with his fingers the way everyone else did, he would
remind himself sometimes, to make his meal more palatable,
that he was the same man who once sat in his high chair at the

table with his family, being a good little boy, spooning his mother's Sunday goulash from his bowl.

JULIUS WAS CONFIDENT that he could figure out the best of his options, and he felt the urgency of his situation, but time seemed to tick by very, very slowly on Madagascar, and soon Julius fell into the rhythms of the island. He found a little hut where he could stay, in a crooked lane at the edge of Antananarivo where goats were tethered, and he paid some men to guard him while he slept, and to guard his things whenever he went out. The first few nights, he was awakened continually by the sounds of geckos scrabbling across the earthen floor, and by the strange chirring sounds of the ring-tailed lemurs who swung from the trees and scampered about the underbrush with strangely graceful leaps, like a little troupe of two-toned, monkey-faced Cossacks.

Orb weaver spiders the size of grapefruits erected elaborate webs across his doorway while he slept, and he was unsettled each time he brushed into one of those webs inadvertently and made contact with the fuzzy scuttling body of its weaver. The hissing cockroaches startled him every time he disturbed one in the night when his bladder forced him to stir from his restless slumber. Julius was reluctant to leave his secret diamond hoard for more than short periods of time, and he knew he had to convert his stones to local currency, but the energies of living each day seemed to soak up all the hours of daylight, and each crimson sunset found him hunkering down for the night once more with nothing accomplished.

Time passed.

He found a woman who would wash his clothes and prepare his food for him in a way that he could eat it. (It helped that she was very beautiful.) Mostly he lived on sweet potatoes, steamed manioc, and *mofo gasy*, a hearth-baked pancake made from sweetened rice flour. Night after night Julius dreamed of the sweet pastries he had served a thousand times in the coffeehouse, each one on a plate with the signature red-and-black-striped rim incorporating the beautiful streamlined logo for Fischer & Czaplinsky, plates they continued to use even after the Czaplinsky name was scraped from the red, black, and gold lettering on the windows and doors. He dreamed of the unsold, stale pastries he had thrown away or given to beggars at the back door of the bakery at closing time night after night. *Kürtöskalácus* unfurled in his dreams, flakey puffs of pastry unwinding from the baking cylinders, dropping in big, buttery curls that he couldn't quite catch before they blackened to ash on the glowing coals.

Months passed before Julius was able to make an approach to a French banker he had been observing in a café, a lonely alcoholic whose misbehavior involving certain accounting irregularities at his previous bank in Paris had led to his exile in this remote French colony. The banker was charmed by Julius, who had the prescience at their first meeting to make a gift of the small bottle of good Slivovitz he had tucked into his baggage and carried all this way and hoarded all this time.

Malagasy wine, which Julius had sampled, tasted like horse piss mixed with vinegar. Perhaps he should start a distillery. Did sufficient sugarcane grow on this or any other near enough soil? Would grapes on vines rot and mold in the humidity or could a vineyard be established, perhaps on the windward side of the island? For modest kickbacks of which Julius was unaware, the banker made introductions for Julius to the right people, who would give him the best prices converting his diamonds to Malagasy francs.

People are people, business is business, money is money. By

the end of 1942, a land broker had secured Julius's rights to some four thousand hectares in the central rain-forest region of the northern part of the island, in the Betsiboka region of the Mahajanga province, where the soil is rich and the humidity high. Half of his hilly lands were covered in a dense pine and eucalyptus forest, while the rest was a crazy quilt of nineteenth-century French plantations fallen into disuse, though they had once yielded rich annual harvests of cacao, coffee, banana, and vanilla.

In Budapest, Julius had struggled to achieve and maintain a modest, bourgeois status. In Madagascar, where the Malagasy people lived a subsistence life on the land, his diamonds had bought such an unimaginable number of Malagasy francs that even after investing in these holdings, he was still an immensely rich man, with more houses than he could count scattered across his four thousand hectares, with dozens of overseers on his various lands, and hundreds of employees grateful for the very small wage he would pay them in exchange for working his plantations or providing whatever services he could possibly want or need. Time slowed and stopped. Time stood still for Julius.

By the spring of 1943, Julius had become the monarch of a small kingdom. The rest of the world seemed very far away. His brilliant strategy had proven to be far more successful than he could have possibly imagined. He was the Founding Jew, the First Jew, the Only Jew of Madagascar! Julius was impatient for the first signs that the transports had begun. Each day he scanned the horizon. The unbroken sea was empty of ships, dotted only by a few of the small square-sailed primitive fishing vessels that went out early every morning to check their crayfish pots along the coastline. Surely they would arrive today, or tomorrow?

Julius didn't consider that in faraway Budapest, time had not stood still. On Kazinczy Street, time had marched along quite briskly.

EVERY DAY JULIUS envisioned himself in his new role as the wise pioneer whose helpful advice would be eagerly sought by his people. He could see himself greeting and providing comfort and wisdom to as many of the newcomers as he could accommodate as they tumbled off the ships by the thousands, day after day, week after week, sailing into every port on the island, from Toliara to Antsiranana, each of them dazed, frightened, staggering under the weight of the few precious worldly goods they would have managed to bring along on the voyage from the Old World to this very New World.

We will begin again! Julius insisted to himself as he sipped the muddy coffee made from his own Caturra beans prepared for him each morning now by his housemaid, and served to him on the veranda of his headquarters, a plantation house that overlooked five hundred acres planted in Trinitario and Criollo and Porcelana cacao. The openwork lace of the early morning mist floated through the tops of the banana canopy that soared over the hodge podge of the cacao trees. He longed for Szilvia, Matild, and Geza. And of course, Ágnes too. He would welcome with open arms any of the Weisz family who wanted to come live on his plantations.

He was deeply moved by his own anticipated generosity as he envisaged himself presiding over his grateful family, perhaps dozens of them, all thankful that he had given them such a wonderful fresh start. He would be the patriarch, providing plenty for all. They would all be safe. They would all be prosperous. They would all be together again.

But the horizon remained empty. The ships filled with the Jews of Europe eager to begin their new lives did not arrive.

Julius had written to Szilvia steadily since his arrival, though the centralized postal service from Antananarivo was erratic at best and a complete disaster at worst, so he hadn't been overly worried not to have heard back from her in the beginning. But now when his letters continued to go unanswered, he began to fret. One morning as he sipped his coffee and gazed out over the treetops of his plantation it suddenly dawned on him with horror that while time stood still in Madagascar, it rushed ahead furiously and tumultuously and disastrously in the wider world.

That day he sent a long letter to the alcoholic banker in Antananarivo by messenger, with specific and urgent instructions for a wire to a correspondent bank in Budapest where the banker had told him long ago he might still have a contact who might be willing to deliver the message to Szilvia, or if that was risky, then to Péter, at the coffeehouse, who would surely be willing to pass a message to Szilvia. Wouldn't any banker in Budapest know Fischer's bakery and coffeehouse, on Kazinczy Street?

The wire Julius sent was three pages of dense advice about obtaining a visa for Zanzibar, traveling on the same route he had followed (whatever that was, let's agree that it's unimportant to the story), using the same sympathetic official as before, Ágnes's supervisor, the man who had approved his traveling documents. Julius's wire enumerated all the contact information he had for every leg of the journey, concluding with the name of the shipping clerk to see at the harbor in Stone Town once they arrived on Zanzibar.

THE ENSUING SILENCE was ominous. Julius had heard nothing for too long. He felt a sudden spasm of terror, and he realized that he had been insanely complacent. Anything could have happened in all this time. He had to do something more, take some kind of action. He could no longer just sit and wait. He set out with one of his plantation managers in the most functional of his three rusting, patched-together Ford Model A trucks, but a summer monsoon had drenched the highlands for days, and after a day of fighting the mud that filled the narrow, winding track that led to his aerie, the truck was hopelessly mired, and they had gone only ten dozen kilometers. Julius had to make the journey to Antananarivo in the back of a zebu cart. The jolting, slow-motion trip took many days, and he arrived feeling quite sick from the rocking of the cart and from the fear that now clutched his heart. How could he have been so blithely unconcerned all these months, months that had turned to years? It was now July 1944.

The dissipated and habitually hungover banker arranged for Julius to use one of the few telephones on Madagascar that could connect him to Budapest, in the central government office across from the bank. Julius had developed a fluent Malagasy-inflected French, and he was able to make his needs understood well enough. It took nearly an hour to make the connection, but finally, miraculously, the series of operators was able to hold all the necessary connections to patch him through to Budapest.

He gave the number to the local operator there in Hungarian, his eyes filling with tears as he spoke the familiar numbers to another Hungarian speaker, but a moment later her faint voice in his ear told him through the echoing static that the number was no longer in service.

Ah, of course, Szilvia was economizing. He begged the operators not to disconnect the line and then he gave the next number that came into his head, for Fischer's. Surely Péter would be willing to relay his message to Szilvia. The call went through more quickly this time, and he could hear the familiar ringing tones echoing faintly down the line.

"Bitte?"

An unfamiliar voice, with the clatter of the coffeehouse in the background. Why answer the phone at Fischer's in German? A wrong number? A bad joke? Julius's mind was racing in slow motion, every thought slippery and ungraspable. In carefully enunciated Hungarian he asked if this was Fischer's and the man said, *"Ja, ja,"* impatiently, before demanding, *"Wen wollen Sie sprechen? Was wollen Sie?"*

Julius switched to his rudimentary German and asked for Péter. The German laughed, a short mirthless bark, and said Péter had gone for a little swim in the Danube, and then he hung up.

Julius didn't know that even while he was still making his way toward Madagascar, the transports of Jews from German territories into occupied Poland had resumed, as had work to complete the fortifications of the Warsaw Ghetto. Eichmann's beloved Madagascar Plan had stalled. Germany had not achieved a quick victory over Britain (the Battle of Britain had not gone as predicted so confidently by the Luftwaffe, despite their colorful maps and pins), and so the British fleet, crucial to the Madagascar Plan, would not be available to ship all the Jews to their island colony in the Indian Ocean after all. There was no alternative means of efficiently transporting four million Jews out of Europe.

In late August 1940, Rademacher begged Ribbentrop to hold a meeting at his ministry so they could revise the Madagascar Plan and put it in motion. Ribbentrop did nothing. Eichmann's Madagascar memo was never approved by Richard Heydrich, chair of the Wannsee Conference. From time to time, one or another official of the Third Reich would raise the question of a future plan for the ghetto colony on Madagascar for all the Jews of Europe, but by early December of that year, it had been abandoned entirely. The Madagascar Plan was stillborn, and the massive logistical quagmire of Jewish deportations would be solved in another, more efficient way. If the Jewish island colony in the Indian Ocean was a First Solution, then the answer to the vexing Jewish Question would be the Final Solution.

I HAVE TO admit the time line is way off here. Why is the sudden and successful British invasion of Madagascar in May 1942 not in this story? I suppose it's not really possible that Julius had no awareness of the stealth landing in Courrier Bay by the combined forces of the 13th Assault Flotilla. He had already been on Madagascar for more than a year at that point. So let's allow for the possibility that he welcomed the British forces. Perhaps he even played a small role, and had a secret involvement in the mysteriously deployed guiding beacons that enabled the invading, unlit British flotilla to glide past the dangers in the shoals of the harbor and land the troops safely in the darkness, while the Vichy slept. That would be good, if Julius did that. It improves the story. Let's say he did.

Soon after the British secured Madagascar, Free French Forces took over from the Vichy government. But looking at Julius's land acquisitions, I have to admit that a less nice version of this story has Julius doing business with the Vichy officials one way or another from the moment he arrives on the island in March 1941. The drunken banker is thick as thieves with them. The Vichy haven't got much to do, governing this godforsaken jungle in the middle of the Indian Ocean, and Julius is an amusement. They are willing to assist this pushy, ambitious Hungarian Jew with his coatful of diamonds in securing a position of power and authority in advance of the hordes. Why not? He will be useful to them.

Perhaps Julius is unhappy to see the corrupt Vichy officials replaced by the Free French officers who now govern the island, as it dawns on him that the chances of the Madagascar Plan's being executed as proposed are dwindling with every passing day. Surely the Third Reich wouldn't want to go to the trouble and expense of delivering the Jews of Europe to Madagascar only to see them pick up and take themselves wherever in the world they pleased after that. Even without knowledge of what has transpired in Europe, it is clear that without the Vichy in control of Madagascar, the plan collapses.

Perhaps Julius recognized then that he and he alone has escaped to Madagascar, while his family, everyone he has left behind, will be swallowed up by the incoming tide of history. Perhaps he never tried to reach them at all. Perhaps he did nothing but cultivate his holdings and wait. He is helpless. What can he do, from here, but hope for the best?

It is established fact that he spent the war years on Madagascar, where he was safe. But he died there, too, of malaria, soon after the end of the war, at the age of forty-two. Julius left behind his beautiful, young common-law wife, Lalao (she had been his housekeeper), and their two children, Darwin, who was two, and Huxley, who was an infant.

I don't really have a good way of telling this story seamlessly. While it is true that it is difficult to reconcile the time line completely, or really nail down the facts one way or the other, how important is that in the larger scheme of things? Can we just skip over these discrepancies? Let's say Julius was isolated on Madagascar from the moment he arrived, and in a way he was a prisoner of his circumstances. The larger truths of this story are what matters, and it would be pointless to get too distracted by details. In fact, a failure of imagination may be the most honorable choice here. Think of it this way: if for even a brief moment any of us could possess the full realization of all the horrors of human experience, how would it be possible to live?

JULIUS HAD NO way of knowing that Germany had occupied Hungary in 1944, when Hungary was on the verge of negotiating with the Allies after the German losses on the Eastern front. Nor did he know that tens of thousands of Hungarian Jews had already been killed in labor camps and deportations even before the occupation.

He would not have been able to imagine that the shul on Dohány Street had been turned into a small concentration camp. Adolf Eichmann himself had taken over the rabbi's office behind the beautiful rose window in the women's balcony. Eichmann organized a Budapest Jewish council to oversee the Jews who remained in Hungary, all two hundred thousand of them, now concentrated in Budapest, crammed into two thousand homes scattered through the city, each designated Jewish dwelling marked with a conspicuous yellow Star of David.

Julius did not know that nineteen people had been assigned to his apartment, and that for several miserable months Szilvia, Matild, and Geza had shared a narrow bed in what had been Matild's room, a room in which four strangers also slept.

Nor did he know that the Arrow Cross Party members had rampaged through the Jewish Quarter, shooting hundreds of Jews and throwing their bodies into the Danube, Péter's among them. Szilvia, Matild, and Geza were among the thousand who lay buried in the mass graves in the courtyard of the synagogue on Dohány Street, just up the street from where Fischer's dry goods shop once did business, before the Arrow Cross burned it to the ground with seven members of the Fischer family, who had refused to wear their yellow stars, locked inside.

Ágnes had been arrested and placed in the Kistarcsa transit camp for two months before she was marched with hundreds of other prisoners all the way to the Austrian border in freezing November sleet. On the third day of the march, when Ágnes was so weakened by a fever that she was unable to walk, she was shot and left at the side of the road.

By the end of 1944, here is what Julius Czaplinsky did know. He was thirty-eight years old. His wife and children were dead. He was rich beyond imagining. He was safe from the turmoil of war. And he was utterly alone. The other four million Jews of Europe weren't coming. There would never be one ship unloading its bewildered cargo of Jews. There would never be a single grateful recipient of all the wisdom and generosity Julius was so prepared to bestow upon his landsmen. The Madagascar Plan had brought only Julius Czaplinsky, the first, last, and only Jew on Madagascar.

9

SHOULD NOT BE held accountable for the Bereavemints fiasco. Why bring this up now? That is simply an unfair piece of Zip's history to lay at my doorstep. And even if I was involved, it was nine years ago. I am perfectly willing to take responsibility for certain poor decisions in the history of Zip's Candies, with Little Susies at the top of that list, but not the Bereavemints. It is true that I headed the product development team at Zip's Candies, but that's just a designation on paper, a fancy way of captioning the management scheduling and availability of our workers and equipment. "Product development team" was really just a bookkeeping term. Who was on that team? Petey Leventhal, a couple of hourly line workers, and me.

And the product was certainly not my idea, let's be clear about that, if we have to talk about Bereavemints. It was Howard's. He should have been identified as part of the Zip's so-called product development team, because it was his product. I encouraged him when I should have been more honest. In truth, I never thought it was a good idea, but Howard was proud of the concept, which he dreamed up after eighteen holes on the Yale golf course with his high school friend Morty Rubin, whose family has run Rubin & Sons Memorial Chapel on George Street for fifty years. It has always struck me as peculiar that someone in Sidney Rubin's line of work would name his son Morton. Morty the mortician thought Bereavemints was a great idea.

Howard came home from his afternoon with Morty brimming with enthusiasm, and I didn't have the heart to tell him what I really thought, which was that this product was not only questionable in concept, but was also neither a good match for the Zip's Candies image nor for our production lines. I was walking on eggshells with Howard by then, and I didn't want to discourage him if something made him happy, even if it meant biting my tongue at moments.

I had counted on Frieda to throw cold water on the idea, but I had underestimated the blinding effect of a Jewish mother's obsessive love for her wunderkind, and though she was a canny businesswoman with a good nose for the candy business, Frieda was impervious to any possible flaws in a new piece that originated with her precious Howdy.

It was 2001, and Sam had been gone for two years. In his lifetime, no problematic product like the Bereavemint could ever have been deemed of sufficient quality or potential value to carry the Zip's Candies name and signature green umbrella on the wrapper. Few people realize that Eli made notes for a fourth line that was never put into production, a wafery, layered buttercookie center enrobed in vanilla icing that he called PanKakes, which was consistent with the *Little Black Sambo* inspiration for each of our lines. Why? "When Black Mumbo saw the melted butter, wasn't she pleased! 'Now,' said she, 'we'll all have pancakes for supper!'"

Bereavemints had no such continuity with our existing lines or potential for brand association. I repeat: it wasn't a good fit at all for Zip's. I would have much rather pursued development of those PanKakes. But Sam was dead and mine would have been the lone voice of dissent while everyone else was so enthusiastic. In retrospect, it isn't clear to me that even if I had made my misgivings known, that Howard would have been willing to slam the brakes on this runaway disaster, in part because the small test batches were fine. It was the one and only production batch that was catastrophic.

ZIP'S BEREAVEMINTS, SMALL, gray, rectangular, molded, spiced peppermints in somber black waxed wrappers printed with discreet green umbrellas, were not envisioned as a retail product in their first production phase, but instead were meant for distribution chiefly to funeral homes, support groups, grief counselors, and religious organizations. The concept was sound enough—something to freshen the breath of funereal personnel and the bereaved alike; it is a regrettable fact that sorrow and halitosis often go together, what with all the coffee drinking, crying, inattention to personal hygiene during the stressful experience, and the ceaseless consumption of funereal carbohydrates.

It was a good idea, in concept, maybe, for some other company, one already running a line of cough lozenges, for example. Perhaps it was even a brilliant idea for a niche product for the right brand, one with a more herbal-supplement sort of profile, but it wasn't for us. I have an intense aversion to the flavor of cloves, which admittedly may have clouded my judgment about the viability of the product in the market, but that has absolutely nothing to do with what happened.

We had to do most of the blending and pouring by hand, using certain processing elements on the Mumbo Jumbo line. That's where we lost quality control. I was specifically concerned that I could not be a good judge of the flavor adjustments, and I had made my limitations known to Howard. He said it didn't matter, but in retrospect I should have insisted that someone else have ultimate responsibility for sampling the test batches more frequently.

Owing to a terrible and significant last-minute miscalculation during production (we used a basic sugar and corn syrup
hard-candy recipe, with cinnamon, clove oil, and peppermint
extract), the proportion of cinnamon, clove oil, and peppermint
extract in that first test batch of Bereavemints was terribly, horribly concentrated. I don't know how it happened. I had tasted a
sample of the batch at an earlier stage of the blending and had
not thought it necessary to do so again. I know that two employees have stated they saw me taste the batch again just before the
pour, and I may have given that impression, but I am certain that
I did not actually taste the batch again.

We wrapped the mints by hand and boxed them by hand,
and then we stickered the boxes by hand with a simple and taste-
ful black-and-white label set in Castine, the font often used on
traditional headstones. I employed Julie and her friend Wendy
to come to Zip's one afternoon right after school and spend a
few hours with green Sharpies, drawing a simple umbrella on
the lid of each box. The Zip's green umbrella, though originally
inspired by Little Black Sambo's green umbrella, has long been
an integral part of our brand identity.

We distributed these inaugural boxes of Zip's Bereavemints
gratis to some forty funeral homes throughout Connecticut.
Within ten days, Bereavemints had caused twenty-three epi-
sodes of choking or bronchial spasm, two of them severe grave-
side allergic reactions.

The consequent cascade of lawsuits was inevitable, given
how disruptive the Bereavemints reactions had been to any
number of funerals and memorial services. Death and the rituals
surrounding death are occasions when people are already very
sensitive. Therefore, as so many documents from so many different law firms throughout the state suggested, if injured griev-
ously by an improperly manufactured hard candy at such a

fragile time, they are especially susceptible to trauma, which can lead to anxiety, sleeplessness, loss of gainful livelihood, diminished capacity for enjoyment of life, and poor self-esteem.

All the settlement agreements (the file, which was incomplete, owing both to the pandemonium surrounding this time period and to Howard's habitual slapdash approach to paperwork, showed fourteen different agreements, but I believe there were closer to twenty) cost Zip's Candies something like half a million dollars. Rubin & Sons was among the litigants with whom Zip's settled.

Never again, declared Frieda, blaming me for the miscalculation with the clove and peppermint formulation, although it was never determined where the error occurred in the mixing of the overconcentrated production batch. Frieda then became weirdly triumphant about this disaster, conveniently forgetting that her precious bumblebee Howdy had anything to do with it, because it offered concrete proof that she was right and I was wrong about the risks of Zip's Candies venturing one inch beyond the familiar territory of Eli's original Little Sammies, Tigermelts, and Mumbo Jumbos.

Howard let her dictate company policy on this. Not only would Zip's never again venture into new product development, but also Zip's would never even consider any brand extensions within the lines. None whatsoever. We had been burned. We had learned our lesson. That was that. No more risk-taking. I should never have repeated to Howard one of his father's favorite remarks about business practice, "It's easier to stay out of trouble than to get out of trouble."

The way Howard wouldn't listen to reason on this subject (meaning he wouldn't listen to me and instead chose to honor his mother's arbitrary edict) created a paralysis that no ordinary board of directors of a small business would tolerate in any corporate plan; shareholders would be indignant. But Zip's has never had any checks and balances. This de facto zero-growth policy remained in place for the rest of Frieda's life, even at the point when she was no longer able to remember her own opinions or understand very much of what was going on around her, and if foot-long, tutti-frutti Tigermelts had been coming off the line it would have been fine with her. But even after her death, Howard continued to coast with this lazy approach, right up to the day he left for Madagascar.

Howard grew bored with Zip's over the past few years, and this restriction has suited his indifferent management style. I cannot emphasize enough just how severely damaging this artificial limitation has been on Zip's Candies' ability to innovate and expand in natural ways. And I am not just making this observation because I am angry and hurt that in this same time period it became more and more obvious that Howard also lost interest in me.

I don't mean that we need to develop entirely new products willy-nilly. Completely new products can be hideously costly for many reasons, especially if they are pieces that cannot be made with simple adaptation on our existing lines, the way Index and Detox, our contract energy bars, are run on the Tigermelt line ten days of the month with minimal retooling. (They are so similar in formulation to each other, there is little adjustment downtime needed between the two runs, which is very efficient for us. The Detox bar has ground flaxseeds and dried blueberries in the base, while the Index bar has acai and goji berries, but their proprietary ten-gram-protein base is identical.)

I am not, despite the insulting language in Irene's ridiculously long-winded and crazy affidavit, trying to run the company into a ditch, and I am not, despite her allegations, proposing the development of any entirely new lines that are not extensions of existing lines. Painful as it is to admit, I do concede that a while ago I was motivated to experiment with brand extensions partly in the hope that a brilliant and successful development might reengage Howard in the business of Zip's Candies. Maybe Howard would have come back to me if Dark Mint Tigermelt Fun Bites had gone into production and had really taken off; who can say? I'll never know.

Zip's Candies has neglected some very obvious brand extension opportunities for decades. Even with stagnating sales—especially with stagnating sales!—we are overdue for some growth in those areas. For example, because the consumer continues to be extremely willing to increase purchases when he sees a familiar piece in a new flavor, I predict that the best growth in nonchocolate and gummy candies will continue to be in the tropical flavor category. This is why we should be making Tropical Mumbo Jumbos (which we could also call Hawaiian Mumbo Jumbos; we would have to pick whichever one tested more positively), in flavors like pomegranate, pineapple, coconut, and mango. We wouldn't have to change anything on the line other than the flavoring and the coloring in the blend to make limited-edition Tropical Mumbo Jumbos, for example, in two different combinations of those four flavors, thereby retaining the familiar two-color, two-flavor pack that consumers know so well in the Mumbo Jumbos. We could do new label graphics like our present design but in tropical colors, with palm trees. Frankly, I can't see how we could fail if we tested Tropical Mumbo Jumbos in movie boxes.

Limited editions are a good way to test a market, because their limitedness makes people rush to buy them before they disappear, and at the same time, if the product is really successful, there is room to keep it going, or at least to bring it back seasonally if that's appropriate. There are so many possibilities for limited editions, too; a Dark Tigermelt, which would be a dark chocolate–coated Tigermelt with a milk-chocolate stripe, for example. Or a White Tigermelt, which would be, obviously, a white chocolate–coated Tigermelt with a dark-chocolate stripe. It would be ridiculously easy to produce Mint Tigermelts, or Almond Tigermelts, or Crispy Tigermelts, with sugar wafers or crisped rice in the mix (either will reduce calories); that's another potential growth area we are neglecting at our peril: the reduced calorie, "light" version of the familiar piece—which can be anything from one-hundred-calorie stick versions with the same formulation to going a half step away from the original piece while developing a related yet distinct new product, like, for example, Annabelle's Skinny Hunk extension from their Big Hunk.

Another option for a Zip's brand extension, though it would be an expensive undertaking (because even with the same ingredients and basic formulation, all the equipment would have to be changed over, as would the wrapping and packaging), would be to introduce different sizes of our existing lines. Historically, Zip's Candies has never had any interest in making Halloween snack sizes. Sam believed that selling snack sizes (or bite sizes, fun sizes, minis, to name some of the common terms) would only be undercutting our own business, offering our customers a chance to go smaller instead of bigger.

Perhaps that was once true, and there is certainly value in driving consumers away from total dependence on Halloween miniatures, or Mars wouldn't have developed their 2008 Halloween campaign featuring the brilliantly manipulative slogan "Really cool moms give full-size bars!" But actually, size change-up attracts consumers, with increased sales of classic pieces when they are offered both smaller and bigger than the original piece. I heard from someone who knows someone who works at Mars that their studies show that when they first tested their bite-size

Snickers, people ended up eating one and a half bars' worth, a bite at a time, even though their written responses immediately after the sampling estimated that they had eaten less than half a bar!

You would think that with all my ambition for change and innovation at Zip's, I might have considered experimenting on some brand extension with myself, changing my hairstyle, for example, or having my colors done, as Marie Smith, one of our bookkeepers, did a few years ago (as a consequence, having discovered she was a Summer, all Marie ever wore after that were outfits in pastel blue, pink, lavender, and red, and what's more her nail polish always matched those outfits). Perhaps I should have done something like that to try to keep Howard. If I had a close friend, maybe this is the sort of thing she would have advised me to do. But I don't have anyone in my life to advise me about things such as this, and I am just not the sort of woman who would make desperate changes to my appearance in an undignified attempt to keep my husband. If that's all it would have taken to save my marriage, what kind of man would Howard have been all along? I didn't want to risk finding out.

In any case, the changes I wanted to make were at Zip's Candies, and I know I am right about this. In this era of chronic dieting and a kind of pseudo health consciousness, people who wouldn't dream of buying a couple of full-size candy bars are willing to take home a bag of minis and work their way through the equivalent of four bars instead. And the truth is, the snack size, fun bite, healthy mini, whatever we would call them, has a bigger markup, piece for piece, ounce for ounce. Tigerbites! Baby Sammies! Mini Mumbo Jumbos! And at the same time, because America loves a bargain and people are willing to consume buckets of coffee and soda when they are offered the chance for a few pennies more than the reasonable-size option, we should be producing larger versions of each of our lines as well. Tiger Kings! Big Sammies! Mega Mumbo Jumbos! Zip's has absolutely got to do this, go small and big. That's where the money is.

The huge growth area in recent years, as we know, is in premium chocolate. Contrary to Irene's insistence that we should be producing an organic, fair trade premium bar, there is no way we can or should extend our brands in that direction. Zip's Candies doesn't make gourmet premium chocolate products. We know who we are. Our customers expect a certain kind of candy from Zip's. I believe it is a mistake to stray too far from our brand identity.

I don't understand why Mars wants to dilute the M&M's line to the extent that they have with those iridescent Premiums. (Which are delicious.) Why not expand the Dove line this way instead? There have been numerous successful M&M's brand extensions, from Almond, to Dark, to Minis, to some innovative limited editions like Mint Crisp and Wildly Cherry. In both cases, the limited-edition product was a great match for the brand for several reasons, one being the logical and pleasing color coordination. But the new M&M's Premiums taste like a Dove product and lack the classic M&M's shell. This, to me, is confusing, and challenges the very definition and identity of M&M's. Why do it?

It is possible to go too far with brand extensions, no question. I am by nature cautious, and I would propose an extension only with much thought and planning. There are some really pointless extensions out there, cautionary exemplars of what not to do, like the Milky Way 2 To Go, which is a king-size Milky Way simple divided into two pieces, making it, what, more portable? So it can be eaten "on the go" without the usual elaborate preparations and accoutrements ordinarily required for the consumption of an unwieldy ordinary one-piece Milky Way? Maybe there is a calculation here that I am underestimating, that people will buy and eat more candy if they tell themselves they deserve it because they are always "on the go," as if the reward for the virtue of busyness is this 460-calorie bar divided into two convenient pieces. Zip's Candies would never insult our customers that way.

But there are numerous good examples for us to consider, from the Sour Apple Abba-Zaba, the Abba-Zaba Chocolate Cream, and Abba-Zaba Mini Morsels, important extensions to consider when you think about how iconic and unchanged that piece has been for decades, to the exceptionally appealing White Kit Kat. (Kit Kat is a bar with spectacular success, especially in the UK, where forty-seven Kit Kats are consumed every second, if you can trust Nestlé Rowntree's statistic.)

And let us pause a moment to admire the outstanding Twix Java, one of the most successful brand extensions I have ever tasted. When will Mars bring that fabulous bar back? How could they be willing to go so far down the wrong road with M&M's, yet throw away the huge success of this Twix extension? In the three months it was on store shelves, more Twix Java bars were probably sold than the total number of pieces we sell in a year, all three lines combined. We live on that, but it's just crumbs off the table for Mars.

ZIP'S IS TOO small to have marketing research, or even marketing. We have no product development like Mars, no matter what the documentation concerning the Bereavemints episode might suggest. The big three have test kitchens ten times the size of our entire operation. We employ forty-seven souls when we're at full throttle. The big three will always have us outranked and outflanked and outspent, they will always command the best shelf real estate, with their endless capacity to pay hideous slotting fees, and they will always outsell us eight ways, with presell deals that really move the merch.

And yet, companies like Mars and Hershey's don't have all the answers. They make mistakes. And we have the advantage, in our smallness, or we should, that we can follow our hearts, we can turn on a dime, and we aren't at the mercy of the vast machinery of a marketing department. I know this sounds immodest, but after all these years at Zip's, I have perfect pitch for the candy business. I can go to a supermarket candy aisle and talk to people about their choices, and with my expertise and experience I can come away from an encounter like that with a useful impression of consumer thinking equal to a six-figure marketing report.

I mentioned the Abba-Zaba, a curious candy, not a personal favorite of mine, but perhaps if I had grown up on the West Coast, I would feel differently. Though maybe not, as I am really not a taffy aficionado at all, and unlike many in my cohort, I harbor no fond yearnings for Bonomo Turkish Taffy or Bit-O-Honey either. When I was six I lost one of my baby incisors in a Sugar Daddy, in the darkness of a movie theater, where I had been taken to see *Mary Poppins*. I will always associate that supremely irritating song about how a spoonful of sugar helps the medicine go down with the shocking sensation of that sudden, bloody void in my mouth.

Abba-Zaba is a strange piece, with a thin peanut-butter core surrounded by unusually chewy taffy, with a dedicated following; it's one of those candies people either love or hate. While today it is made by the Annabelle Candy Company, Abba-Zaba was first produced by the Cardinet Candy Company around the same time Eli was starting Zip's Candies. Cardinet also produced the U-NO; Annabelle bought them in 1978 and now produces both, along with their flagship bar, Rocky Road, and their Big Hunk and Look! lines, acquired in 1972 when they bought Golden Nugget.

Abba-Zaba shares more than vintage with Little Sammies. It also had a problematic icon. The original wrapper featured a savage-looking, almost simian jungle baby with a bone through the topknot in his hair, in silhouette, hanging from a vine. The Abba-Zaba jungle baby has vanished from the official story. According to Julie, who looked into this for me, a couple of candy blogs mention this and report that the company will only say that the design of their Abba-Zaba wrapper hasn't changed since they started making Abba-Zabas. Which is perfectly true.

I like the spirit of the Annabelle Candy Company, which was founded by Sam Altshuler, who came to America in 1917 from Russia, and was next headed for years by his daughter, the eponymous Annabelle. It is now run by his granddaughter Susan Karl, an energetic former prosecutor who took over running the business from her brother a few years ago (she's something of a role model for me). I have wanted to raise the delicate subject of the original Abba-Zaba wrapper when we meet at conventions, but I haven't yet found the right moment.

It seems likely to me that the name of the candy itself, when Cardinet started selling it, was probably somebody's idea of made-up African lingo. Possibly it was the Abba-Zaba baby's own utterance in the early brand concept. But that's just a guess. Perhaps the creator of this image was influenced by Kipling's *Jungle Book,* or by the popularity of Josephine Baker's Cuban- and African-inflected repertoire of jungle songs and dances, some of which were rendered with scat syllables.

Which is not to say that America invented this particular sort of casual racism. The French embraced Josephine Baker, and they still exhibit an unabashed nostalgia for their colonialist relationship to Africa. Jean de Brunhoff's *The Travels of Babar,* published in 1932, featured some wild cannibals dwelling on a remote island who resemble the Abba-Zaba creature. On French supermarket shelves today, there are all sorts of food labels featuring black Africans, including the Y'a Bon Banania man, a grinning Senegalese soldier who has been featured on the label of the Banania chocolate and banana breakfast drink in various versions since 1915. ("*Y'a bon*" is meant to represent his pidgin French for "It's good.")

From Rastus on the Cream of Wheat label to Uncle Ben (Uncle Ben's rice is owned by Masterfood, which is to say, Mars) to Aunt Jemima (who has been around since 1890, and who bears an uncanny resemblance to Helen Bannerman's 1899 illustration of Little Black Sambo's mother, Black Mumbo), there is something in our white American culture that has long made us want to associate plain, comforting foods with the suggestion that they are being provided to us by jovial black people. Let's not forget the Oompa-Loompas, who love their work so much. (Question: Why weren't there any dark-skinned winners of Willy Wonka's golden tickets?) Privileged Caucasians seem to have an abiding fantasy that the dark-skinned people who prepare and serve our food to us are actually quite fond of us and love feeding us.

I can offer no excuses for our own Little Sammies, which had been in production at Zip's Candies for more than fifty years before I arrived. It is beyond question that by the mid-1960s, if Little Sammies hadn't already been established as a successful brand, there is no chance they could have possibly seemed like a good idea to anyone.

Is *Little Black Sambo* truly racist? I could argue for its being naive rather than truly racist. Sambo is an adventurous child who survives his encounter with the vain and rapacious tigers who compete with one another for grandeur in their bits of clothing stolen from Little Black Sambo. His doting parents, who have provided him with his colorful outfit (the entire family dresses in a stereotypically riotous mix of colors and patterns), also feed him lovingly, while taking smaller helpings for themselves. Black Jumbo brings home the pot of melted butter made from those whirling tigers, which is poured over the "huge big plate of most lovely pancakes" Black Mumbo prepares for the family. So they are industrious, and are certainly not clichéd lazy Negroes. The story, which has the timelessness and simplicity of a fable from start to finish, concludes with the three of them sitting down to supper. "And Black Mumbo ate Twenty-seven pancakes, and Black Jumbo ate Fifty-five but Little Black Sambo ate a Hundred and Sixty-nine, because he was so hungry."

Helen Bannerman, a devout member of the Free Church of Scotland who lived most of her life in India and believed that blacks and whites would meet in heaven, probably didn't think that people with black skin were intrinsically inferior to people with white skin so much as she held them in her imperial British gaze as less fortunate Others. Eli the immigrant (whom she also presumably would have regarded as an exotic, less fortunate Other), eager to get ahead in his new American life, read her little book over and over as the train carried him from New York City to New Haven, finding in those pages his inspiration to make sugary treats based on what he thought was a simple American folktale. He didn't understand what he was looking at any more than Helen Bannerman did with her white dissecting gaze that sliced and fixed the specimens under that confident and superior microscope. Yet each of them in their misguided way made something beloved and enduring.

❀ ❀

BEFORE I GO into detail about what happened with Little Susies, let me explain a few more things about brand extensions. One of the brand extension areas that has been quite successful for a lot of established lines is a white-chocolate version, from White Chocolate Kit Kats and White Chocolate Twix bars to Reese's White Chocolate peanut butter cups. I have always been ambivalent about white chocolate. It is so often really terrible and cheap, very sugary and often gritty or chalky, with a predominant lingering flat note, that harsh telltale artificial metallic vanillin aftertaste. It isn't "real" chocolate. That's what so many people say, which is correct, though in true white chocolate there is substantial cocoa butter, and it is the cocoa liquor (this is the paradoxical term for the crushed and ground chocolate mass) that is missing. Unless it has been adulterated with vegetable fat swapped for the cocoa butter (which is actually a common practice, and makes for what is technically candy, not chocolate), true chocolate has a melt temperature that is almost the same as our body temperature. This, I believe, is one of the reasons we love chocolate so much—it loves us back. It melts from the heat of our tongue. Of course it's sexy.

I have tasted my share of white chocolate over the years, but since I have mostly been unimpressed or disappointed, in recent times I have chosen to avoid it. As I have gotten older, I have learned from experience and I have a greater willingness to offend rather than suffer. Like dubious hollandaise sauce that's been sitting for hours on a brunch buffet, or any item on any menu that begins with the three words *twin baked stuffed,* white chocolate is usually just something you're probably better off not putting in your mouth.

But then at last year's All Candy Expo in Chicago, I had an epiphany. I was taking a break from our booth, wandering the aisles, sampling a little more than I had intended to (it's pretty hard to resist nibbling, even for those of us who work in candy factories; you become immune to your own lines, but that doesn't mean you don't succumb to all kinds of candy outside your own product range).

My weakness is always the gummy aisle, and I would do well to avoid it altogether at trade shows. It's true that Mumbo Jumbos are technically gummy, but I hardly ever eat them, and I have to admit that for years I have preferred the aroma that comes off the mixtures as they are being molded to the experience of putting a Mumbo Jumbo in my mouth. The vast Haribo space was especially alluring, and I lingered there awhile, admiring the jewel-like mounds of Gummi everything; I admit to an intense relationship with their red and black nonpareil raspberries.

I spent some quality time at the Goelitz candy corn display. Fresh candy corn is such a different experience from stale candy corn. While I wasn't tempted by Farley's & Sathers's Jujyfruits, Now And Laters, or Jolly Ranchers, I did have a few Lemonheads at the Ferrara Pan space before going for a visit with my good friends at Just Born, who make Mike and Ike and Teenee Beanees as well as Peeps.

I had worked my way through a lot more sugary sampling than is a good idea, and I suddenly realized I was feeling lightheaded and jittery. I suppose I should have been carrying an Index bar, but since our contract work is confidential, I wouldn't ever want to be seen in public with an Index bar or a Detox bar in my hand. It would be too risky, especially at a candy show, where people could put two and two together. I suppose it is widely known in candy circles who makes what for whom, but that is still a confidential agreement, and I am an honorable person who means to respect not only the letter of the law, but also the spirit of the law.

I knew my sugar rush would be followed by a crash, and I was feeling worse by the minute, so I headed to the meat snack area, where I usually never bother to set foot throughout the three days of All Candy. I helped myself to some venison jerky, which saved me. When a candy show includes other snacks (like nuts, chips, dried fruit, cookies, and meat snacks), the meat snack and chip areas are always a strange departure from the festive, carnival aesthetic of the rest of the show. In meat snacks, most of the vendors are men. And a lot of them are burly lumberjack types dressed like Paul Bunyan, which makes sense, since a candy and snack show is our one point of intersection, and the rest of their trade-show calendar consists of gun shows, boat shows, and camping and hunting shows.

Having reached the end of the fortuitous meat snack aisle, I cut across the chips and nuts area and was on my way back toward the Zip's Candies booth when I stopped at the Green & Black's booth to see what they had going on. There I talked with the guy who designs their bars, whose cards say "Head of Taste," which is a cute term for product development manager. I admire the way Cadbury has strategized this brand since they bought it in 2005, letting it be independent and focused on quality, in much the same way Hershey's has managed Scharffen Berger and Dagoba since it made those acquisitions in 2004 and 2006. (Most casual consumers have no idea that these three companies are no longer the artisanal start-ups they once were, which is no accident.)

The Green & Black's guy was passionate and persuasive about his products. He had samples attractively laid out, and he was cutting up bars as he talked to a couple of buyers and a journalist about how the company sources the entirely organic ingredients and how they balance the cocoa mass and the cocoa butter for best mouthfeel. Since I was standing there with them, it would have been rude for me to refuse the proffered samples, so I nibbled on each as we discussed their lines, planning a return to meat snacks for some teriyaki turkey jerky I had espied, to balance this latest sugar infusion.

Then we got to their white chocolate. He spoke of the clean and fragrant taste of the Madagascar vanilla they use exclusively. I said, No thanks, I don't like white chocolate, and he laughed at me, holding out a small square on the tip of his knife, which I took. I put it in my mouth. Ecstasy! Revelation! Incredible mouthfeel! Creamy vanilla pleasure flooded through me. The intense chocolateness of this ambrosial substance was hidden in plain sight. He laughed at me again, holding out another square on the tip of his knife.

Even though Zip's Candies takes one of the smallest possible spaces at the expo, the expenses for us to show our three little candy lines at this annual event are horrendous, more than twenty thousand dollars, and so we usually bring along only a couple of employees, and we like to have a strong family presence in the booth. I notice that other family-owned candy companies do too, and sometimes you talk to a third- or fourth-generation family member who is attending law school or who lives across the country from the family business and isn't involved in the day-to-day operations at all but who shows up at times like this. It's good for the company image.

I had never done Chicago without Howard before, and even though I was of course very angry that he had left me and gone to Madagascar to live his authentic life, I missed him incessantly for those three days of the show. It was so different, being there without him. I had a hard time smiling and giving vague answers when people asked for him. Everyone expected to see that nice guy Howdy Ziplinsky at the Zip's Candies booth the way they always had. Howard loved this show. It's a schmooze-fest, and that's the part of the business at which he excelled. I had never appreciated how good for business it probably was that Howard had an uncanny ability to remember every name and every face (a skill he honed at Yale fulfilling his pledge require-ments at DKE, when he memorized the names of every frat brother).

It was even harder to carry on imperviously when people we've known for years at these shows—lots of buyers, but also some of the perennials from our tribe, the other small, family-owned candy companies (like the Sifers family, who make those quirky Valomilks in Kansas; or the Sioux City–based Palmers, who make Twin Bings (and even *they* have ventured into an extension with King Bings), or the Wagers, who make the Idaho Spud Bar, the Old Faithful Bar, and the Cherry Cocktail Bar)—didn't ask for Howard, because they had heard through the grapevine that he had left me. I am sure there was a buzz of speculation about the future of Zip's Candies as well. But isn't this always the question for every small family-owned candy business in its third or fourth generation, how long they will hold out before selling?

In 2003, when we were in Chicago and everyone was talking about Just Born having bought the fourth-generation Golden-berg Candy Company (makers of Peanut Chews in Philadelphia since 1890), I overheard Howard telling a buyer that he was hop-ing that one of these days Just Born or Annabelle would make him an offer he couldn't refuse. I didn't say anything until the show was over and we were at O'Hare and checked in for our flight to Hartford. When I finally confronted Howard about what I had heard him say, we had a fight, right there in the boarding area. Our seats were in different rows on the flight home; Howard had assured me he had booked our seats together, but he neglected to follow through on that, and neither of us attempted to swap with other passengers in order to sit together.

AFTER MY WHITE-CHOCOLATE epiphany in the Green & Black's booth, I asked Julie to scout out some other white-chocolate samples from around the show, and back at our hotel that first night, we spread them on a clean towel on the bedspread and sampled our way through them. You know these brands, all the usual suspects. Most of them were terrible. A few were barely acceptable. Nothing was good. I took out the Green & Black's white-chocolate bar I had helped myself to after that transcendent taste; we swigged some water to clear our palates, and then we each took a bite. What a significant contrast to everything we had just tasted. It was rich and creamy, and the vanilla was powerfully fragrant. It was the combination of the high-quality vanilla from Madagascar and the very pure cocoa butter from their high-quality organic Trinitario cacao beans, which are from Belize or the Dominican Republic.

"We could do this," Julie said, licking some crumbs off the wrapper. Between us we had devoured the entire hundred-gram bar. I asked her what she was thinking. "Couldn't we do something with white chocolate, like White Tigermelts?" Perhaps this was it, a white-chocolate product extension as the optimal first step for Zip's. We could do something with Little Sammies or Tigermelts and high-quality white chocolate, without losing our identity, without getting too fancy. I looked at the array of undistinguished white-chocolate brand extensions strewn on the towel, each one missing a sampled corner. They were each bitter, chalky, or harsh, with that chemical telltale aftertaste of vanillin, the cheap and artificial vanilla substitute that Zip's Candies has never used and never will. (Most months now we go through three fifty-gallon drums of Czaplinsky's Pure Madagascar Vanilla, which has always been an ingredient in both Tigermelts and Little Sammies, and is now a significant flavoring in our Bao-Bar as well.) In contrast to the creamy luxe taste and mouthfeel of the Green & Black's white bar, there was no comparison. This is how you figure out what not to do, sampling this way.

It was nice to have Julie at the show that year especially, and it was a rare moment for the two of us to share a hotel room and spend some time alone, since Julie and Kelly are very rarely apart. That was the same trip when Julie suggested to me that I should consider becoming a situational lesbian because I would have more options for finding a new partner after the divorce. I didn't and don't see it, but in a curious way her thinking about me this way was flattering, like an invitation to join an exclusive guild.

That night I had one of my Zip's dreams, as I often do when I am just falling asleep or am on the verge of waking up. I think there is something about the endless repetitive movements and sounds of the factory that penetrates my unconscious mind and manifests as complex and fantastical machinery that is often out of control, with switches I cannot reach, and dials and indicators I cannot read. There are weirdly intricate and clearly sexual images of things with apertures closing to slits and opening to quivering gaping orifices, and there are often strange cylindrical objects being thrust into slots and receptacles, over and over and over, with an urgent mechanical insistence; often, too, there are disturbing mucilaginous substances being extruded in menacing coils, or oozing out of or into places they shouldn't. Sometimes I don't recognize the viscid matter at all, but other times Little

Sammies are piling up uncontrollably, or enormous Mumbo Jumbos are rolling toward me like runaway wagon wheels. I start awake from these dreams tasting a faint note of chocolate, cherry, and anise in the back of my throat. Dr. Gibraltar once told me that my dreams like this are probably not really dreams, but are more likely hypnagogic or hypnopompic hallucinations. Whatever—they're vivid and exhausting. Mornings after those nights, I feel as if I've worked an overnight shift.

This was a Little Sammies dream, but the Little Sammies were white.

IT WASN'T VERY difficult to make Little Susies. The most challenging element was creating a new mold that had a little less volume than the Little Sammies, but was clearly a girl in a dress, with more feminine features. The figures are pretty blobby anyway, so the details of the head didn't matter as much as the shape of the body. The Halloween crisis of 1981 had taught me how to hand-dip Little Sammies, even though in the end that got us nowhere close to an approximation of the panned hard, shiny shell. But Little Susie, as I conceived of the product, our first brand extension, wouldn't be panned at all. Even if we could match the shell coating, it wouldn't have enough thickness to give a real white-chocolate flavor, and I didn't want just an appearance of white chocolate, I really wanted that flavor to come through. Little Susies would be dipped in white chocolate.

The slightly smaller interior core of the same fudgy mixture as the Little Sammies (the core ingredients for Little Sammies are sugar, corn syrup, molasses, partially hydrogenated soybean oil, condensed skim milk, cocoa solids, whey, soy lecithin, salt, and vanilla) would allow the finished piece to match the Little Sammies and fit in the packaging, because the balance of the thickness would be added with the pure white-chocolate enrobing.

Little Susies would offer a pleasing contrast to Little Sammies. Little Sammies are boys. They're shiny; they're fudgy. Little Susies would be girls, with creamy smooth white chocolate on the outside, but with the familiar Little Sammies recipe core. How could this not be a winner? It was innovative, but still familiar. I wished Howard could be a part of this, sharing with me the birth of Zip's Candies' new baby. If only I had thought of Little Susies sooner. I believe it would have been a bond between us.

I WORKED FOR the next couple of months with Jacob and two of my most loyal and experienced employees, Petey Leventhal and Sally Fernstein, developing the Little Susies slowly and carefully, troubleshooting batch by batch. We figured it out, and began our laborious production in earnest. In the last hour of each Little Sammies shift, we made cores for Little Susies, and then the four of us would do the white-chocolate enrobing dip, sixty at a time.

In this way we began to build some prototype stock in order to have samples for CandyCon at Javits, in September. It's the other big show we do, every fall. It's a little smaller than All Candy, but it's a bigger show for us—we take a bigger space and have more people on the floor, because we can truck everything down from New Haven instead of airfreighting our stock and worrying about Tigermelts melting and resolidifying out of temper along the way, and we don't have to rent as much furnishings for the booth, either.

It was now August. We hit our stride and were able to produce a consistent product, batch to batch. My plan had been to sample Little Susies at the Con and get enough orders to pay for a proper line setup, and to develop a design and print the new labels we would need. I had a vision of something that would mirror the Little Sammies wrapper, but in contrasting colors and with the words *white chocolate* on the green umbrella. Once they were in production, I could see running the Little Susies on the Little Sammies line every third or fourth day, and then, who knows, if sales were significant and sustained after the true roll-out, we would consider a dedicated line.

The white chocolate cost Zip's—well, a lot. More than I want to say right now. If there is going to be a forensic accountant reviewing our books anyway, fine; let him hunt for that information if it's so important to Irene. It was a reasonable decision. In the press of those hectic weeks, I made the choice to triage our energies and go with a sure thing, knowing that at a later stage we would have to develop our own white-chocolate enrobing recipe. We used Green & Black's white chocolate for our Little Susies prototypes. It tempered beautifully. Well-tempered chocolate is glossy, breaks with a clean, crisp snap, and has a molten mouthfeel. Badly tempered chocolate feels gritty and crumbly in your mouth. It is the taste of failure, disappointment, and broken promises.

The Little Susies were perfect, if I do say so. It was a great combination, the soft fudgy core, identical to Little Sammies except, going for a contrast with Little Sammies, and also following Sam's advice, with a slightly saltier formulation, which played beautifully off the nicely tempered white chocolate. The proportion was very good. Little Susies were a great innovation. Fantastic mouthfeel, tremendously appealing in alternating bites with Little Sammies. A brilliant product extension. This is undeniable.

❋   ❋

WE HIT A snag when we realized that we really didn't know how to put Little Susies in the hands of buyers at CandyCon in an advantageous way. They didn't look good enough to display on plates or in bowls—Little Sammies would also look like nothing much if displayed that way. The packaging is important. Who would want naked Idaho Spud Bars? Unwrapped, they look . . . well, I don't want to say how they look; it would be disrespectful. (Unwrap one yourself, if you're curious.) Anyway, if you think about it, out of the wrapper, all the bestselling bars are just five indistinguishable inches of lumpy brownness. Once the buyers walked away from the booth with some unwrapped Little Susies, what would they have? A one-page handout and some pathetic bare samples in a plastic bag? We would have to do better than that. We needed to launch Little Susies decisively.

In any case, although I had envisaged Little Susies being packaged three to a pack, just like Little Sammies, I was reluctant to give our precious handmade prototypes away three at a time, which is what we would have to do if they were packaged in a standard pack. What had we gotten ourselves into? We had already invested an insane amount of hand labor at each stage of production along the line in order to create a finished product that could pass as a manufactured candy already in production. Even if we had enough stock, we had a wrapping problem. I couldn't just put Little Susies into Little Sammies wrappers, and we didn't have a Little Susies wrapper. We weren't prepared. We had to think fast. The Con was now ten days away.

Jacob and I were dipping what would have to be the last batch of Little Susies on our own, and the third shift was leaving. We worked together without speaking, and then he said quietly, as we moved a completed tray of sixty Little Susies to the drying rack, "I have an idea." He cocked his head for me to follow him, and after the tray was locked in place, I did. He led me to a worktable where he had laid out a row of some thirty alternating Little Sammies and Little Susies. Jacob explained that he had just been fooling around at first, but now he wondered if this might be the answer. We could package Little Susies in with Little Sammies in specially marked packs as a promotional gimmick at the CandyCon.

Of course! It was perfect. I loved the way they looked lined up that way. Together, he and I created another row, and another, in reverse alternation so as to form a checkerboard pattern of Little Sammies and Little Susies. It was striking, and it would be perfect for our Little Susies display strategy in the Zip's booth at CandyCon. Jacob took a Little Sammies cardboard sleeve and placed two little Sammies on either side of a Little Susie. The three fit perfectly together. We could run these through the usual wrapping machine, and then get some rush-printed "Little Susies" stickers that we could slap onto those Little Sammies packs to distinguish them from the regular stock. The stickers would have the added ingredients of the white-chocolate enrobing in agate type running around the "Little Susies" lettering. We certainly weren't going to identify the source of the white chocolate, so we decided simply to list the ingredients (cane sugar, cocoa butter, milk powder, soy lecithin, vanilla extract), omitting the organic designation, since there is nothing organic about our products ordinarily, and that term, while true for the time being about the enrobing, wasn't our kind of word. So that's what we did.

WE DROVE DOWN to the show in a convoy of Zip's Candies trucks and vans, with our usual show stock and twenty boxes of the specially stickered Little Sammies/Little Susies packs, forty-eight to each box. We had almost a thousand Little Susie

giveaway packs, and we had about fifty more Little Susies to display in a glass countertop flat case, which Jacob would set up
with that striking checkerboard arrangement of Little Sammies
and Little Susies.

Julie brought Kelly along, with a Zip's employee badge for
her, which was slightly awkward because she was overwhelmed
by all the candy and wasn't as helpful with our setting up as she
could have been. Most people go into a Stendhal candy swoon
the first time they attend a big trade show. It's understandable,
but we needed all hands on deck, and I was annoyed that Julie
didn't even try to reel her in, but seemed charmed every time
Kelly staggered back into the booth with more booty from
around the floor, giddy as a child having an ultra Halloween
experience. I felt myself being quite irritated with the two of
them giggling together and littering our booth with wrappers of
other candy brands, which I kept picking up with exaggerated
efficiency, but they were too entranced with each other to take
my irritable tidying as personally as they should have. Kelly
watches me closely when I am speaking to Julie, and I often feel
that she is observing me in order to give Julie advice about how
to handle her problematic mother.

Jacob has made the point to me that I would probably be
more welcoming and flexible if he brought a girlfriend along as
often as Julie brings Kelly. I know he's right, but it isn't likely
that he would have a girlfriend with such a passive-aggressive
vibe. Anyway, Jacob doesn't let me meet his girlfriends, a regrettable and unfair policy based on his erroneous belief that I am
"intrusive" and "controlling" and "don't respect boundaries,"
which was perhaps somewhat true when he was younger and
less mature, but it is not a fair characterization. I don't press him.
I am optimistic that one day soon, when Jacob is ready, I will
meet Becky, the girl he has been seeing for a while now. (A law

student at Yale, a runner and a devotee of early music, she is very articulate and intelligent, and quite devoted to Jacob, based on the emails I read over a few months' time, before Jacob changed his password. He uses "jakezip" for so many of his passwords, though I have advised him repeatedly that diverse passwords are far more secure.)

CANDYCON WAS LIKE any candy show; it was hectic and crowded, and there were problems with the electrical supply and confusion over the rental delivery, but we got set up. Jacob had burned a CD from Howard's old Everly Brothers album, so we had "Wake Up, Little Susie" playing, we had organized our space according to our usual show planagram, and Jacob and Julie had done a great job with the displays. We had order sheets with our usual lines and a new space for Little Susies orders, with some special show discounts and deals for orders placed at the booth.

There was some Little Susies buzz even before the show doors officially opened; lots of nearby vendors had checked us out, drawn by our music, plus we had better real estate on the floor than ever before. Instead of being shunted off among the start-ups and really small companies like the nice Glee Gum people from Providence, or those ambitious Sweetriot women from New York, for once our space was in the middle of the action, across from Tootsie Roll, which may have suited us a little more than it suited them, since there is that slightly uneasy kinship between Little Sammies and that primal Ellis Island Tootsie Roll of Eli's. Call it the anxiety of influence. But they're enormous and we're small, and they've been in business since 1896 and we started in 1924, and they can afford to tolerate our existence.

The morning went well. There was a good, upbeat atmosphere at the show, and everyone was psyched for what felt like a strong back-to-school and Halloween season. A number of vendors greeted me with real warmth, and a few told me it was good to see me at this show, because they had heard that things were up in the air at Zip's. I knew they were speaking of Howard's departure from our marriage, which had fueled the inevitable speculation about the future of the business. All the more reason to have a strong presence, with a new product to showcase, to make it clear to everyone across the industry that Zip's Candies was doing just fine, better than ever.

In a momentary lull, I had an intriguing conversation with a reporter who was interested in the Little Susies, though she admitted she wasn't really there to cover the show, and was actually writing a novel about a candy company. She quizzed me rather insistently on my thoughts about Jewish family-owned candy companies. Why did I think so many had been founded by Jewish immigrants: Sam Born, who came to America in 1910; Sam Altshuler, who arrived in 1917; Eli Ziplinsky, who landed in 1920; Nathan Radutsky, who started Joyva halvah, who arrived in 1907; David Goldenberg, who invented Peanut Chews, who came in 1880; and so on.

I thought about what she was asking. Perhaps the candy business was one that offered opportunity to immigrants with few resources. What other product could be developed for a few pennies and made in a pot on a stove, or at a kitchen table, with everyone in the family helping to do something, stir the pot or wrap the finished pieces? They might have recipes from the old country that would appeal to people from the same background living in their neighborhood, and they could sell their product on the street with no overhead. I had never considered the pattern in quite this way before.

After lunch there was a flurry at our booth, with a lot of people specifically coming over to grab a Little Sammies/Little Susies pack. Because we didn't want to run out of stock on the first day, we had to be selective about giving them out. At any show you waste a certain amount of product on giveaways to other vendors, or to people with press passes who aren't going to be writing about your product, or to bloggers who might be planning to rave about your product or diss your product but who are also cruising for free samples they can then offer up in giveaway contests on their blogs. A certain amount of that is fine, and all of it is ordinary and expectable at a trade show like this. We tried to get selective and target the buyers without being rude to anyone who really wanted a Little Sammies / Little Susies pack. The booth was now weirdly mobbed, with a lot of younger people, a lot of journalists with blog and website credentials. Julie was looking unhappy and overwhelmed, trying to deal with people. Two of our new, young workers had not come back from lunch on time, and we were shorthanded, struggling to keep up with samples and questions. The hundredth repetition of the Everly Brothers singing "Wake Up, Little Susie" was getting on my nerves, and it was making me miss Howard, too, which also got on my nerves. I turned down the sound a little. Why were we getting slammed all of a sudden?

The reporter who was really a novelist was back. She semaphored urgently to me over the heads of the buyers and journalists thronging our little counter area, and I waved her to come around the side into the booth and talk to me. Did I know about the live blogging, she wanted to know. I didn't have a clue what she was talking about, but I thought Julie might, so I asked her to repeat her question to Julie, and a moment later Julie was sprinting off to the exhibitors' break room, where she could go online. When she returned, she looked stricken.

❊ ❊

To PUT IT bluntly, the white Little Susie snuggled in between the two brown Little Sammies apparently struck a certain snarky culture blogger with a devoted following as a representation not only of tawdry, three-way sex, but also of tawdry, three-way, mixed-race sex. Candy miscegenation. I pushed my way through the people standing expectantly around the Zip's Candies booth and reached into one of the open boxes under the counter for a pack of Little Sammies/Little Susies. I turned away and opened it, trying to look with the eyes of a stranger, to see how it would strike me if I had never laid eyes on them before. I was startled.

They were wedged together shoulder to shoulder, Little Sammie/Little Susie/Little Sammie. It did sort of look as if they were three in a bed. I tried to see it the way the blogger had apparently seen it, the innocent, creamy white Little Susie, lying there, flanked by glistening black savages. Was it obscene? Did it really seem like an erotic representation of what he was calling a "chocolate sandwich"? Another blogger was apparently analyzing the "Wake Up, Little Susie" lyrics line by line, to demonstrate our intentional erotic message.

I know I made a terrible mistake, not anticipating the error in our packaging presentation, but none of us had seen it. When you are overly focused on your product, you lose the ability to view it with fresh eyes, the way the public might see it. Two years ago, Mill Farm Gummi Lighthouses got a lot of unwanted candy blog attention because somebody noticed that if you turn them on their sides, each one looks like a colorful penis and testicles, which was presumably not something the Mill Farm people had ever considered or aspired to. But when you look at them now (on the Web), you can hardly believe they shipped them.

I realize our packaging decision seems utterly foolish in retrospect, but I can only say again that not one person who handled the packaging as we made those prototype handouts for CandyCon anticipated how a white Little Susie would look nestle between two brown Little Sammies. Let me be really clear about this: nobody who was aware of the time and energy and money that were poured into the Little Susies development could possibly think that I had anything but the best interests of the company at heart. I know it was a good brand extension. I know what my state of mind was, and it is deeply insulting to suggest that any action of mine was deliberately calculated to drive down the value of Zip's Candies just as it was under consideration by a serious buyer in ongoing negotiations with Howard's duplicitous lawyer. Since this possibility, the potential takeover of Zip's Candies, had been actively concealed from me, it is an outrageous suggestion, accusing me of having acted with that knowledge to sabotage a potential sale of the business. I am the betrayed, not the betrayer. I know what Sam would have said: your best teacher is your last mistake.

I TRIED TO remain calm. Surely this blog thing was not a major problem? Anyone who thought the sight of these candies lined up together was suggestive would presumably go into spasm over the incipient orgy in a tin of sardines. Was it possible the bloggers weren't serious at all, they were just having fun, doing what they do, riffing on the material? Candy bloggers can have a certain sardonic tone, as we well know. (I think Mumbo Jumbos deserve more than a 2.5 on the AndyCandy scale, for example.

And I think Sugarbomb was unnecessarily harsh about the occasional summer leakage problem in Tigermelts.)

Julie couldn't be calm with me. She was convinced that once something like this gets onto the Web, it is linked and repeated everywhere, and you don't know who is going to take it seriously as a deliberate statement on our part. After all, think of all the people who fall for stories in *The Onion*. Kelly, who had now rematerialized breathlessly, amped up on sugar and toting a bag spilling over with samples from all over the show, reported that Little Susies were being talked about everywhere she went on the floor. In a good way? I asked optimistically. She said she thought we were in deep shit. She's immensely irritating, but she was right.

Within the hour Julie reported that there were more than three hundred new posts on the Little Sammies forum, and her mailbox was flooded with questions and comments of one kind or another from our website form. Our website server crashed at some point later that day, the traffic was so intense. And we hadn't even had time to update the site with an image of Little Susies, though we had intended to, so the only mention was the teaser Julie had added a few weeks earlier, about how anyone attending CandyCon in New York would meet the newest member of the Ziplinsky Candy Family, come see us at the show! So people hoping to find a picture of this controversial candy artifact were frustrated, and they left a lot of angry and obscene comments.

It took only a few hours for the viral tsunami to hit. Of course it jumped from the blogosphere to television and print media, especially since everyone is always looking to cover a trade show like this with a new angle. They had found their story. What followed with the wire stories, all the press coverage, was a terrible déjà vu of the Blessed Chocolate Virgin coverage, which was of course among the first items anyone searching for references to Zip's Candies would find, which in turn led to yet another airing of the fire story from 1975, and how I was once known as Arson Girl (the way it might be said of someone that she was the Munger Potato Festival Queen of 1975). Add to that an endless exponential web of interconnected blog and Internet mentions that persist to this day.

You can find references to Little Susies and Little Sammies on websites devoted to preserving the purity of the white race; you can find references on numerous sites that also use the key-word *kike* (given the Ziplinsky heritage, I suppose that was inevitable). There is a website with lyrics for a version of the Little Sammies jingle that begin "Little Sammies are for you / If you are a hook-nosed Jew." Some of the white supremacy web-sites have put us on a list of companies whose products should be boycotted permanently. (Did anyone seriously believe that Zip's Candies was using this product launch to subversively put forward a positive image of mixed-race threesomes?)

There are some pornographic images on the Web, involving a sex-crazed Little Susie with two very well-endowed Little Sammies having their way with her. Julie tells me Little Susie threesomes will be on the Web until the end of time. They are horribly easy to find now, in any case. There are endless numbers of obscene videos of crudely animated Little Sammies and Little Susies in motion, on YouTube and elsewhere, and there are thousands of images on the Web that all seem to follow the same format, with one white something between two dark somethings (kittens, shoes, cows in a field, wine bottles, cars, etc.), captioned with the implicitly suggestive punch line, "Say, Dat's Tasty!"

Some of the videos of animated figures remind me of the awk-ward Claymation of *Gumby* television shows of my childhood.

(Gumby's mother was Gumba, and his father was Gumbo.) If you soften Little Sammies briefly in the microwave, they become temporarily pliable, though the coating will lose its gloss when it cools. I imagine this is what was done for the porno Little Sammies; their fudgy genitals were sculpted out of parts of other Little Sammies and stuck on their bodies while they were still warm.

Loose Little Susies and unopened Little Susies–stickered Little Sammies packs that we gave away at the CandyCon were a hot eBay item for a while, and there were even, weirdly enough (think of the effort involved), some counterfeits.

The blogger who started the whole thing—Leonard Blatt is his actual name, but being an ironic hipster with literary pretensions, on his blog, Kretschmar's Lunch, he is known as Vivian Darkbloom—has made quite the name for himself with his particular brand of deadpan prudery. At the peak of the Little Susies nightmare, he wrote me an email to tell me that he had really enjoyed Little Susies, and was very sorry that his actions had contributed to their being unavailable indefinitely. He offered to begin a "Bring Back Little Susies!" blog campaign, but I emailed him back to tell him he had done enough.

IO

She saw every relationship as a pair of intersecting circles. It would seem at first glance that the more they overlapped the better the relationship; but this is not so. Beyond a certain point the law of diminishing returns sets in, and there are not enough private resources left on either side to enrich the life that is shared. Probably perfection is reached when the area of the two outer crescents, added together, is exactly equal to that of the leaf-shaped piece in the middle. On paper there must be some neat mathematical formula for arriving at this; in life, none.

—Jan Struther, *Mrs. Miniver*

WE DID NOT HAVE enough private resources, Howard and I, to enrich our shared life. I loved him with all my heart, such as it is, but he never loved me with all of his. Howard chose to reserve his most private and precious resources a world away, while I poured my heart and soul into Zip's Candies and the Ziplinsky family, thinking we were in it together, for life. The maintenance of an enduring marriage is a process sensitive to both time and temperature. You have to balance and maintain the heat over the years. Too much heat can melt even tigers, as we know. But we had a good, rich life, one that could have endured. Of course, over time, there are infinite adjustments to make, and make again. It always comes down to time and temperature. Good tempering is essential for durability. A badly tempered marriage becomes dull and brittle, and then it breaks.

HOWARD, HOWARD, HOWARD. The love of my life is a shmuck (who taught me the word *shmuck*). The love of my life turns out to be Carson McCullers's "most mediocre person," who can be the object of a love which is "wild, extravagant, and beautiful as the poison lilies of the swamp."

I AM SORRY about the Little Sammies I put in the gas tank of Howard's ridiculous Porsche Boxster in the Zip's Candies parking lot the week before he left. I take full responsibility for the expense involved in replacing all the engine parts that were clogged when the dissolved Little Sammies passed through the fuel injector as Howard was driving on the Wilbur Cross Parkway. However, I take no responsibility for the added inconvenience and expense of the car's breaking down inside the West Rock Tunnel, which would not have happened if he had followed my advice to avoid the parkway, especially in the late afternoon, and instead, when driving from East Rock to the Yale Golf Course, always to take Morse Street to Fitch Street to Fountain Street. How many times have I told him that this is the best route?

Also, I shouldn't have put Howard's Patek Philippe watch in the Cuisinart. I was frustrated, but it was wrong. I will pay for another if it is important to Howard that even if he no longer cares to know the day of the week, he has an insanely overpriced watch that offers "timeless aesthetic perfection," and is "not merely a method of telling time [but also] a silent statement about your values," a watch that has "the ability to create an emotional response." Instead of, you know, a Timex or something.

My willingness to accept responsibility for these two uncharacteristically destructive and immature actions, which I took at a moment of extreme emotional distress, should be considered further proof of my honesty and integrity.

The most fundamental business philosophy Sam ever told me to write down, "We'll cross that bridge when we come to it" and "There's no use crying over spilled milk," are useless beliefs when it comes to running Zip's Candies. Our philosophy must be: first cross every possible bridge in your imagination. And spilled milk is the only kind worth crying over.

HOWARD TOOK A little more than four hundred thousand dollars of company funds out of the business over the last four years. He tried to hide this theft and spread it around through various accounts, but after he left for Madagascar, the company books turned out to be a big, sugarcoated mess. After one meeting, I cut loose Howard's sleazy friend and accountant (and accomplice), the despicable Marty Shapiro, and hired a new accountant as part of my effort to pull Zip's Candies together.

Casper Weisswasser is probably a high-functioning autistic of some kind. He's a cross between Kaspar Hauser and Casper the Friendly Ghost. Large and pale and awkward, he seems surprised by ordinary clichés, as if he has never heard anyone say anything like "When it rains it pours" or "If you can't beat 'em, join 'em." He was amazed when I told him his name means "white water." He speaks in a slightly loud monotone, as if making announcements in a bus station through a PA system, and he identifies himself to me in full every time he phones, even if we have already spoken several times within the hour. Casper has that perfect accountant's obsessive ability to make order out of disorder. Order, disorder, counterorder. That's what Sam always said when a line broke down. That's how I live my life.

The money Howard took apparently seeped into his Madagascar bank accounts in increments, laundered through various Czaplinsky accounts, with padded billing and duplicate payments. I am not going to make any claims about the money now. I don't want to hurt the Bao-Bar venture, and the business relationship between Ziplinsky and Czaplinsky interests is too valuable to damage that way. The money signifies to me (the way a dagger in the heart signifies), because it tells me how long it has been since Howard had any intention of staying here, in his Connecticut life with me. I now realize that he left me long before he actually left.

The stolen money is spilled milk, a minor spill in the larger scheme of things, the kind worth shedding just a few tears over, to be sure, especially when I think about the ways I have juggled shifts to keep the lines running at maximum efficiency, and shaved expenditures all over the plant, and bargained with all of our suppliers so hard that Manny Feldman, who sells us our corn syrup and sugar complained to me a few months ago, "You really Jewed me down on that last order."

SAM SUGGESTED THAT I become a notary public, which I did, twenty years ago. It's a useful thing for any business, having an in-house notary. He also encouraged me to learn how to do his signature perfectly, which was useful for signing checks, or if anything else came up requiring authorization, when he and Frieda were in Deerfield Beach every February for so many years. You see how much he trusted me? It was our little secret.

❊ ❊

THE ZIP'S CANDIES fire occurred on a Sunday, when I knew I was unlikely to be detected, because I wanted to burn a large quantity of papers efficiently and discreetly. I used two of the three empty fifty-gallon drums that were on the loading dock. I didn't use the third one because it had a couple of inches of liquid in the bottom, which I assumed, erroneously as it turned out, was rainwater. It is beyond obvious that I was not in any way trying to cause damage to the premises of Zip's Candies, or I would not have set a fire out on the loading dock when I had full access to every corner of the building and could have in fact burned the place to the ground very efficiently if I so chose, by setting the fire in the basement.

When the third drum blew up, igniting everything on the loading dock, the only damage to the building was to the roof overhang on the loading dock, which was in terrible condition anyway, and had been patched and patched again over the years. A mess of framing and plywood with several layers of buckling tar-paper patches laid down haphazardly for quick rainwater leak prevention (Howard's management style, not mine), the roof got scorched when a stack of wooden pallets ignited.

I have had an intention for quite a while now to reroof our entire premises with standing seam metal, perhaps in a cheerful green to echo the Zip's umbrella, which is of course an echo of Little Black Sambo's green umbrella. The cost of new roofing would be approximately a hundred thousand dollars, however, and it is not in our budget at this time. We lost the original Zip's Candies "Say, Dat's Tasty!" sign, too, the only serious loss from the explosion. I do think the fire would have burned out on its own even if the fire department hadn't responded to a 911 call from someone who saw the black smoke rising and thought the empty Bigelow Boiler complex beside us was on fire.

The Zip's Candies building stands on ground with an ironic (to me) history. The corner of James Street and River Street lies at the edge of a filled swamp old maps call Grapevine Point. This very corner was the site of the administration building for Camp Terry, which was a compound of nine barracks erected to house Connecticut's two Colored Civil War Regiments, the 29th and the 30th, while they were trained for battle. (Today the parade ground is Criscuolo Park.) Governor William Alfred Buckingham brokered the sale of the land to the U.S. Army by Yale University, in order to avoid the risk of colored troops, armed with rifles, being drilled on the New Haven Green, where many other Connecticut regiments had been trained. After the war ended, the army disposed of the property, and the Bigelow Boiler complex of buildings was erected on the site. Thirty years later, the Peet brothers bought one of the smaller Bigelow buildings for their short-lived enterprise.

THOSE FIFTY-GALLON DRUMS had held Czaplinsky Pure Madagascar Vanilla, which is highly inflammable, being two-hundred-proof ethyl alcohol. The drums should not have been left on the loading dock like that, especially not unrinsed, and with one of them containing several inches of vanilla extract. It was an extraordinarily careless waste of one of the most expensive commodities we use, and I am conducting an investigation to find the person who deemed that drum empty. The stacked wooden shipping pallets should have been disposed of properly or recycled, not left to pile up like that on our loading dock. Also, the decaying roof on the loading dock should have been replaced with a standing seam metal overhang years ago, even if we weren't ready to reroof the entire building, but Howard kept deferring the expense.

That all these elements of danger were present on the loading dock demonstrates to me that I have failed to maintain the high management standards that should always govern Zip's Candies. It should have been perfectly safe for me to burn documents in those two drums, undetected, without mishap. The material safety data sheet on Czaplinsky's Pure Madagascar Vanilla says: "Pure vanilla has a flash point of 60 degrees Fahrenheit. The flammable limits are in the upper 19 percent. The product is highly flammable in the presence of open flames and sparks. The risks of explosions of the product are low. Containers should be grounded. Vanilla extract may burn with a near-invisible flame. Vapor may travel considerable distance to source of ignition and flashback."

Admittedly, I wasn't thinking about that when I lit fire to those papers. But I maintain that if all three drums had been empty and rinsed, the fire would have burned uneventfully, and my actions would have gone undetected. I take full responsibility for the fire getting out of control as it did. There are no bad soldiers, only bad officers.

Not that anyone other than Julie and Jacob has asked, but I was not on the loading dock when the explosion occurred, because my BlackBerry signal was weak and I had jumped down into the parking lot to get more bars so I could look at my email while the papers burned. So I wasn't injured.

If anyone is going to be accused of acting with fraud and malice, it shouldn't be me. (And in memory of Miss Solomon and in honor of all that she taught me, I would like to point out that one doesn't act "with fraud and malice," one acts "fraudulently and with malice.") There is no extant evidence that I have done anything malicious or fraudulent. And despite the explosion, everything I wanted to destroy was in fact successfully incinerated. I could have spared myself all the ridiculous attention this fire has brought if I had only used our shredder. It would have taken me a few hours, and that would have been that. But there is no beauty in shredding, no grace.

WHAT I BURNED: all the documentation and correspondence I have described in this affidavit, and much more that I haven't described. All the significant files of Zip's Candies, going back to 1924. I'm not crazy. Nothing that affects day-to-day operations is gone. Copies of our tax returns and current personnel files have been retained. All the invoicing, all the billing, accounts receivable, everything to do with the ordinary business of the factory, that's all intact. All current contracts and documentation pertaining to the plant operations are untouched.

I burned every scrap of paper about the numerous lawsuits over the years, all the litigation, all the settlement agreements, all the correspondence about stolen recipes and agreements of nondisclosure with Hodgson relatives and a few others. I burned the stolen Peanut Charms recipe scribbled in pencil in Eli's slashy scrawl on a yellowed Hodgson Sweet Shoppe envelope. I burned all the drafts of wills, letters of intent, promissory notes, agreements about company loans to family members that were never repaid. I burned all the notes about the creation of the Ziplinsky Family Trust (a highly ironic name for a legal instrument, when you think about it).

I burned the agreement between Howard and Sam, promising Howard the business if he married me and stayed in New Haven until he was forty-five years old.

I burned all the blackmailing letters with pretty Madagascar stamps on the envelopes from Huxley to Sam, starting with infant photos of Newton in 1976, the ones from 1982 with photos of Edison, and the more recent ones as well, with photos of Howard and his sons and their mother, his second cousin Huxley, who claimed, in childish print on the back of the photo, to be the true love of his life. May I just say that even though it's not literally incest, surely this attraction is a little incestuous? Maybe if you're a Ziplinsky, nobody but family is ever really good enough.

I burned all the correspondence from 1946 concerning a planned agreement between Julius and Eli, granting each a 25 percent interest in the other's holdings. This was to be the first step in Eli's ambitious plan to follow the Hershey's model of ownership interest in suppliers. The Ziplinsky/Czaplinsky brothers would form a mutually beneficial alliance. If Milton Hershey found it worthwhile to grow sugarcane in Cuba, then Zip's Candies would have its own cacao and vanilla in Madagascar. Sam told me about this. He found both copies of this agreement on Eli's desk the day he found Eli dead in his office. Eli had just signed and dated the documents earlier that same day, a few minutes before closing time, on that Friday afternoon, with Rosalie Fleischer, his secretary in those years, domiciled at 266 Orange Street, New Haven, Connecticut, as his witness. Sam never sent Julius his executed copy, though Julius outlived Eli by two years.

Sam buried the contracts in the safe, and when Julius wrote in response to the news of Eli's death, inquiring about the agreement they had made, Sam took his time writing back, and when he did, he was deliberately vague, saying he didn't really know much about this matter but would look into it, and then he made sure to put inadequate postage on the letter, which he addressed with slightly wrong spellings. The delay in the correspondence bought several months. Julius wrote again, and Sam replied just as slowly and vaguely. He really hadn't decided what to do, Sam told me, he just hadn't yet come to any conclusion about whether or not it was in the best interest of Zip's Candies to honor the agreement, and so there were a few more such letters back and forth, and then Julius died.

Sam didn't destroy those contracts when he should have. And so I have done it for him. They're gone now. Everything is gone, everything on the loading dock burned to ash in that aromatic, white-hot blaze.

FIRE DESTROYS. BUT fire also can cleanse and purify. Fire is life, but fire also is damnation. We speak of fiery passions, fiery tempers, flaming arguments, flaming assholes, flaming homosexuals. Ellie Quest-Greenspan said that Jung saw fire as a symbol of transformation. Dr. Gibraltar told me that Freud believed fire symbolizes the libido. Well, duh. Freud thought that human beings were wired to piss on flames, only some of us end up being relegated to the domestic sphere because we can't. He wrote that it is "as though woman had been appointed guardian of the fire which was held captive on the domestic hearth, because her anatomy made it impossible for her to yield to the temptation of this desire."

LANGUAGE HAS THE ability to express and to conceal. The sentence is one of the great inventions we've got, as elemental as fire and the wheel. Sentences like the ones I have been using can enlighten and enhance meaning, or deny it and undermine it. Sentences such as the ones Irene has used to level all of her baseless, mendacious accusations tell her story, not mine. Irene calls my words wild. Are my words wild? I certainly hope so. Keynes said words ought to be a little wild, for they are the assaults of thoughts on the unthinking. Think! Think, Irene! This, *this* is my story.

I HAVE BURNED all the documents, the real ones and the ones I made up. Trust me, or don't trust me. Either way, they're all gone now. According to some sentences I have been reading, Alice Ziplinsky embellishes. She is unreliable and she makes things up. She has a distorted sense of the events that surround these conflicts, and she has acted with fraud and with malice. She was responsible for fiscal mismanagement over the past decade when in a position of unwarranted authority. Alice Ziplinsky is unwilling to turn over documents and threatens to destroy them. Her actions have caused the company to lose value at a sensitive time when potential buyers will be alienated, thereby precluding the completion of a preliminary agreement for an unnamed large corporation to make an offer to shareholders for the purchase agreement concerning Zip's Candies premises as well as full license to produce Little Sammies, Tigermelts, and Mumbo Jumbos.

If I am that Alice Ziplinsky, then perhaps there never were any documents such as the ones I have described. Who knows what I burned? Maybe I have made it all up. Maybe I'm losing it, like Frieda, and all I burned were old meaningless invoices and bills. Nothing of what I have described in all my many precise sentences is legally binding without documentation.

Where's the evidence? Am I reliable, as Sam asked me that

first day? Who has been more reliable over these years? Who, who has ever been more loyal to Zip's Candies and the Ziplinsky family?

Nobody will ever know which signatures of Sam's are really mine. Comparisons of everything he signed in the last twenty years of his life would be meaningless. Whose signatures match, his to his, mine to mine? The testamentary Ziplinsky Family Trust instrument has been accepted by the Probate Court of New Haven. The appeals were denied. What's done is done.

HOWARD OWNS 15 percent of Zip's Candies. I own 35 percent. The Ziplinsky Family Trust owns the other half of the business. Samuel Ziplinsky's grandchildren share equally in the Ziplinsky Family Trust. That is the letter of the law, but it is also the spirit of Sam's intentions. How many slices of this pie are there?

It's not three, Irene; it's five. Each grandchild—Newton, Ethan, Jacob, Edison, and Julie—owns 10 percent of Zip's Candies. Whether we agree in the end that Howard is the third trustee of the Ziplinsky Family Trust or I am, the five grandchildren are the beneficiaries, and in this Howard and I are in rare agreement. Did you believe, Irene, that you could count on my rage over Howard's betrayal to blind me to fairness? Did you think I would be as greedy on behalf of my two children as you have been on behalf of your son? That greed by proxy has no influence. Fortunately Ethan doesn't support your position. Nobody does. And beyond my sense of fairness, my clarity on this matter is that much sharper because of my unwillingness to agree with you, Irene, about anything at all, if I can possibly help it.

Newton and Edison are Howard's children, Howard's issue. The trust language could only have been clearer if Sam had named each of his grandchildren individually, but that's not relevant. There are five grandchildren, five living issue of Sam's two living children.

And as to your outrageous, faux-generous "offer"—can't you see it's not yours to offer, Irene?—that Newton and Edison could share a quarter interest in the trust? That's absolutely out of the question. Either they are Howard's issue, or they are not, and since they most certainly are (and your suggestion that we demand paternity testing is pathetic and mean and pointless; just look at them!), they are each entitled to full recognition as a grandchild of Sam Ziplinsky's, and an equal share in the Ziplinsky Family Trust, whether you like it or not. I would have thought you would be pleased to have two brown nephews. Apparently, when it gets personal, your greed trumps your sanctimonious virtue.

Sam recognized that giving Newton and Edison their fair share would be the best way to bind Howard to Zip's Candies, if not to me and to his life here. Ownership of Zip's Candies binds us all together, except for you, Irene, and you've been fully compensated. These were Sam's intentions for his family and for his business.

Can we move on now, with malice toward none, with charity for all? Can we strive to finish the work we are in, to do all which may achieve and cherish a just and lasting peace among ourselves, as Abraham Lincoln suggested so long ago in an admittedly different but certainly not ungermane context?

WHICH BRINGS ME to a significant Zip's Candies decision. And in case it isn't clear by now—we're not selling! With my 35 percent ownership plus Jacob and Julie's combined 20 percent, we three Ziplinskys control more than half ownership of the company. They don't want to sell. Not now. The Bao-Bar is a huge success, with exponentially increasing sales every month. It's not clear how much longer we will be able to keep up with orders at this rate, and the time is coming very soon to expand our production capabilities. As it is, we're running Tigermelt production on that line only two or three days at a time every fourth week. The Bao-Bar has become the tail wagging that cat. It's an exciting development for Zip's Candies, both because it's extremely profitable and because it's a completely new product developed by the fourth generation of the family, who are prepared to take Zip's Candies into the future and make it their own.

WHEN PRESIDENT OBAMA was sworn in, and I watched George W. Bush as he stood there during the ceremony, grimacing and smirking and shifting his weight like a child enduring church, I found myself thinking about Howard's unconscionable breaking of his word to me in 2000 that he wouldn't send his DKE brother those congratulatory Little Sammies. And as Julie and I watched the inaugural pageant on television over our reheated leftover vegetable chow fun, seeing those two little girls with their mother gazing adoringly at their father, feeling the weight of that historic moment, like so many of us who felt betrayed for so long by the policies and actions of our government, I was moved, and I was proud. Dignity and grace have been missing for too long.

Julie, well aware of the history of that inscribed photo of W. on the wall in my office, asked me if I was thinking of sending some candy to the White House to welcome the Obama family. We looked at each other for a long moment. How could I? And I came to a realization. I have been thinking about it ever since that January day. Now, seven months on, I am certain. The time has come to end production of Little Sammies.

Of course it has. I have discussed this with Julie and Jacob, who agree. It's become an embarrassment to pretend they're fine, to act as if those who perceive Little Sammies to be racist and vulgar should lighten up and not be so PC. For all these years as a Ziplinsky, and as a representative of Zip's Candies (Sam used to tell every employee and every family member that we should never forget that every day, in every way, we were each Zip's Candies ambassadors), I have taken the position that Little Sammies are amusing, they're retro, it was Eli's innocent misperception, of course we're not racists, so how can our candy be racist?

But Little Sammies are really not okay. "Say, Dat's Tasty!" is not an acceptable slogan any longer, and it hasn't been for years. It's time to put Little Sammies on the shelf next to Amos 'n' Andy and Al Jolson in blackface. We've had a good run, but it's over. We are better than that. We can do better than that.

We won't simply stop production of our most successful line. This is the perfect moment to introduce a new product. We won't have to start from scratch. We have almost everything we need to go into production very quickly, after announcing the end of Little Sammies, and before we do that, we should run a final production limited edition of a few hundred thousand, with a commemorative wrapper designation, 1924–2009, which will sell like hotcakes.

The farewell to Little Sammies will be an excellent platform for the launch of our new line, which we will be able to run on the Little Sammies equipment. If our wholesalers and retailers aren't smart enough to make big buys of our new line, we can scrounge up some slotting-fee money to get the product out there in key markets, and I am certain it will succeed. I have an instinctive feel for these things. It shouldn't be difficult to generate excellent publicity for this transition, with Julie and Jacob speaking for the company as the next generation. It becomes a human interest story, a classic American success story. Eli's great-grandchildren take Zip's Candies into the future. I will announce my intention to step down within the next five years. We will court the candy bloggers. Julie will know the best way to do that.

Jacob will delegate some of the Bao-Bar production supervision in order to work with me on refining the manufacturing recipe so we can go into production. There is no reason to jettison the humanoid form. We can modify the Little Sammies mogul molds to make something more modern and streamlined in shape, genderless and featureless (a bit like the Academy Award Oscar statuette, but plumper and smoother), but within the same basic Little Sammies dimensions and specs.

What I envision will be a pair of pieces that will be packaged together. The first one will have a solid white-chocolate core, a white chocolate as good as we can make it, using pure Czaplinsky vanilla and high-quality cocoa butter. Frankly, I would want to aim for something very equivalent to the Green & Black's white chocolate, with as comparable a flavor and mouthfeel as we can achieve. But, in memory of Sam, ours will be just a little saltier. We will pan this piece with the Little Sammies coating, so they will have that same familiar, shiny finish, but perhaps with a darker chocolate, one with a lower sugar content in keeping with contemporary taste.

The second piece will have the identical form, but the core will be an increment smaller, and it will be made with our original, fudgy Little Sammies recipe, which will give this new line the familiarity and continuity of a brand extension, and will appease those aficionados who will mourn the end of Little Sammies. (If only Peter Paul had offered something similarly compensatory to the Caravelle mourners!) We will coat this piece in white chocolate. In other words, we will use the Little Susies formulation, but the two pieces together will match, and will share this new, identical, genderless shape. We will package them as a pair, and by selling two instead of three in a pack, we can keep the unit pricing in the Little Sammies range, despite the higher-quality ingredients, which will cost us more, piece for piece. They will be delectable. This new line will be what Sam, and Eli before him, would have called a true confection.

Of course, in the most basic sense that matters most to the consumer, this new piece isn't exactly new, but has the appealing blend of familiarity and newness, since it is in some ways a reintroduced upgrade of Little Sammies. I am reminded of the brilliant Post Shreddies campaign that Ogilvy & Mather started a couple of years ago in Canada. Shreddies is a shredded-wheat square breakfast cereal that was cleverly relaunched with a tongue-in-cheek campaign promoting new Diamond Shreddies, which were simply the same old square Shreddies viewed from a different angle. (The Third Reich did precisely the same thing with the traditional swastika form by turning it forty-five degrees.) They even marketed boxes promising a "combo pack," with both square and diamond Shreddies in equal proportion. Sales, which had been stagnant, exploded.

For the new wrapper, I'd like to keep the continuity of a Zip's umbrella, but without color, with the name of the candy in white on a black umbrella, against a checkerboard background, all in black and white (a subtle tip of the hat to the Abba-Zaba checkerboard border, to be sure, but surely they can't copyright such a universal design as a checkerboard). I think the time is just right in our history, as a candy company and as a nation, if I may say that without sounding too grand, for a black-and-white contrasting piece such as this. And I mean black and white in every sense.

During the Little Susies crisis, Julie told me that the term "white chocolate" is ghetto slang for two things with opposite meanings. Intriguingly enough, the term can be used to deride a black person who acts white, and it can also be used to deride a white person who acts black. Surely this is an excellent moment for this paired candy piece with something to say, one white on the outside and brown on the inside, and the other brown on the outside but white on the inside.

I have been thinking long and hard about what to name this new line, and I believe I have come up with the perfect name, one that has a friendly and cheerful sensibility, yet sounds timeless and classic, like Oh Henry! Julie and Jacob have agreed to it, if Howard doesn't object. It will be in his best interest not to object. Who knows, he might even like it. We will call this new candy the Say Howdy!

WHEN I WAS pouring starter fluid on the papers, and when I struck the match, and as I fed the sheets to the flames, I found myself, college degree or not, thinking about not just the selflessness but also the literariness of my act. I did, after all, intend to major in English at Middlebury, and as these pages should have made abundantly evident to any reader, despite the turns my life has taken, I have educated myself. And I thought about how Thomas Carlyle's only copy of the manuscript for *The French Revolution,* which he had sent over to his friend John Stuart Mill, was thrown in the fire by Mill's maid. Carlyle rewrote it. So many other significant pages have gone up in smoke. Thomas Moore burned Byron's memoirs. Jane Austen's sister Cassandra burned her letters. Henry James burned . . . well, we don't really know what he burned.

Kafka wanted *The Trial* burned, but he was thwarted. If Nabokov was serious about wanting his last, unfinished novel to be destroyed, he should have done it himself. It is rare to find sufficient loyalty when it comes to honoring such a request. Miss Tita, though a fictional character, is an example to emulate, burning the Aspern letters one by one as she did, in order to honor her aunt's intentions. I believe that my burning of all the old files and documents at Zip's Candies was the best way I could honor Sam's intentions. And that's the truth.

"Truth is truth to the end of reckoning." That's Shakespeare, Irene, *Measure for Measure,* which I happen to know you have never read or probably even heard of because you haven't been curious about what you don't know for a very long time, not since college. And even then, when that expensive education was at your disposal, when you could have done anything, gone any-where, studied anything, thought about anything, you didn't have time for Shakespeare, because you were too busy reading about gendered space in the workplace and the sociology of het-erosexuality and feminist environmentalism.

HOWARD ZIPLINSKY MADE me a member of this family, and now he is living a world away, where he is the Grandest Tiger in the Jungle, even though he left most of his beautiful shirts behind. He believes he has changed himself into the person he was always meant to be by living that life. Maybe I have changed myself, too, by finally accepting that I am also living the life I was meant to live.

I will end my affidavit here. Leonardo (it is as erudite to call him by his first name as it is uneducated to call him "Da Vinci") said that art is never finished, only abandoned, and I can only add that most everything important in life is never finished, not just art. Julie and Jacob are coming over for dinner so we can work on the details of the Say Howdy! launch. Madagascar is eight hours ahead of us, so if we wait until midnight, when it is his morning, they can call Howard and talk to him about the name of our new candy line (if they can get through to their father on that primitive telephone connection). It will be just the three of us on our own, like old times, when Howard was in Madagascar, and I would let the children stay up until midnight in order to call him while he was having his breakfast, because we missed him. Surely it's a perfect night for a breakfast-dinner. I have flour and eggs and milk and butter. I will make a huge big plate of the most lovely pancakes, as yellow and brown as little Tigers.

WITNESS MY SIGNATURE THIS FIFTEENTH DAY OF AUGUST, 2009
SIGNATURE OF DECLARANT:

About the Author

KATHARINE WEBER is the author of the novels *Triangle, The Little Women, The Music Lesson,* and *Objects in Mirror Are Closer Than They Appear.* She lives in Connecticut with her husband, the cultural historian Nicholas Fox Weber, and teaches in the graduate writing program at Columbia University.